EAGER FOR THE AIR

The Lizzie's War series

Kevin O'Regan

Core Books

Published by Core Books

Paperback edition ISBN: 978-1-7392206-4-8
A CIP catalogue for this book is held by the British Library.

CONTENTS

Title Page

Chapter 1   1

Chapter 2   8

Chapter 3   15

Chapter 4   22

Chapter 5   29

Chapter 6   36

Chapter 7   43

Chapter 8   50

Chapter 9   56

Chapter 10   63

Chapter 11   71

Chapter 12   78

Chapter 13   85

Chapter 14   92

Chapter 15   99

Chapter 16   106

Chapter 17   113

Chapter 18   120

Chapter 19   128

Chapter 20   136

Chapter 21   143

Chapter 22   150

Chapter 23   158

Chapter 24   165

Chapter 25   172

Chapter 26   179

Chapter 27   186

Chapter 28   193

Chapter 29   200

Chapter 30   207

Chapter 31   214

Chapter 32   222

Chapter 33   229

Chapter 34   236

Chapter 35   244

Chapter 36   251

Chapter 37   259

Chapter 38   266

Chapter 39   273

Historical Note   279

Also by Kevin O'Regan   281

Acknowledgements   283

Prologue

Like water, we take freedom for granted when it is plentiful and only realise its importance when we are in danger of drought. In places where oppressors and tyrants hold sway, the freedom to be oneself, to make one's own decisions is restricted or lost. But, in so-called free countries there is a more subtle tyranny: those who take licence whilst espousing liberty. Perhaps a country can only be judged to be free if the rights and liberties of everyone are protected from those who would trample on them. Seek always the fresh air of freedom; it is something worth fighting for.

"There is more than one kind of freedom," said Aunt Lydia. "Freedom to and freedom from. In the days of anarchy, it was freedom to. Now you are being given freedom from. Don't underrate it.
The Handmaid's Tale, Margaret Atwood

In memory of the women of the Air Transport Auxiliary, pioneers not just in flying but also in the role of women

and in memoriam
the dead, the injured and the bereaved of
the Grenfell Tower fire
RIP

CHAPTER 1

Lizzie watched the Tiger Moth approaching White Waltham airfield where she stood with the other trainees and two instructors. The pilot seemed to be having difficulty keeping the plane from rolling and yawing. The jovial atmosphere amongst the group turned to consternation when the aircraft was some half a mile from the boundary fence of the airfield and started dropping to the ground. It was still yawing, twisting from side to side.

"For God's sake don't put it down like that." Roger Carlisle breathed. Lizzie glanced at the anxiety on his face.

"It is daunting making your first landing."

"There speaks an experienced pilot." Carlisle smiled.

"I'm lucky. I learnt to fly in Tiger Moths a couple of years ago when I was eighteen. Legacy from my grandmother, God rest her soul."

Carlisle twisted one end of his handlebar moustache. "And what did your parents make of that? Young lady learning to fly?"

My mother couldn't understand it...still can't. As far as she's concerned, a young lady should be preparing herself for marriage that's all. My father was okay about it, especially when my brother - he's a couple of years older than me – joined the RAF. He's now flying Spitfires."

They fell silent when the aircraft was a few feet from the ground. It touched down with both main wheels, the tail skid dropping almost immediately afterwards. The aircraft veered off course and described a circle on the airfield.

"The Moth does tend to do that of course," Carlisle said. "Perfectly understandable for a trainee pilot."

Lizzie breathed out. "I think it's more worrying watching than actually flying."

"It certainly is if you're a capable pilot…as indeed you are Lizzie. Your landing was perfect."

"So it should be. I've landed enough times already." Lizzie appreciated the compliment especially coming from Carlisle. Many men would try to belittle any female achievement. He was in his fifties, she guessed, a veteran of the Great War in which he had flown Sopwith Camels amongst other aircraft. At the first briefing, he introduced himself as old school. He loved the open cockpit of the Tiger Moth, the wind in his face, 'flying by the seat of your pants'. He was certainly a superb pilot, the aircraft seeming to be almost an extension of his body as if his arms were wings. A former Flight Lieutenant in the RAF, he was now a pilot instructor in the Air Transport Auxiliary which she had joined just one week before.

The Tiger Moth bumped over the grass until it had reached the apron and came to a stop close by the group of observers where the engine was cut. The silence was wonderful. The mid-May morning was full of the promise of Summer, warm with the lightest of breezes and high cirrostratus clouds a wash over the infinite blue of the sky. Flying in an open cockpit was still cold even on such a day but was much more comfortable than on a frosty Winter morning when even thick gloves and a flying jacket seemed inadequate.

The instructor, Commander Trueman, climbed down from the aircraft followed by the trainee who jumped down awkwardly and ripped off his helmet.

"Where are the bloody ground crew? That aircraft has a faulty rudder." The voice was that of a wealthy, former public-school boy. Before anyone could stop him, Edward Melford had stormed off into the nearby hangar, his limp even more pronounced than usual.

"Mr Melford," Trueman called after him to no avail.

2

Carlisle signalled to Trueman that he would deal with it, turned and started to follow Melford. Lizzie, unsure what to do, walked slowly behind. In the hangar, Melford was confronting one of the ground crew who looked baffled at the sudden onslaught of words.

"What are you trying to do? Kill us? Hitler's doing that, we don't need people like you joining in."

The mechanic wiped his greasy hands on a piece of cloth. His face turned from bewilderment to anger. "I don't know what you mean…Sir."

"That bloody Moth I've just flown wouldn't stay straight. And when I landed, the damned thing turned in a circle. There must be something wrong with the rudder."

"All the aircraft are checked daily. If there was something wrong with the rudder, we'd have fixed it."

Melford's voice dropped low and he jabbed his finger at the unfortunate mechanic. "I don't need your insolence. Check that bloody aircraft again. What's your name anyway?"

"Hale…John Hale. And what's yours?"

"Bloody cheek. All you need to know is that I'm more important than you."

"I think that's enough Mr Melford." Carlisle reached the two men and placed himself between them. "Come with me and I'll explain something about the Tiger Moth." He placed a firm hand on Melford's shoulder and moved him towards the entrance of the hangar.

The mechanic turned away and threw the rag down on a workbench. "Bloody arrogant bastard," he hissed.

Lizzie felt for John Hale. "I'm sorry about that Mr Hale. It's just quite a strain when you're learning to fly. Mr Melford was just feeling the pressure. I'm sure he will apologise to you later. I hope you don't think we're all like that. We do appreciate the work you do, keeping all the aircraft in tip-top condition."

Hale said nothing for a moment. "Thank you Miss. I appreciate that. Glad you're not all like him."

When Lizzie walked out of the hangar, Carlise was

locked in conversation with Melford. He seemed to be getting somewhat heated himself. "For the last time, Melford, the tendency to yaw is a feature of the Moth. You just have to learn to deal with it. If you're not straight when you land, the tail skid will cause you to turn in a circle."

"I think there was something wrong with that aircraft and nothing you say will change my view. The ground crew made me look a complete idiot in front of everyone."

"No one, Mr Melford, no one who has flown a Tiger Moth would consider any novice pilot to be an idiot because of what happened. Put it behind you. Next time, I'm sure, you'll bring it down perfectly."

Melford was not convinced and walked away in injured silence. He joined the rest of the group as did Lizzie and Carlisle. There was that moment of embarrassment when no one really knew whether to say anything to him or not. Trueman stepped in.

"Right everybody, stow your parachutes, helmets and goggles and then make your way speedily to the Briefing Room." He glanced at his watch. "We'll start in ten minutes."

They all walked away. Lizzie fell into step beside Kasia. "How did your flight go?"

"Was okay but, you know, landing for the first time was difficult. I made an approach but then Stephanie Garrett, my instructor, told me to go round again before I touched down. Not happy with my approach."

"There's bound to be tricky things at first but I'm sure you'll master it quickly."

Kasia said nothing but it was clear she was not convinced. Her dark hair, released from the flying helmet, fell in thick curls onto her shoulders and set off the dark brows and striking features of her face.

"I think you're Polish aren't you?"

"Yes. I come from near Warsaw. When the Germans invaded last September, we thought our army would be able to defeat them. But then the Russians invaded from the other side.

Our forces were beaten at the Battle of Bzura. It was the middle of September. We knew then we had to get out."

"Would it have been dangerous for you to stay?"

"Of course. My family are Jewish. We knew what the Germans had done to the Jews in their own country. It would have been no different in Poland. But there are so many who were not able to leave or perhaps did not want to. Leaving your home is difficult."

"I can believe that." Lizzie thought of her own comfortable home in the village near Dorking in Surrey. At this time of year, the trees, the shrubs, the flowers were bursting forth with new life. Her parents' garden was rich with scents and with birdsong. How hard to have to leave all that behind for a foreign country. "Did you speak English already?"

"Yes. As you can tell, I not good but getting better."

"How did you get out of Poland?"

"Ship. We travelled North to Gdansk... Baltic coast...and found a ship coming to England. It was full of us refugees."

"I'm so sorry that you have had to endure that, Kasia, but very glad that you are here and safe. It's wonderful that you want to play your part in our campaign."

"Hitler must be defeated before he murders thousands of innocent people."

"Amen to that."

◆ ◆ ◆

Inspector Daniel Hawkins closed the folder and put it to one side of his desk. He was troubled. Why was it that people were so unpleasant to those who had fled Nazi Germany and Austria? Surely it was the British way to help those in trouble and who could blame people for wanting to escape the tyranny of Hitler's Third Reich? He looked at the folder with concern. It was becoming thicker weekly with new cases of refugees being abused and in one case physically attacked.

He sighed deeply, sprang out of his chair and opened the office door. "Drake...have you a minute please?"

Sergeant Drake left the front counter and entered the office. Hawkins motioned for him to close the door and to sit at the chair by the desk. Hawkins slid the folder across to him.

"Take a look, Drake. Yet another report of a refugee being abused."

Drake opened the folder and read the crime report on top of the pile. "I remember this one, Sir. PC Teal took down the details."

"And has he investigated it Sergeant?"

"There was no real way of doing so, Sir. The refugee who reported it could not describe the perpetrator. Apparently, he was wearing a hat pulled low on his head. As you can see, Sir, the complainant was able to give height and build but nothing else. It could be almost any man in Maidenhead... except those who are very over-weight."

"I understand that, Sergeant, but it may be that we have a very small number of people who are doing this. Have you or Teal looked at similarities between cases?"

"Yes, Sir, course we have. But other than the cases being unprovoked, there seems to be nothing to link them. They're in different parts of the town like, at different times of day. I mean we could follow some of the victims, see if it happens again but that could be a wild goose chase."

Hawkins nodded. "I just don't understand it Drake. Why can't our people realise what it must be like for a refugee? You might be German or Austrian but it doesn't mean you like what Hitler is doing and, if you're a Jew, you have every reason to get out."

"Some of the abuse has been directed at Jews, Sir. But there's also rumours going round that some of the refugees are actually German agents who will be spying for Hitler and waiting to help out in the event of an invasion."

"Rumours, yes, rumours but no evidence for that is

there?"

"Not that I know of, Sir, but it's a possibility."

"Yes but if we have evidence of any refugee spying, we can arrest him or her. Until then, we must treat them as bona fide refugees."

"Sir."

"I'm wondering if we should ask the local newspaper to run an article, perhaps focusing on the stories of one or two refugees."

"Might be worth doing, Sir, but I doubt any of the refugees would agree to be part of that…might just lead to more abuse."

"True Drake." Inspector Hawkins sighed again. "We live in very troubled times, Sergeant, very troubled times."

"I won't argue with that, Sir. I don't think it was ever like this back in Wales during the last war. I'd just started with the Force at the end of it."

Hawkins nodded again. "Ok Drake, let's hope we get a lead of some kind."

CHAPTER 2

Commander Trueman now stood at the front of the briefing room to address the recruits in Lizzie's batch. As head of The Air Transport Auxiliary, he had given a short account of his working life at the first briefing. His career started as a banker but his enthusiasm for aviation involved him in joining British Airways which had now become the British Overseas Aircraft Corporation. Lizzie had been impressed by the clarity of his thinking and his commitment to the Air Transport Auxiliary. He had stressed how important this new organisation was to the war effort. "Every ATA pilot frees up an RAF pilot for combat," he had said.

He was a tall man, imposing, and commanded respect yet he seemed to Lizzie to be thoughtful and approachable. "As soon as you have satisfied your instructor that you can fly the Tiger Moth – and those of you who joined us as trained pilots have reached that stage already – you will begin training on the next aircraft which is the Miles Magister, a single-engined monoplane. Most people find that easier to fly than the Moth."

"You can't beat a good old bi-plane," chipped in Carlisle.

"As you can see," Trueman smiled, "nostalgia is alive and well and living at White Waltham."

Carlisle beamed and there was a mock cheer from some of the recruits dispelling any gloom that had arisen from Melford's outburst.

Trueman continued. "You probably already know that we have six different groups of aircraft, each larger than the lower group. Once you are deemed capable of flying one aircraft in a group, you are authorised to fly any aircraft in that group. But it is important that you read up as much as you can about all the aircraft. We will give you notes but the more you know about the aircraft the better."

A hand was raised. "When do we get to fly a Spitfire, Sir?" There was a boyish eagerness about Graham Swinburne the questioner, his fair hair combed neatly to one side. Lizzie guessed he was about mid-twenties and she wondered why he was not in the RAF. She was beginning to realise that all the men in the ATA were there because they had a condition or age which made them unsuitable for combat duties. 'Ancient and Tattered Airmen' was the rather offensive interpretation some had given to the ATA.

"That will depend on how you do but the Spitfire is Class Two - advanced single-engined planes." The smile on Trueman's face disappeared. "But put aside thoughts of joy-riding. We have an important job to do and we pride ourselves on delivering aircraft in A1 condition, on time."

"Of course, Sir. Wouldn't dream of doing anything untoward." Swinburne chuckled and looked sideways at Olivia Hulett whose face broke into a huge smile. Lizzie's eyes followed his. Olivia was beautiful, quite delicate looking with fine features and blond hair that fell in luxurious curls past her shoulders. She was a dancer and a more unlikely pilot recruit one could not imagine. Her sister, Laura, sat beside her. She was very different, attractive certainly, but her dark hair, tied tightly at the back, made her face rather severe and signalled a more serious disposition. Older than Olivia, she spoke little and had a determination about her that suggested she would achieve whatever she set out to do.

From the corner of her eye, Lizzie could see Edward Melford who looked troubled at Olivia's response to Swinburne. However, the scowl on his face suddenly disappeared and the characteristic twinkle returned to his eye. Nothing like a little rivalry to snap someone out of a bad mood.

His hand went up and Trueman nodded to him. "Sir, I just wanted to apologise to everyone for my outburst this afternoon. I'm afraid the pressure got to me a bit. Won't happen again."

"Thank you Mr Melford, that is very generous of you. I understand that one of our ground crew took the brunt of your displeasure; I hope you will find an opportunity to give him a suitable apology too."

Kasia was sitting beside Lizzie. "Was that genuine apology you think?" she whispered."

"Not sure, but I suppose we all get angry some times."

"I think he should save his anger for Hitler."

Mark Sanders, who was sitting in the row behind with the red-haired Patrick Kenny, leaned forward. "I couldn't help hearing that. I agree with you totally Miss Michalski."

Lizzie turned around and smiled at him. She guessed he was in his forties, lines beginning to crease his face, but he looked quite athletic. As she and her instructor had watched him landing that afternoon, Carlisle had told her Sanders was an experienced pilot also. He had learnt to fly the previous year with the Civil Air Guard. "Like you Lizzie," Carlisle had said, "he'll soon progress. We do like to put everyone through the basic flying training on the Moth though so we can assess their capabilities."

Trueman looked around the room for further questions. No hand was raised. "Right, that will be all for today. Well done everyone. Have a very enjoyable evening and a relaxing Sunday and we'll resume on Monday morning."

Olivia sat at the desk that doubled as a rudimentary dressing table, applying make-up with great care. Kasia had said she was not bothering with make-up; Lizzie and Laura had put on a touch of powder and lipstick and were now dressing. Kasia, having changed from her flying clothes into a dress, had been flicking through a magazine that Olivia had brought with her. She dropped it open on the foot of her bed.

"Look at that advertisement for beauty products. 'Beauty is your Duty' it says. Why they think we have time to worry about beauty?"

Olivia, still in her petticoat, turned away from the mirror and picking up the magazine, looked at the advertisement. She smiled. "Well I for one am not going to lose my femininity just because I'm doing a job that is considered a man's preserve. I shall do the job as well as I can and still try to look as beautiful as possible."

In truth, Olivia needed to make very little effort to be beautiful. She was tall and slim with a natural elegance and her vivacious nature gave her eyes brilliance.

"The expectations that everyone has of us puts us under the pressure." There was no frivolity in Kasia, no softening of her sharp features; she seemed unable or unwilling to relax.

Lizzie decided that was something she would try to help her with; it was not good for Kasia to allow herself no relief. "It's important that we don't try to ape the men. We are as good as them and we should do the things that make us women. I'm with you Olivia." Lizzie spoke as reasonably and gently as she could. She did not want what she said to be a rebuke to Kasia. "In some ways, I think we need to be very feminine, despite the flying suits we wear."

"Those are for practical reasons though." Laura, who had been fastening her stockings, lowered her hem and looked up. "Apparently, at the start, they expected the women to wear skirts when flying. Stephanie Garret pointed out that skirts were too cold and besides you couldn't hold the joystick between your legs with a skirt on."

Olivia and Lizzie burst out laughing and even Kasia smiled.

Laura continued. "Yes, she said you need both hands at certain points like landing and so you have to hold it between your legs."

"Well that's something to look forward to!" All four young women laughed at Olivia's quip.

"I do hope we have a decent meal tonight."

"I'm more concerned, Lizzie, that there'll be no fun to be had afterwards. We are rather stuck in the sticks out here and I don't suppose Maidenhead has much to offer in the way of nightlife."

"Olivia is a party girl, aren't you Sis?"

"Absolutely. We may be dead tomorrow so today must be lived to the full." Olivia walked over to the wardrobe she shared with Laura and selected a dress which she stepped into and pulled up, buttoning the front. It was a gorgeous green satin which emphasised the curves of her figure. She checked herself in front of the mirror and then put on a gold necklace with a diamond pendant and two hanging diamond earrings. She turned around, struck a pose and said, "How do I look girls?"

"Stunning Olivia. Absolutely stunning. If you fly as well as you look, you'll put us all in the shade."

"Thank you Lizzie." Olivia made a small mock curtsy. "Shall we go down and cheer up the chaps with our dazzling presence?"

Her exuberance was infectious. She had a vivacity, a lightness, a warmth that brought joy to anyone who was in her presence. Lizzie could tell that even Kasia was infected. Perhaps she was revising her previously expressed views. Lizzie wondered if there were any rivalry between the Hulett sisters. Beauty such as Olivia's could easily create jealousy in an older sibling but Laura seemed free of that; instead she sensed a desire to protect Olivia.

The four young women sat around a low table in the comfortable White Waltham lounge, one wall of which boasted shelves lined with books, another a large noticeboard dominated by the ATA motto which was above it. They had had to persuade Kasia to have something alcoholic – a sherry like Laura and Lizzie. Olivia opted for a dry martini but was disappointed that they did not have a proper cocktail glass at the bar.

"I can't stop thinking about what Stephanie Garrett

said about the joystick." Laura's usually serious face cracked in a smile and the other three broke into laughter again.

"I hope I'm not interrupting a private conversation. It sounds pretty racy to me." Edward Melford lifted a long and expensive cigarette to his lips, drew on it and blew smoke into the air.

"Nothing to get excited about Eddie...we're just talking about the joystick."

"So that's not a euphemism. How disappointing."

Edward Melford pulled over an empty chair, sat down and leaned forward over the table. His eyes were glittering and he spoke as if revealing a secret. "I've had an excellent idea. After dinner, why don't we all zoom off to a club...Soho or somewhere. I could do with a bit of fun."

"Ooh yes let's do it. I so want to dance again. I miss it so much."

"Do you have anywhere in mind?" Laura seemed unconvinced by the plan.

"I have just the place. It won't take us long. Only thing is we won't all fit in my motor so we need to find another chauffeur." He looked around the room over one shoulder then the other. "It's a question of who has a motor car."

"I not go so that will be fewer people."

Lizzie wondered if Kasia's unwillingness was due to a lack of money. She felt for her but did not want her to miss out.

Olivia spoke before Lizzie had formed something suitable to say. "Oh but Kasia, you must. It will be fun. Eddie, do you have somewhere in mind?"

"I was thinking the Café de Paris. Excellent dance band there and all the best people go. I'm a member."

"I know of it of course but it sounds expensive." Lizzie glanced furtively at Kasia, sure that Eddie's suggestion would convince her that she should not go.

"It's not too bad but, anyway, it's my treat. You ladies will pay nothing." Eddie lowered his voice. "The Pater, you know, looks after me well. Just changed his main car and gave me his SS

Jaguar two and a half litre. It's stunning and goes like a bomb...
sorry that's an unfortunate expression these days."

Lizzie turned to Kasia. "Do come, Kasia. It will be good to
have a break from training and, as Eddie said, we have a rest day
tomorrow."

"I don't know." Kasia looked at the floor, some internal
struggle clear on her face. "It's seems wrong somehow...you
know...we out enjoying ourselves while others are suffering."

"You staying at base will not make a scrap of difference
to the suffering of those in Poland or the Lowlands nor
even Germany for that matter." Laura spoke firmly, her voice
betraying no criticism of Kasia but stating a blunt truth.

Kasia looked uncertain. Lizzie laid her hand on her arm.
"Please come Kasia. It won't be the same without you."

She looked up and full into Lizzie's eyes. Lizzie hoped she
would read there the genuine warmth she felt; Kasia came to a
decision. "Okay. I will come but I insist I pay for myself."

Eddie shrugged. "Well that's settled then. Let's order some
wine for dinner." He raised his hand and clicked his fingers,
looking over at the bar where Arthur Bloom, the steward,
was serving someone else. The smile disappeared from Bloom's
face and was replaced by a scowl. He continued serving the
gentleman at the bar and then, in as unhurried a fashion as
possible, approached Edward Melford. During the transaction,
Bloom did not look Melford in the eye and no smile broke his
stern features, except when he looked towards Kasia.

CHAPTER 3

The three ATA instructors working with the new recruits had just enjoyed an excellent meal provided by Richard Trueman's wife, Felicity, with the considerable assistance of Mrs Brown, the housekeeper. They were now sitting in the elegant drawing room with coffee before them, the two gentlemen sipping brandy and enjoying cigars.

"When I've had my coffee, I'll leave you to your discussions. I'll subside onto the settee in the snug and listen to the wireless. Saturday evening usually boasts a play which is a great distraction from everything that's going on in the World." Felicity fingered the beautiful golden necklace which set off her handsome face. Her hair was meticulously groomed and her nails painted crimson to match her lips and her dress.

The room looked out over the river as the house, a substantial Edwardian building, was on the south bank, the Berkshire side of the Thames. One could see the top of Windsor Castle clearly from the first floor rooms at the back Felicity had said earlier. Now the sun was nearly gone, the light on the water gentle and making a beautiful display of the weeping willow in its fresh coat of new leaves. The river flowed softly, as if not to disturb the inhabitants of Windsor. A pair of swans glided down majestically and skimmed the water to land out of sight upstream. One could not imagine a more tranquil scene, something worth preserving at all costs from the mindless destruction of Hitler's jack-booted thugs.

There was a tap on the door. Mrs Trueman called 'enter' and a stout woman of about forty-five waddled inside. She was wearing a coat and hat beneath which her plump face looked flushed. "If there's nothing else Mrs T, I'll be off. My Sidney does get right grumpy if I'm too late. Oh I left him his dinner so he's got nothing to grumble about but you know how it is with some men. Ooh he doesn't half go on sometimes. You should hear him sometimes at the news on the wireless."

"Thank you Mrs Brown. That will be all tonight. And thank you again for such a lovely dinner."

Stephanie Garrett added her thanks. "I wonder where you learnt to cook so well, Mrs Brown."

"Oh that's kind of you to say Madam. I was in service before I married so I learnt a great deal. It was at a big house in Mayfair in London. I was so lucky to get the position. I was never the cook, of course, nothing as grand as that but I was in the kitchen and Mrs Chandler, the cook, really brought me on, always showing me things. Course then I married my Sid and he lived here in Windsor so we came here."

"Yes thank you Mrs Brown. I'm sure Miss Garrett and our other guest don't wish to detain you longer, interesting though it is."

"Oh it's ok Mrs T. Sidney can wait a bit."

"I don't think you should keep him waiting any longer Mrs Brown. Thank you for an excellent dinner. I wish you a very pleasant evening. You should be able to walk home in the light still." Richard Trueman stood and with great courtesy showed Mrs Brown to the door. When he returned, he took up his cigar again and chuckled. "She is a very good person is Mrs Brown though she does tend to talk for England. The house she was talking about in Mayfair was the London home of Sir Oswald Mosley, the fifth Baronet and the father of the current Sir Oswald Mosley."

"I wonder how Mrs and Mr Brown met... perhaps both worked for Oswald Mosley." Roger Carlisle sipped his brandy meditatively, his other hand resting on his ample stomach.

"Possibly, but that would have been the current Mosley's father. It would probably have been over twenty years ago when they met and the current Oswald Mosley was still a young man, a Conservative MP; he married Lady Cynthia Curzon in 1920."

"It was not clear from Mrs Brown's statement what her Sidney 'goes on about' when the news is on. Presumably, he is as appalled as most of us are about the things Hitler is doing. Extraordinary isn't it how Hitler has generated such hatred for the Jews and how some Germans are able to mis-treat others they don't even know?"

"I agree, Roger. It seems that some have a need to despise and hate others. But we should discuss our recruits. I'm rather pleased that we have four men and four women."

As the soft daylight faded, Trueman turned on the lamps and closed the curtains which added further to the feeling of comfort in the room. They began to discuss the recruits one by one, starting with Edward Melford.

"I am certain he will make a perfectly good pilot – he was fine for most of the flight, seemed to take instruction and was keen to do well. But the tirade you said he gave Hale in the hangar is most concerning." Trueman looked to Roger Carlisle.

"Very worrying. I hung back a little to see how he would deal with it but I had to step between them. Melford was really quite nasty – asked Hale's name and when Hale asked for his in return told him he was being insolent. I think Lizzie Barnes had a word with Hale afterwards, tried to mollify him a bit but I could see he was angry."

"It is worrying." Stephanie Garrett spoke carefully, her shrewd intelligence evident in her measured comments. "We need relations between aircrew and ground crew to be as cordial as between pilots. The ground crew are essential to our operation."

"Precisely Stephanie. I think we need to keep an eye out for any further examples of that. If he has a temper which he can't manage, he could be dangerous at the controls of an aircraft. Imagine he is ferrying someone important who says something he doesn't like."

"I fear that Mr Melford is from a family who expects everyone to doff their caps to them. It's not so much that he's arrogant, more that he has a set of assumptions about his position in society."

"I think you're being too kind, Stephanie." Roger Carlisle put his brandy down with a clatter on the table. "I think he's a cocky bastard who needs taking down a peg or two. Doubtless the training programme will reveal to him that he is not anything special."

"I did meet his father once - I can see where he gets the arrogance from – I came under a lot of pressure to assign him a single room" Trueman sighed. "Let's see how he gets on. Did anyone else come to your attention today either because they excelled or because they caused concern?"

"No concerns. Obviously people like Lizzie Barnes flew very well indeed but so she should really - she's already a trained pilot, " said Carlisle.

"Likewise Mark Sanders – Civil Air Guard. He seems a very steady man, calm, thorough…just the sort of person the ATA needs," Trueman offered.

"The two sisters Laura and Olivia did well. Laura is more practical I think but Olivia is no fool. She presents herself as someone a bit girlish and flighty but I think she has a serious determination to do a good job."

"Interesting observation Stephanie." Trueman made a note in his book. I went up with the Polish girl, Katarzyna Michalski. Prefers to be called Kasia. She was very impressive and is very determined to learn quickly. Can't wait to be doing something useful for the war effort. There is a darkness in her though. I do hope she lightens up a bit when she gets to know people better."

"Her name in Polish means 'pure' apparently. Let's hope she is."

"Now, now, Roger." Trueman wagged his finger at Carlisle. "I hope you're not harbouring suspicions. She was thoroughly checked out by the Ministry when she applied to ATA."

"Graham Swinburne took to it very well. I am sure he will

make a good pilot. It's a shame for him that he has that spinal injury - playing rugby at school apparently – he would be an asset otherwise in the RAF. But still," Stephanie smiled, "their loss is our gain."

"And finally, Patrick Kenny, our Irish firebrand."

"He's not actually Irish is he? His Liverpool accent is very strong."

"He is of Irish parentage," Trueman explained. "I have to confess to being a little unsure of where Irish sympathies really lie. They don't seem to be completely behind our attempts to defeat Hitler."

"There's plenty of Irish in this country who've signed up. 'By their deeds shall ye know them.' Let's judge by what we see of him. So far, so good." Stephanie Garret returned her cup and saucer to the table beside her. "I think he knows his own mind, perhaps a bit outspoken, a bit dour at times, but he will make a good pilot. He's another one who's a bit too old for the RAF."

The drawing room door opened and Felicity Trueman stepped into the room. "I'm sorry to interrupt you but I thought you may wish to know. The BBC has announced that Neville Chamberlain resigned late yesterday as Prime Minister and Mr Churchill has been asked by the King to form a government. He'll make his first speech to the House of Commons on Monday."

"That's good news. Churchill will give much more decisive leadership to the Country." Trueman drained his brandy.

The waiter had pulled two tables closer together so all eight of them could sit as a group. Edward Melford had ordered two bottles of champagne and glasses for everyone. The protests that Kasia and Lizzie had made he waved away and Lizzie felt it would insult him to press further. He was either generous or perhaps he liked to flaunt his wealth. The waiters treated him with deference; he was clearly known well at the club.

"It pays to have connections," he said to Lizzie quietly. Now he relaxed back in his chair and drew on his cigarette before leaning forward to stub it out in an ashtray. "Let the dancing commence," he announced, rising to his feet and offering his hand to Olivia. She stood and accepted it with a glowing smile. They made a good-looking couple, Melford suave in his evening suit despite the increasing flesh around his mid-riff.

Graham Swinburne invited Laura to dance but Mark Sanders and Patrick Kenny, with whom they had driven up to London in Mark's car, did not issue invitations. Perhaps being older men they felt an advance from them would be unacceptable to younger women. Lizzie contented herself watching others dance. The band was playing a Charleston and Lizzie's eyes were drawn to Olivia as were the eyes of many people still seated. She was brilliant, stunning, her movements absolutely capturing the spirit of the dance and her legs swivelling with a precision and elegance unmatched by the other dancers. There was a freedom, a joy in her dancing that was uplifting.

Lizzie turned to the others. "Come on, let's join them." She stood and held out her hand to Mark Sanders. He looked a little shy as he took her hand and led her onto the dance floor. Patrick Kenny needed no other prompting to take Kasia's hand. The band finished the Charleston and began to play a waltz.

"This is more my style," Mark said. He took Lizzie in his arms. She felt the excitement and euphoria fill her as it always did when she danced. Such a wonderful feeling of lightness and being carefree, the sort of freedom she experienced when flying.

They danced to several tunes, swapping partners so that everyone had danced with nearly everyone else in their small party before they collapsed into their chairs. Lizzie noticed that Kasia and Melford did not dance together and there was a moment when Patrick Kenny and Laura were facing each other but both turned away, avoiding an encounter. Olivia seemed to be the only one who did not need to rest but, as they sipped their champagne, she declined the numerous offers she had from men who sidled by, drawn to her like proverbial moths to a flame.

One of them, with black, tightly-curled hair and a prominent nose was a little more persistent. As politely as she could, but clearly becoming irritated by his persistence, Olivia said, "I'm talking with my friends at the moment and do not want to dance but thank you."

The young man opened his mouth to protest but Edward Melford suddenly stood up. "Can't you take no for an answer? The lady does not wish to dance with you. Now go away."

The last words were almost shouted. Melford watched the man skulk away casting hostile looks back at him before he resumed his seat. He smiled. "Some people just don't know when they're not wanted." He picked up his glass. "Probably a damned Jew by the look of him."

Lizzie's mouth opened with shock and her eyes turned to Kasia who was suddenly on her feet. "And what if he is a Jew?"

CHAPTER 4

"Sidney...Sidney." Mavis Brown was puzzled. "Where's he got to?" she muttered to herself. "Must be up the pub."

She took off her coat and shoes and put on her slippers. She was tired and looking forward to nestling in a comfortable armchair to listen to the Saturday play on the wireless. She looked at the kitchen clock as the kettle was heating. Just twenty past eight. In good time for the play which started at eight-thirty.

The Truemans were a nice couple to work for. They were always very appreciative of what she did - nice to have compliments from their guests too – and they paid her well, especially on a Saturday. When the tea was ready, she poured it into a mug and took it through to the sitting room where she turned the knob on the wireless until it crackled into life. She flopped into the armchair and put her feet up on the little footstool which was covered in a cross-stitch she had done herself years before when they first married.

She managed to finish her tea and put the mug down on the little table beside her before her eyes drooped. The play was not as good as usual and was failing to keep her fatigue at bay. She did not sleep though, not really sleep. Her thoughts, a little jumbled, turned to her children. The house was quiet without them. William had joined up. Part of her wanted him to stay at home but that was not really a possibility for a self-respecting young man. 'What would people say about me if I did that?' he had said. It wasn't just about doing his bit though. It was the adventure, the excitement. Of course, at nineteen, he was not old enough to remember the last War. Anyone who remembered the appalling suffering of that time would not be eager to be part of it again.

And Sheila wanted to do her bit as well. Training as a nurse now in the King Edward VII Hospital in Windsor no less – on nights at the moment. Hard work but at least there was little danger of her getting killed – provided of course the Germans didn't invade like everyone expected them to when we declared war on them. Still, they might yet have need for the gas masks they'd been issued with last September. Sid never took his when he went out. She did nag him sometimes but he took no notice.

Her increasingly muddled thoughts took her to her younger days, prompted no doubt by mentioning her first job in domestic service earlier that evening. She had loved it there. The work was hard but Mrs Chandler, the cook, was good to her and she had learnt so much. She remembered the day she been sent into the outhouse to pluck pheasants for dinner. They'd been hanging there for several days, tied by the legs upside down. It was an awful job, feathers flying everywhere, and it took ages. Mrs Chandler had come in wondering where she'd got to. Mavis was nearly in tears.

"Why do these damned birds have so many feathers?" she'd wailed.

Mrs Chandler burst out laughing. "So they can fly you silly girl." But she had shown her how to hold the bird and how to pluck the feathers. The next one she did, took hardly any time at all. "It's all about the knack, you see. If you know what you're doing, jobs are easy. Watch and learn Mavis, watch and learn and before long, you'll be cook in a big house."

Mavis smiled to herself and let her mind wander through the many rooms of her memory. She was asleep.

Even Edward Melford looked stunned by Kasia's reaction but he rapidly regained his composure. "Nothing in particular…just mentioned that he looks Jewish."

"You said he's probably a 'damned Jew'. That word tells me your attitude to Jews."

"What's it to you? Do you know him?"

Kasia pointed at herself, her eyes blazing. "I am a Jew."

Melford spread his hands and shrugged his shoulders. "I didn't know." He sat down and picked up his glass.

"That's not the point. What is wrong with Jewish people that you describe that man as 'damned'?"

Melford's mouth twisted into a snarl. Lizzie had seen it that afternoon in the hangar where he had revealed a nasty side to his character. He presented himself as charming, easy-going and generous but…

"Well if you really want to know. They control everything, they're sweeping up all the money everywhere, they're secretive, corrupt…"

Kasia laughed, a loud, humourless bark. "What evidence do you have for that? Isn't it bad enough that Hitler is driving them from their homes, murdering them, taking their possessions? Is that right you think?"

Lizzie stood and put her arm around Kasia, hoping to calm her or move her away but Kasia shook her off roughly. The rest of their party were transfixed at this sudden explosion of anger on what was supposed to be an enjoyable evening.

"Look just forget it will you?" Melford turned away from Kasia and forcing a smile to his face asked Olivia to dance. She stood and took his hand but there did not seem to be the enthusiasm she had shown earlier.

Suddenly the mood had changed and the club no longer seemed to promise laughter and joy. The majority of people there had not of course noticed the contretemps. The band still played with as much vigour and passion, dancers spun on the floor, the wider ballroom dresses of the ladies ballooning out as they twirled. There was laughter, glasses being tipped up and drained, re-filled. For most people, the atmosphere remained wonderful, exciting, but Melford's outburst and Kasia's response had dampened the spirits of their party.

"Sit down Kasia. You mustn't take any notice of what he said." Lizzie knew it was going to take time to soothe Kasia. She looked towards Laura who seemed frozen in her seat.

"Would you like to leave Kasia?" It was Mark Sanders. "If you do, we can go now…that's provided Lizzie and Patrick don't mind."

"No, no. I be alright. Please just leave me to sit for a while until I calm down."

On the dance floor, Olivia was attempting to teach Edward a swing dance but he didn't seem to be grasping it very well, his bad leg a definite disadvantage. Other couples were displaying superb skills and the party mood had definitely not been affected by the disagreement at their table. Lizzie did wonder about Edward Melford. Was he one of those who despised Jews? She knew there had been attacks in England on some Jewish people, something she could not understand. How could there be such hatred of people one did not know? How could people persist in those attitudes, knowing what Hitler had done to the Jews in Germany?

She moved away from the table a little; Mark Sanders followed her. She said, "What do you know about Melford, apart from the fact he is very rich?"

"Not much, I'm afraid. I remember reading somewhere that Melford's father went to school with Oswald Mosley. They are perhaps still friends. I hope it's not the case, but maybe Melford is a sympathiser with Mosley and his blackshirt thugs."

"Good grief. I do hope not. Do you think we should say something to Trueman about that? I mean, he could be a Nazi sympathiser and hence a spy."

"Let's see how he is over the next couple of days."

Lizzie watched the dancers for a while. The band once again started playing a waltz. "Perhaps you should persuade Kasia to dance again. Might lighten her mood."

Mark Sanders returned to the table and sat next to Kasia. He spoke with her for several minutes before she agreed to dance. Laura Hulett was already on the dance floor with Graham Swinburne. Lizzie watched them for a while. Laura was a talented dancer but less demonstrative than Olivia and hence in her shadow as, it seemed to be, with everything else. She seemed content with that and showed only an older sister's regard for her younger sibling.

"Are you going to ask me to dance?" Lizzie looked at Patrick Kenny and smiled cheekily.

He returned the smile, stubbed out his cigarette and took her hand without saying a word. Once in hold, Lizzie asked him if he knew Edward Melford.

"I don't know him at all...never met him before this week. I think our spheres are very different and I'm from a different part of the country although I've lived in London for a while."

"He appears to dislike Jews."

"Yes...not sure what that was about but I fear he may be a Mosley supporter. Quite a few of the upper classes are or at least were. I mean take the Duke of Windsor. He had lots to do with Hitler before the war started. It's a worry."

Grenfell Road, in a quiet residential area of Maidenhead, was dark as blackout regulations permitted no street lights. Though shielded by cloud, some light from the moon penetrated and made it possible for the two figures to walk along the pavement. They wore hats pulled low on their heads and scarves which covered the bottoms of their faces. One carried a bottle, holding the bottom so that it was largely hidden behind his sleeve. The other carried an open pot of red paint from which a brush protruded.

They walked in an unhurried fashion, ensuring that their heels made little sound on the hard pavement and watching carefully for anything that may trip them. At the corner with South Road, opposite a shop, they stopped and listened for a full minute. Whilst doing so, they checked both directions of Grenfell Road and along South Road.

In the distance, they could hear footsteps approaching on South Road. They both stooped quickly and put down what they had been carrying right against the wall so their legs and shoes concealed the items. The taller of the two men took out a packet of cigarettes, offered one to his mate and put one between his own lips. From his pocket, he withdrew a box of matches and lit both.

"So what d'you think of Arsenal's performance this season?" He asked quietly.

"Not as good as I could have hoped."

Between puffs of their cigarettes, they maintained a hushed conversation about football, listening to the ring of heels growing louder. At last, the owner of the footsteps reached the corner opposite the shop and turned. He waved vaguely in greeting and walked on. They maintained their conversation, watching the departing figure surreptitiously.

In the dim light, they could make out the sign over the shop front. "Feingold's Store." In the daytime, there would be wooden racks outside laden with goods, but they had all been taken in for the night. The shop window displayed a range of household goods and several tins of food.

The taller of the two men nodded to the other who retrieved the can of paint and crossed the road to the shop door. With some degree of care, he took the brush and began to paint something on the door. It took only a minute. He stood back to check his handiwork and crossed back over the road to re-join his mate. He, the taller one, waited another minute, listening for any sounds and peering at the upper windows to make sure no one had been aroused. Once satisfied, he crossed the street carrying the bottle. With a final check in all directions and looking at his mate for confirmation, he put the bottle on the ground. Removing the top and taking an old rag from his pocket, he pushed it into the neck of the bottle. He tilted the bottle a few times so that the contents soaked the rag and then he returned it to the ground. Once more, he withdrew the matches, took one and struck it. Holding the burning match in one hand, he lifted the bottle with the other and lit the rag. It took a few moments to light but as soon as it did, he swung back his arm and threw it as hard as he could into the shop window.

He was already halfway across the street when the bottle struck and both men were running hard. They glanced back at the crash of glass and witnessed moments later the burst of flame that shot from the broken window. They ran.

CHAPTER 5

It was nearly eleven when Mark Sanders led the way out of the club onto Coventry Street with Lizzie, Kasia and Patrick Kenny following. Patrick had seemed unconcerned about the incident with Melford; his face held a constant smile, almost a grin and his eyes always glittered. Lizzie could not decide whether it was a fixed expression concealing deeper thoughts or an uncomplicated delight in everything he encountered.

Once the car had left the kerbside, Kasia cleared her throat and spoke. "I sorry about spoiling everyone's evening."

"You didn't spoil it Kasia and you said what you felt needed to be said." Lizzie laid her hand on Kasia's thigh and rubbed it gently. Kasia put her hand on top of Lizzie's and smiled her thanks.

Lizzie watched the darkened shops passing the window. There were a few pedestrians about but not many and very little other traffic. Coventry Street brought them to Piccadilly Circus and the statue of Eros on top of the Shaftesbury Fountain. It was ghostly in the dim light, conveying none of the romance normally associated with it. They drove down Piccadilly, the grand Georgian buildings impressive in their statuesque silence, past Hyde Park Corner, now empty, and along Knightsbridge. So strange to see the big shops, usually so garishly lit, now dark and sombre. Once they had driven through Kensington, Lizzie lost track of the areas they passed through.

There was little conversation on the way back to White Waltham, just the occasional subdued question and answer between the two men sitting in the front seats about the direction and the car. "It's basically a straight road all the way to Maidenhead…as long as we can find the Bath Road that is."

"Your knowledge of London's geography is impressive, Patrick, for a Liverpudlian."

Patrick Kenny laughed briefly. "I made a careful mental note of the route we followed on the way here that's all."

They remained silent for a while before Patrick Kenny said, "Nice little car this. Did you buy it from new?"

Mark Sanders humphed. "You must be joking. I'm not made of money. No I've had it for about a year…it was four years old when I bought it. Needed to take my poor old Mum out. She's on her own…my father died a few years back."

The density of building started to thin and Mark Sanders called back. "Do you mind if I smoke, ladies? I'll open the window."

"Not in the least," said Lizzie looking to Kasia who signalled her agreement.

Mark Sanders exhaled out of the open window but Lizzie was glad when he had finished and wound the window up again. The evening air had a chill to it even though the days were warm. Lizzie felt sleepy. She looked at Kasia whose eyes were closed and whose upper body was sliding towards her. Lizzie put her arm around Kasia's shoulders and they cuddled together; within minutes, Lizzie recognised in Kasia the breathing of a sleeper.

Their route took them through the centre of Maidenhead. Before they had left it, Patrick Kenny pointed to a red glow to the South of the road. "Wonder what's going on there?"

"Do you want to go and see?"

"I don't think we should. Looks like a fire…quite a big one to make such a glow in the sky."

Lizzie was instantly alert. "Do you suppose it was a bomb?"

"Doubt it. There's not been any talk of German air raids. Probably just a house fire, sad but it happens." Mark Sanders kept glancing towards the red glow, even when he was having to turn his head slightly backwards.

They approached a junction with a road that went left and Lizzie recognised it. "Isn't this where we turn off to White Waltham?"

By then the car had passed the junction and Mark Sanders brought it to a halt. "Are you sure?"

"Pretty sure but let's check before we end up in the West Country."

Patrick Kenny offered to walk back to have a look but Mark Sanders performed a neat three point turn in the road and, reaching the junction, said, "You're right Lizzie. This is definitely it. I was too busy watching the fire."

"You can always trust a woman you see."

"Of course. I've always known that."

Inspector Hawkins surveyed the scene. The fire crew were still dousing the flames with water but had nearly put it out. He glanced at his watch, twisting his wrist to see in the beam from the headlights of the fire truck. It was one o'clock in the morning and he should be in bed. He had discovered that everyone was out of the building now, but the elderly mother of Mrs Feingold had been taken by ambulance to the hospital in Windsor suffering from smoke inhalation; the local cottage hospital was not deemed suitable. Her infirmity had meant her family had not been able to get her out quickly; they had managed to support her down the stairs and out of the back of the building and then to save themselves.

He had been called because the fire crew had been told by Mr Feingold that a large 'J' had been painted on the door of the shop. The door was now hanging from its hinges, the glass panel shattered but the remnants of that red letter were still visible. The family had been taken in by the next door neighbours but Mr Feingold stood huddled in a greatcoat staring at the scene of destruction. Hawkins approached him.

"Inspector Hawkins, Sir, from Maidenhead Police Station." Mr Feingold said nothing but looked at him briefly and returned his eyes to the shop. "I'm so sorry to hear about your mother-in-law. I am told that none of the rest of the family were injured."

"No physical injuries but…is there any future for us here?"

"I see there are still some traces of what was painted on the door."

"J for Jew. It was what the Nazis did in Germany. You remember Kristallnacht I'm sure."

"I do. You think this is a copycat action?"

"Of course. There are Jew-haters in this country as well as in Germany. What is happening there is emboldening the Nazi sympathisers here."

"Have you had any threats or damage prior to this?"

"No damage but occasionally insults. You know the sort of thing…go home filthy Jew…you're taking our jobs…that sort of thing. It's only very occasionally though. Most people here are very kind."

"I'm pleased to hear that. Is there anyone who repeatedly insults you?"

"Not really. None of my regular customers would say such things."

"Have you lived here, in Maidenhead that is, for long?"

"Ten years nearly. We moved from Golders Green in London to set up the shop here. My brother-in-law and his family live next door to us. He works at the airfield."

"White Waltham?"

"Yes."

"Thank you, Sir. Will you and your family be able to stay next door until…until the building can be repaired?"

"I think so. They are good people and, you know, we Jews support each other."

Inspector Hawkins left the poor man to his thoughts and judged that things were sufficiently under control to talk with the fire chief. He found him by the fire engine supervising the winding up of the hoses. "Inspector Hawkins from Maidenhead Police. Any thoughts about how it started?"

"You'll need this as evidence." The fireman held out a broken bottle in a brown paper bag. "Petrol bomb I'd say thrown through the shop window. It would have set things off within seconds. If you like your prunes well cooked, you'll find a few tins in there." The fireman gave a grim laugh. "As if we haven't got enough to do with normal house fires without people going around lighting them deliberately."

"Thank you Chief." I'll examine the scene outside and then go inside when you give me the all clear."

"Rightio Inspector. Could be anyone though couldn't it?"

"I'm afraid it looks at the moment like a case of needles and haystacks but you never know." There was too much debris immediately outside the shop so Inspector Hawkins began his search on the opposite side of the road. He took his torch from his pocket and began walking slowly along the pavement, shining the torch downwards and from side to side. There was no sound of aircraft so it was quite safe to do so. After a few paces, he stopped and stooped to the ground. Two cigarette stubs lay discarded on the pavement and a single match. Why would there be two cigarette stubs unless there were two people or one person standing at that spot for some time who smoked two cigarettes? Someone waiting for the right moment?

In either case, one person or two, someone may have seen them there.

Kasia had fallen asleep almost the moment she had laid her head on the pillow. Lizzie was unsettled and knew she would not sleep for a while. Laura and Olivia had not yet returned and she wondered how much longer they had stayed at the club. The evening had started with such promise. It had not been a complete disaster but the brief row between Eddie and Kasia had certainly created a tension that was impossible to dispel. Edward Melford had a darker side to his character, a rather vicious streak. She had seen it twice that day, surfacing suddenly and unnecessarily.

Kasia could clearly be fiery too but Lizzie knew there was good reason for her anger. In the darkness of the dormitory, she listened to her breathing, regular, slow and peaceful. Lizzie was glad she could sleep so soundly after such an upset.

She walked carefully in her bare feet to the window and pulled back one edge of the blackout curtain. Peering through the criss-cross tapes on the glass, applied to prevent the window shattering in the event of a nearby explosion, she looked out. A figure was standing smoking just below their window looking out over the darkened airfield. In the glow from the cigarette when sucked, she could just make out that it was Mark Sanders. He was presumably enjoying a final cigarette before turning in. She liked him. He was pleasant, unassuming and had a regard for others. She remembered him asking if Kasia wanted to leave and then talking with her and persuading her to dance again. A real gentleman.

She noticed car headlights approaching the building at some speed. The car turned into a parking space and the engine was cut. It was Melford's Jaguar. The four doors opened almost simultaneously and Melford, Swinburne and the Hulett sisters climbed out. Although she could not hear any conversation, the two women seemed to be thanking Melford and Swinburne for taking them to the club, smiling their gratitude. They then turned and started to walk away but Melford grabbed Olivia's hand and pulled her sharply towards him. She stumbled and fell against him – tipsy perhaps; his arm slipped around her waist and held her tightly against his body.

Olivia threw back her head and laughed. She wriggled and pushed herself free from Melford though he took her hand again. Swinburne waved a good night and walked into the building with Laura. Melford whispered in Olivia's ear and she shook her head though she then smiled at him. After a minute or so, they both walked into the building, Olivia's hand still held by Edward.

Mark Sanders remained standing where he had been and must have witnessed the incident. He now dropped his cigarette and extinguished it with his foot, kicking the butt into the border.

Lizzie eased the curtain back into place and shuffled over to her bed. She did not want to be at the window when the sisters came into the room. Climbing between the sheets, she lay down waiting for them. Curiosity gnawed at her mind; what had Melford been saying … though she was certain she could guess? Listening for footsteps in the corridor outside that would signal the girls returning to the room, she waited. No sound came for a while and then she heard a single set of steps on the boards of the corridor.

The door opened with a soft creak and Lizzie recognised Laura's silhouette against the landing light. "Kasia's asleep but I'm wide awake," she whispered. "Did you stay at the club much longer?"

Lizzie detected some agitation in Laura despite her whispered response. "Not much. He drives very fast does Edward so it didn't take long to get back here either."

"You enjoyed yourselves I hope."

"Yes but…oh well it doesn't matter."

"Shame about the row between Edward and Kasia."

Laura was slipping off her clothes. "Yes, both are quite quick-tempered I think." She slipped her nightdress over her head and slid under the covers. "Goodnight Lizzie."

"Goodnight." Lizzie knew that Laura was not happy about something but now was not the time to ask her. She herself was now thoroughly awake and she lay on her back listening to the sounds of the building settling down for the night.

CHAPTER 6

Arthur Bloom hugged his sister "You stay here as long as necessary."

Wiping her eyes, she pulled away and went to check on the children, huddled top and tail in one bed whilst their two cousins were in the other. They were not yet asleep and he watched through the open door as, crooning softly and stroking their heads in turn, she soothed them until they drifted off. Children seemed more able than adults to deal with such traumas though he knew from his own experience that such events would haunt them in later life.

"You must sleep yourself now, Hilda."

"Where is Benjamin? I must go to him."

"No, I will find him and bring him in. There is nothing he can do out there now. You go to bed." He hugged her again briefly and tramped downstairs to find his brother-in-law. He saw him staring forlornly at the burnt out shop, a blanket pulled over his shoulders for warmth. Arthur himself shivered. It was not just the chill in the air but the scene of desolation. Within him, something stirred, an anger that was part of him and every Jew, born from the centuries of hatred and mistrust they had endured.

"Come Benjamin. You cannot do anything out here. You must now think of Hilda and your children. Come." He put an arm around Benjamin's shoulders and steered him gently towards his own house, thankfully unscathed by the fire in the shop. He was not easily persuaded to go to bed but eventually Arthur prevailed and saw him slide into bed beside Hilda. He bade them goodnight and joined his own wife, Golda.

"How is he?"

"Very shaken...difficult to say. At the moment, he looks broken. We must sleep. I have to be at work early." He turned and kissed Golda on the lips. "Let us pray that our mother recovers and may God punish those who have brought this terror to our doors."

Arthur turned out the light. He did his best to sleep but knew at the most it would be fitful. He felt anger welling up inside him. Why did some people hate Jews so much? That question had been asked so many times down the centuries but there was no real answer. He lay in bed wondering about the kind of people who could have carried out such an attack. What was it in their minds or backgrounds that produced such hatred, that enabled them to perpetrate such acts of violence? If he passed them in the street, would he see that viciousness in their eyes or would they look like everyone else, going about their usual business?

He tried to push the thoughts out of his mind and think of happier times, the birth of their two children, the days of family rejoicing, the major events each year at the synagogue, the friends they had and yes, the many good people he met every day who were not Jews but harboured no evil towards his kind. There was good in the World but there was evil and he knew that he would have to find a way of repaying that evil: "An eye for an eye, a tooth for a tooth," he mouthed silently.

His work was generally satisfying and the people were friendly and kind. But...he thought of the arrogant gesture from that young man Melford earlier that evening, summoning him as if he were a lowly slave to come at his beck and call. Those were the people that he disliked. There was something about that young man that he did not trust, something that made him think that he could, in some complicated way, be connected to the attack on the shop. Then a memory slid into his thoughts... a few days ago...Melford with a piece of paper. Arthur Bloom started to feel better as an idea took shape in his mind. He must be at work good and early so now he must sleep for a few hours.

◆ ◆ ◆

Lizzie was still awake when she heard hurried steps in the corridor. It sounded like someone stumbling. And then she heard the sobbing. She sensed rather than saw Laura sit up. Lizzie was out of bed immediately and Laura followed. Outside the room, the corridor was lit by a single bulb. In its harsh light, the sight that confronted them was horrific. Olivia was stumbling towards them, clutching a handkerchief to her face, her whole frame convulsed with huge sobs and, between them, she was gasping for air as if drowning. Both Lizzie and Laura rushed to her and supported her.

"Livvy, what's happened?" Laura pulled the handkerchief from Olivia's face.

She said nothing but continued to sob. Her lipstick was smudged, distorting her soft mouth into a grotesque mask, her mascara had run down her cheeks, the tears causing black streaks that made a frightening contrast to her bright crimson lipstick. The top of her dress was open, the elegant buttons that had fastened it gone and one stocking appeared to have come adrift, crumpling down her leg.

Laura hugged her sister and Lizzie put her arms around both. They stayed there in the corridor for some time, frozen in that position. At last, Olivia's sobs began to subside and Laura, shushing her still, began to guide her towards the bedroom.

"Perhaps Olivia needs to talk about what's happened," Lizzie said. "We could go elsewhere so as not to wake Kasia."

Olivia shook her head and moved towards the bedroom. "I just want to go to bed."

Laura helped her sister undress and took her into her own bed where they hugged each other. Olivia sobbed a little more and then started to whisper in little short bursts. Her head was cradled against Laura so Lizzie could hear nothing other than the soft murmur of their voices. Gradually, even this faded and sleep seemed to take both the sisters.

Lizzie could not sleep. What had happened? The last time she had seen Olivia, she was with Melford and appeared to be laughingly resisting his advances. A cold hand clutched Lizzie's heart. Had Olivia suffered what she herself had done all those years ago? The feeling of revulsion was replaced by anger. Was it Melford or was it one of the others?

Slipping out of bed, Lizzie found her dressing gown in the dark and put it on. She did not know what she was expecting to find or what she would do if she did find something but she felt compelled to go looking. She tip-toed to the door and, as quietly as she could, turned the door knob. The door opened with the softest creak and she closed it again after her with the same care. She padded along the corridor to the top of the stairs. The men's rooms were along the corridor opposite. She stopped and listened. She could hear two voices talking quietly somewhere below and she crept softly down the stairs, one step at a time.

The door to the lounge was ajar and, now at the bottom of the stairs, she could hear the voices more clearly. Mark Sanders and Graham Swinburne. Their conversation seemed harmless enough. Sanders was talking about his life as a boy. Lizzie listened. She gathered that he had grown up on a country estate on the edge of Cheltenham where his father was on the staff, an under-Butler. He talked about how proud his parents were when he secured a place at Cheltenham Grammar School.

"I suppose it was there that I developed an interest in aviation. One of the former pupils was Handley-Page the aircraft designer and another was Gordon Lewis who designed the Olympus and Pegasus aero engines. So when I went to University, I studied engineering, although my first passion was really Botany."

"Fascinating isn't it how certain things in youth influence one's choices?"

"And how about you Graham?"

"Oh well, not much of a story really. I went to Eton because my father and grandfather had gone there. Then I went up to Cambridge…studied Law which I know is an unlikely background for a pilot. I started in my father's law firm after my degree but, you know, I had a hankering for something more exciting."

"And I assume you were not able to join up with the regular armed services."

"No. Rugby injury from school…damaged the old spine you know. In reality, it doesn't stop me from doing anything though I have to be careful but the MOD decided it made me unfit for active service."

"But no more rugby presumably?"

"No indeed, spend my spare time in amateur dramatics actually. And what's your passion?"

"Still Botany…I'm fascinated by the enormous variety of plants."

Interesting though it was, there was nothing happening which suggested either Sanders nor Swinburne had done anything that would have caused such upset to Olivia. That left Melford and Kenny. She knew it was Melford. Everything she had seen of him indicated an arrogant disregard for others. He had drunk quite a lot, was clearly feeling amorous and attracted towards Olivia. She shuddered at the scene that was forming in her mind.

Should she ask Mark Sanders and Graham Swinburne if they knew what had happened? Would they be having such a calm, ordinary conversation if they had witnessed the kind of scene that would have caused Olivia such distress? She thought not.

Nothing to be done until the morning light, hopefully, brought clarity.

❖ ❖ ❖

In his torchlight, Inspector Hawkins examined the two cigarette butts. Both were filtered and he could just make out printed above the filter what he thought said 'Du Maurier'. The posters advertising that brand of cigarettes came to mind. Nearly always, they featured elegant and wealthy women – attractive of course – the cigarette cocked prominently between slender fingers with brightly coloured nails. 'Filtered for perfection' the adverts often said under the main caption.

But these had not been smoked by women. There were no tell-tale signs of lipstick on the butts and no woman of the sort who would smoke such a cigarette would be out on the street without lipstick. In fact, no woman of that sort of class would be hanging around on such a street at night. Du Maurier were of course smoked by men too but their cost made them the preserve of the wealthy. What would a rich man or men be doing on this kind of street at night?

He was intrigued. Those butts could be a very important clue.

Deep in thought, Inspector Hawkins turned his attention to the shop itself. The fire chief waved him in and he trod gingerly over the broken glass and smouldering pieces of wood. It was a sorry sight. Some of the shelving had collapsed, burnt through, but much of it was still in place though the products on the shelves had either been destroyed or badly damaged. There were tins with the labels blackened and illegible and some had even distorted in the heat. The building itself looked sound – something the fire chief had confirmed earlier – but it would need a lot of work, expensive work, to put it right. The main shop window onto the street had gone, presumably broken by the bottle thrown through it.

What kind of person could do that? How could you fling a petrol bomb through a window knowing that a family was upstairs sleeping after a long day in the shop? Hawkins shook his head. He would have to send Drake out in the morning to have another look as it was too difficult to see. He was not sure that anything of use could be recovered from the scene but they had to look thoroughly.

Hawkins turned towards the street and imagined what the assailant must have done. He must have stood some yards from the shop, probably in the middle of the road in order to fling the bottle without injuring himself. It was just possible that someone had been looking out of the window and seen what had happened. House to house search in the morning then. PC Teal would have to forego his Sunday off and wear out some shoe leather.

It was the worst incident they had had so far, by far the worst. Things were getting very serious.

CHAPTER 7

Lizzie opened her eyes. The blackout curtains had been pulled aside a little, letting a shaft of early morning sunlight stroke the end of her bed. She fumbled for her watch on the small bedside cabinet and blinked away the sleep so she could read it. Just approaching seven hundred hours. Looking around the room, she could see that Kasia's bed was already empty, Olivia's bed had not been used and it looked as though only one person lay in Laura's. Pulling her legs up, she swung her feet to the floor.

She tip-toed over to Laura's bed; the figure lay almost completely covered, blankets pulled up over her head, but a strand of blonde hair had escaped: Olivia, still sleeping soundly and Laura up and about. In her mind lay an image of a figure silhouetted against the landing light leaving the room after she herself had returned. Was it real or a figment of her troubled brain?

Swinging her dressing gown around her shoulders, she left the room and stepped quietly along the corridor to the bathroom. It was not long before she was back in the room dressing. It should be a lovely, relaxing day but the events of the previous night troubled her. She wanted to find Kasia to make sure she had been able to sleep for a sensible amount of time after her row with Melford and, even more, she wanted to find Laura to find out what had happened to Olivia. Her thoughts were running wild and she hoped that her fears would not be confirmed.

Kasia was in the lounge reading a manual of aircraft. She seemed calm – perhaps too calm – and Lizzie wondered if this was an attempt on her part to prevent herself crumbling.

"Did you sleep, Kasia?"

She looked up from the book. "I did thank you Lizzie."

"I was glad to see you went to sleep quickly...I thought after the evening you may have had difficulty."

"I would not let someone like Melford trouble me. He is just a pompous, spoilt boy."

There was anger behind the remark despite the sentiment expressed. Lizzie decided to leave it be and sauntered into the mess to see what time breakfast would be served. Arthur Bloom, the steward who had served in the bar before dinner the previous evening, was setting the last table. Placing the cutlery on the final cover, he looked up.

"Morning Mr Bloom. Looks like another fine day."

Bloom's eyes darted to her face and to the window. He seemed restless. "Very pleasant Miss." His face had a look of severity, the cheek bones prominent and the nose quite pointed. No smile softened the contours of his lips nor lit his eyes. He said no more and began to walk towards the kitchen where someone was whistling and clattering saucepans.

"We have a rest day, today...no flying. I'm looking forward to it."

Again he said nothing and disappeared into the kitchen. The whistling stopped. Lizzie was bemused. She had not got as far as asking what time breakfast would be served. She hovered in the mess, looking out over the silent airfield - so peaceful, a few birds chattering in the shrubs close to the building but no other sound. The sun was already well into the sky, ducking behind the occasional puffy, white cloud as if playing hide and seek. It was a perfect day for flying and, much as though she was looking forward to a day off, she would have liked to be up there, feeling the wind in her face and hearing the growl of the engine.

The kitchen door opened and Bloom returned to the mess carrying a jug of apple juice.

"Ah, Mr Bloom, what time will you start serving

breakfast?"

He glanced at his watch. "Should be eight o'clock on Sunday." Again no smile accompanied his answer, his face remaining impassive and his eyes cold.

"Thank you." Lizzie returned to the lounge where Kasia was still engrossed in her aircraft manual. Laura had joined her but was standing at the other end of the room, looking out across the airfield. Lizzie approached her but she seemed deep in thought.

"Good morning Laura."

She turned briefly, looked at Lizzie and resumed her study of the airfield. She seemed to be looking at nothing in particular. "Morning."

"Was...is Olivia alright?"

"She was still asleep when I left the room."

"Did she...say what had happened?"

"Yes."

Lizzie waited but Laura said nothing more until Lizzie had turned to walk away from her. Then Laura added, "It's sorted out now anyway."

Lizzie did not know what that meant. Perhaps it was that Olivia had got over whatever upset she had had; perhaps Laura had tackled the person who had upset her. It was clear that Laura was going to say no more and Lizzie had to stifle her curiosity. It was strange though, how the three people she had seen so far that morning seemed so cold, uncommunicative, troubled.

The back door banged shut and Mavis Brown looked up. Her daughter, Sheila, flung her bag onto the kitchen top and shook her hair.

"Busy night, Love?"

"Wasn't it just. We had an old lady brought in about

midnight who had been rescued from a fire in a shop in Maidenhead apparently. She was not in a good way, poor old dear. Smoke had got to her. We made her as comfortable as we could but her breathing wasn't good."

"Dear oh dear, that's terrible. Anyway, you go and sit down, Love, and I'll make you some breakfast. You can get that down you and then have a good sleep."

"Thanks Mum. Is Dad not up yet?"

"Nah, not 'im. You know what he's like on Sunday morning...probably too much to drink last night. I didn't hear him come in. I'd gone up and was fast asleep."

"Course you had a busy day yesterday didn't you? Did it go off alright?"

"Yes. Mrs T and her guests were very complimentary." Mavis Brown put a steaming mug of tea on the table by her daughter in the back room. "There y'are Love. Drink that while I make you some bread and dripping. You can have a good sleep today so you're ready for tonight. Goodness it's a hard life isn't it?"

"Yeah, it is but I'm doing my bit, that's what matters."

"You are, Love. No one can say that this family isn't doing something for the war what with William fighting and you nursing. As long as they don't send you out to France or somewhere to look after the injured there."

Sheila slurped her tea. "No danger of that while I'm still training. By the way, I'm going out later this afternoon."

Mavis Brown came through from the kitchen again. "Where you going then?"

"Going for a walk by the river."

"Mmm. Interesting. Who with?"

"Now that would be telling wouldn't it?" Sheila grinned cheekily at her mother who decided she would pursue that later. Sheila couldn't keep a secret for long.

PC Brian Teal sighed deeply as he leant his bike against the wall. This was supposed to be a day off. He had plans to walk by the river later in the afternoon with his new sweetheart, Sheila. She was lovely. Met her a couple of weeks ago at a dance. He pictured her pretty face and the way her hair swung around her as she danced. And such a dancer! He couldn't believe his luck when she agreed to him walking her to the bus stop. Lived in Windsor but that wasn't far away, just a short bike ride. He had asked her out to the pictures and again she had agreed, readily and with a lovely smile. In truth he had always been shy around girls, but with her it was different.

He couldn't bear to wish her goodnight and leave so he had hovered, uncertain, until the bus had drawn up. She'd stood on tip-toe, leaned forward and kissed him on the cheek. "Night, night," she'd said and turned quickly to hop on the platform. As the bus had pulled away, she'd blown him a kiss and given him a dazzling smile. God she was lovely.

It would be something special to walk along the river at Windsor with such a lovely girl and he dreaded the thought that he may not get done in time to cycle over to Windsor by four o'clock. He glanced at his watch. Only eight o'clock so he had plenty of time. She worked nights at the moment so she would get home, have a few hours kip and then meet him. A couple of hours together and she would have to have a meal and sort herself out ready for work.

He looked one way up Grenfell Road from the burnt out shop and then the other way. South Road would also need to be dealt with as it joined Grenfell pretty well opposite the shop. He sighed. "Best get to it," he muttered

Holding his notebook and pencil in one hand, he knocked on the first door beside the shop on the section of Grenfell Road that led towards the station. At first there was no response but, at the second knock, he heard feet shuffling inside. The door was opened by an elderly man.

"What is it?"

"PC Teal from Maidenhead Police, Sir. We're investigating the fire at the shop last night. Did you see anything out of the ordinary, anyone hanging about outside, that sort of thing? Probably quite late, maybe eleven o'clock last night."

"We were in bed Constable so saw and heard nothing. Didn't know what was going on until I heard the bell on the fire engine. Sorry, can't help you."

"Thank you anyway, Sir."

PC Teal proceeded down the street. Drake had told him to go about a hundred yards each way from the shop and the same down South Road. Most of the houses were terraced so no long driveways thankfully. No one had seen nor heard anything. It seemed to be turning into a wild goose chase. He worked his way back up Grenfell Road and then turned into South Road. Still nothing. He returned to Grenfell Road, moving in the opposite direction to earlier and starting at the corner with South Road. The last house he tried, the furthest from the shop on that side was a trim, well maintained house with some nice flowers growing in the tiny patch of garden at the front.

Pad and pencil at the ready, he knocked. The door was answered by a middle-aged woman. He posed the same question as he had already asked dozens of times.

"Oooh terrible thing that fire. Was it started deliberately? It's awful…such lovely people the Feingolds. No, I didn't hear anything but my husband came in quite late last night, I'll just get him."

The man that appeared in the doorway was small and alert. He held a newspaper in one hand and a pair of glasses in the other. "Yes Officer. I came home at about eleven o'clock I'd say from the pub. Met a couple of friends there."

"Did your route take you by the shop, Sir."

"Yes, I came up South Road."

"Did you see anything out of the ordinary, anyone

hanging around?"

"Well it wasn't that strange but there were two men standing on the corner having a cigarette and talking about football. I wished them good evening and carried on. They'd probably been to another pub somewhere and were having a chat before going their separate ways home."

PC Teal seized eagerly on the information. "Did you get a look at them, Sir? Did you recognise them? Would you know them again?"

"No Officer, I'm afraid not. Thing is they had hats on, pulled low, and scarves around their necks but pulled up to their chins. I suppose that was a bit odd because it wasn't cold last night. One was about my height, the other was taller."

PC Teal wrote down the gentleman's name and his address. "That is very helpful, Sir. If you think of anything else, please get in touch with the station."

"Will do, Constable."

A result! PC Teal questioned the remaining residents of Grenfell Road with brisk efficiency but there was nothing more to add. He was not concerned – he had as much as could reasonably be expected from a house to house about events late at night. He would report to the Inspector or Sergeant Drake and perhaps he could then slip off to see his new sweetheart. He smiled to himself at the thought of her lovely face and cheeky smile. She was gorgeous. He swung his leg over his bicycle and pedalled off whistling happily.

CHAPTER 8

Kasia smiled. "I could not go to Synagogue yesterday so I come to your church."

"That would be lovely, Kasia. According to Bloom, it's a bit of a walk but it's such a lovely morning."

Laura came down the stairs, the same cold expression on her face as earlier but Lizzie was pleased to see Olivia behind her. Her face had been made up, she was, as always, dressed impeccably but the playful light in her eyes, the vivacity that characterised her, had gone. The beautiful lines of her face were set in an unflinching mask, a warning that she was closed to questions.

"Just Graham to come now." The four young women waited in the foyer in silence. Lizzie was dying to ask Olivia what had happened but again she stifled her curiosity. Watching Olivia's face carefully, she said, "I haven't seen Melford this morning yet. Have any of you?"

Almost simultaneously, Laura and Kasia said "No" with an abruptness that surprised Lizzie. Olivia's expression did not change, not the slightest flicker of anxiety in her eyes. Perhaps Melford was not her tormentor.

"Probably had too much to drink last night." Lizzie laughed but no one joined her.

Graham Swinburne jumped down the last two steps of the stair. "Sadly Sanders is not coming with us so we will have to walk. Kenny's borrowed a bike and gone into Maidenhead to find a Catholic church. So let's go."

Laura and Olivia walked arm in arm and Lizzie linked her arm with Kasia but Graham Swinburne said it wasn't fair that he was left out. Lizzie broke free of Kasia. "Come on then you poor man, you can have two of us." She linked arms with him and he took Kasia on the other side. She and Swinburne chattered about their homes and families but Kasia could not be persuaded to join in. She walked in silence, seemingly locked in her own thoughts.

The church of St John the Baptist was set some way out of the village of White Waltham and had clearly been built as part of a country estate. The manor house was not far away and had that look of solidity one always associates with the English countryside. The church itself was beautiful, built with stone quoins and walls of knapped flint. It was not large but had a pleasing symmetry.

"I have no intention of getting married," announced Lizzie, "but, if I do, I would like it to be in such a church."

Graham Swinburne laughed. "And why, pray, are you so sure that you will never marry?"

"I have no intention of being at the beck and call of any man. I want to do a job and keep myself. I want to have my own identity, not just be someone's wife."

"Well that's clear enough."

Kasia spoke for the first time since leaving the airfield buildings. "There are men who would respect your independence, Lizzie."

"Perhaps, but it's finding one."

"I beg to offer myself as a supreme example of the enlightened male."

"I don't wish to offend you, Graham, but from what I've seen, those sentiments tend to get forgotten very quickly once the ring is on the finger."

"I wonder, Lizzie, if there is something more to your antipathy towards marriage?"

Lizzie could feel the eyes of everyone on her. She felt a coldness creeping through her, a danger of revealing too much. Part of her wanted to shout an explanation, allow that bottled anger to explode but she knew she must not. She must keep control. She had vowed to herself that no one would know and she was determined to keep it that way. "No more than I've already said. I want to keep my independence."

They filed into the church which was already reasonably populated with mainly elderly people. A village church, with many men off at the fighting, would have depleted numbers. They took an empty pew towards the back, Graham Swinburne graciously ushering Kasia in first, followed by Lizzie, Olivia and Laura. He took his seat next to the aisle.

It was a communion service. When they reached the point in the service for the sermon, the rector, a scholarly man with glasses in his early sixties, climbed the steps to the pulpit. "My dear friends, you have heard me say before that we live in troubled times. I received news this morning that, last night, a small shop in Maidenhead – what we would call a corner store though not strictly on a corner – was attacked. Someone, unknown, threw a petrol bomb into the shop, causing a fire." There was a muffled gasp from the congregation.

"The shop owners, a Jewish family, lived above the shop. Fortunately, they were unharmed except for an old lady who is now in hospital suffering from smoke inhalation. Today we celebrate Whit Sunday, the time when the Holy Spirit descended on the Disciples which was the subject of our first reading. Today's Gospel from John comes at the Last Supper when Jesus is preparing to leave his earthly life. It has several messages starting with those well-known words, 'If ye love me, keep my commandments.' The sixth commandment is clear enough – thou shalt not kill – but we are also instructed in an earlier passage from John's Gospel to love our neighbour as ourselves. Such an act of violence as was perpetrated last night surely breaks everything that Jesus stood for. We must hold fast to Jesus's instruction to love one another, whether that be Jew, Pole or even German."

Lizzie's mind wandered to the horror of an attack at night and she realised that the glow in the sky they had seen as they drove through Maidenhead probably came from that fire. She imagined the burst of flame as the petrol bomb exploded, the raging inferno, the smoke. Kasia, sitting beside her, went rigid. When she looked at her face, it was full of anger, the mouth drawn tight and her dark brows deeply furrowed. Lizzie's hand crept onto Kasia's which was balled into a fist on her knee. She enclosed it and squeezed gently. Her attention returned to the sermon.

"That same lesson also contains the line, 'Let not your heart be troubled, neither let it be afraid.' How can we not be troubled, not be afraid? God is asking something of us that is hugely difficult, that is to trust Him when the World seems determined on destruction. I do not pretend it is easy but we must try to be like the child in distress who is gathered into its mother's arms and is completely sure that the pain being experienced will be taken away. I suppose it is asking us not to worry about what happens on Earth, because the life we need to focus on is in Heaven." The Rector turned over a page.

"Today's Gospel assures us of a comforter being sent who is the Holy Spirit – a sign within us of God's presence. The passage of course also includes those wonderful lines, 'Peace I leave with you, my peace I give unto you'. It is hard indeed in these times to see where that peace may be obtained but it will come, my friends, it will come." The rector made the sign of the cross and carefully stepped down from the pulpit.

Lizzie saw that Olivia, sitting on her other side, was hugging herself, her face pulled tight, preventing a tear squeezing from her eyes. Laura's arm went around her shoulders and Lizzie slipped her arm around Olivia's waist. They held her between them until her body relaxed.

After the service, they were all in sombre mood. They walked back along the lane to White Waltham in silence. Lizzie was walking close to Olivia who at last spoke. "You will naturally want to know what happened last night, Lizzie. Let me just say that Edward Melford made advances that were unwelcome."

"I feared that was the case but I hope...I hope you were able to get away before anything..."

"Not quite."

Lizzie realised she did not wish to say more but she herself was plunged into anger again despite the Rector's sermon. What was wrong with men? Why could they not accept that women did not always want to receive their sexual attentions. She tried to push from her mind the experiences she had herself endured but the fury remained. She had made herself strong, had always been determined that no man would ever again subject her to anything that belittled or diminished her. She knew at times around men her tongue could be acid but better that than have unwelcome comment or attention. She would like to give Melford a verbal whipping and perhaps the chance would arise.

When they arrived at the airfield, the recruits and two of the instructors, Roger Carlisle and Stephanie Garret, were gathered in the lounge enjoying a drink before Sunday lunch. "Ah, here come the church goers. Good service?" Carlisle had not picked up the serious expressions on their faces.

Lizzie offered an explanation though she knew that it was not a full account of the sombre mood of her fellow women. "The service and the church were both lovely but the Rector gave some very disturbing news at the start of his sermon. A fire was started deliberately at a shop in Maidenhead last night…we saw the glow of it as we drove back. It was owned by a Jewish family."

There was a crash of glass from the bar and everybody turned to see Arthur Bloom in his steward's white coat. "I do apologise ladies and Gentlemen. I'm not quite myself today." He bent to pick up the pieces of glass from the floor and fetched a dustpan and brush for the small slivers. Lizzie could see his face. The troubled expression he had worn that morning had not disappeared; if anything, he looked more agitated… hence the dropped glass.

"In Maidenhead? Good grief. We have come to expect such atrocities in Germany but Maidenhead!" Stephanie Garrett expressed the shock those hearing the news for the first time felt.

The four young women left the lounge to put their coats back in their room. Lizzie was last to leave the room and, as the others began to climb the stairs, she heard Swinburne's voice and lingered on the bottom step.

"Still no sign of Melford?"

"I've not seen him at all this morning." She could just see Mark Sanders lower the newspaper he was reading and respond. "Probably sleeping off the drink…he had quite a bit last night."

Swinburne laughed. "I'll pop up when I've finished my drink and tip him out of bed."

"Why not let him sleep if he wants to?" suggested Sanders.

"Not good for a chap to sleep half the day…makes the hangover worse in my experience."

Lizzie caught up with the others just before they reached the room. Once inside, she threw her coat on the bed. Olivia sat at the mirror to check her make-up while Laura hovered behind her, making encouraging noises and complimenting her. Kasia went to visit the toilet.

"I'll see you down there girls," Lizzie called. "We might have time for a sherry before lunch is served."

As she approached the top of the stairs, Graham Swinburne was coming towards her from the men's corridor, his face ashen and his mouth open. "Lizzie…Lizzie…" he pointed down the corridor.

"What is it Graham?" She held his upper arms and shook him.

"Come and see…no it's perhaps too unbearable."

"I can deal with anything that you can Graham."

She turned Swinburne around and followed him down the corridor. Slowly, as if they might be confronted by a wild tiger, he turned into a room on the left. He pointed to the bed. Edward Melford, still clothed, lay there, a small silver-handled knife protruding from his stomach. A little blood had soaked into his shirt and had darkened as it had congealed. Lizzie took two rapid paces towards him and felt his neck.

There was no pulse; he was stone cold.

CHAPTER 9

"So Teal, you've got some useful information?" Sergeant Drake looked at the Constable's youthful face and remembered the excitement he had once felt at discovering something that could be helpful to an investigation. "I think perhaps you should report to the Inspector directly. Come on."

Sergeant Drake tapped on the office door and walked in. Inspector Hawkins was behind his desk staring at two cigarette butts, a used match and a broken bottle. He looked up.

"Sir, PC Teal has picked up something from the house to house on Grenfell Road."

Brian Teal flipped open his notepad and checked the name. "A Mr Arnold Foster of Grenfell Road was walking home from the pub last night and passed two men who were standing opposite the shop, on the corner of Grenfell and South Roads. They were smoking and talking about football. Couldn't give a description other than one was taller than the other. They both wore hats pulled low and scarves up around their chins."

Hawkins looked thoughtful. "Two men smoking rather than one man waiting for some time while he smoked two cigarettes then. Did your Mr Foster say anything about accents? Were they foreign, were they working class, middle class?"

Teal looked a little crestfallen. "He didn't say, Sir....sorry."

"You'll need to go back and ask him. I suppose tomorrow will do. We're not going to get very far today."

"Looks a bit like a needle in a haystack again, Sir, doesn't it?"

"It does Sergeant except we do have these. Something very curious. These cigarettes are du Maurier – that's quite an expensive brand and one that is often advertised to women as being classy and elegant though of course it is smoked by men too...but I would guess wealthier men. These are not what your average man smokes. Our two possible attackers were clearly men according to Mr Foster. This bottle is or was, according to what is embossed on the base, a bottle of IPA from Thomas Wethered's Brewery in Marlow."

Teal and Drake were engrossed as neither would have thought to give such items that degree of scrutiny. The Inspector continued. "We should be able to find out tomorrow which pubs or off-licences are supplied by Wethered's with this particular beer. It may be quite a few but you never know."

"Sir, will you need me for anything else today...it's just that I've..."

"No thank you Constable. Well done this morning and thank you for coming in on your day off. You can take time in lieu or put in for overtime."

"Yes Sir. Thank you Sir." PC Teal was out the door before Hawkins thought of something else for him to do. A quick cycle home, grab something to eat and change and he'd be over at Windsor in good time. As he left the building, he heard the telephone ring.

Lizzie and Graham Swinburne stumbled down the stairs and into the lounge. Lizzie did not wait but blurted out the news. "Melford is dead...he's been stabbed."

The room went silent, faces turned towards her and someone repeated "Stabbed!" not even a question. Mark Sanders had said nothing but had stood up in silent shock. The three women whom Lizzie had left upstairs entered the room quietly, sensing something terrible had happened.

"We need to call the Police," Lizzie added.

"I'll do that," Roger Carlisle took charge. "No one must

go near Melford's room." He bustled away to the office to make the calls. He telephoned the Police and straight after telephoned Trueman who said he would come immediately. Inspector Hawkins from the Police was very clear that no one must enter the room. Carlisle explained, of course, that two people had - that's how the body had been discovered - but they had touched nothing.

Whilst he was out of the room, questions started to be asked, slowly, hesitantly. Graham Swinburne seemed unable to speak so Lizzie explained how he had gone to Melford's room to get him up only to discover the body. He had bumped into her when he was staggering along the corridor outside and the two of them had entered the room.

"I checked for a pulse in his neck but there was nothing. I was not surprised because his shirt was stained with blood."

Olivia stifled a cry. Her hand went to her face and she fled from the room, followed by Laura.

"But who would do such a thing?" Patrick Kenny asked of no one in particular.

"Perhaps an intruder...someone from outside." No one responded to Sanders' suggestion. "Just a guess." He shrugged.

Roger Carlisle returned and repeated the instruction regarding entering the room...not that anyone had any intention of going in. "The Police will be here as soon as possible. In the meantime, no one must leave the building. I realise you may not have any appetite but I think we should have the lunch that has been prepared for us. Please follow me. I assume we are ready Mr Bloom."

"Yes Sir. Everything ready as one would expect." Bloom seemed to have regained his composure though when Lizzie smiled at him, he averted his eyes.

There was little conversation over lunch. Before the soup was served, Laura brought Olivia by the hand into the mess and they sat at the same table as the previous night with all the new recruits, except of course Edward Melford whose chair remained vacant.

Patrick Kenny finished his soup and looked at Melford's empty chair. "It's like Macbeth – Banquo's ghost."

No one laughed. "Perhaps a little in poor taste old boy," said Graham Swinburne.

"Yes perhaps. At least no one is acting strangely like Macbeth. Probably means we're all in the clear."

Olivia lifted her hand to her face and Laura gripped her arm. She seemed to fight with herself and then relaxed enough to continue dipping her spoon in the soup, though she did not appear to be consuming any .

"What happens now?" Mark Sanders asked.

"The Police come, examine the crime scene and then interview everyone who was in the building at the time of death...if they can establish when that was." Graham Swinburne's face was still pale from the shock of the discovery.

"I suppose it must have been someone who was here overnight, unless of course it was an intruder, as Mark said. I think the sleuths always try to work out who was the last person to see the victim alive"

"That's the tricky bit though isn't it and, until we know when he died, there's not much point in speculating? Let's leave it to the Police." Graham Swinburne had recovered but still looked shaken. Lizzie looked around the table. Olivia may have been the last person to see Melford alive but, as Graham Swinburne said, when was Melford killed? It could have been late the previous night or it could have been early that morning. She began to run through events in her mind involving Edward Melford: the incident with John Hale the member of the ground crew yesterday afternoon, that tiny incident in the bar before dinner with the steward, Arthur Bloom, something that perhaps no one else had noticed but the way Melford had clicked his fingers at him and the look he had given in return. But could such insignificant sleights as those result in murder? Surely not? She looked around the table. She knew nothing really about Graham Swinburne, Mark Sanders and Patrick Kenny. What connections may there be, what animosities?

And then there was Kasia, deep, silent, a terrible anger locked inside her. It was Kasia who troubled Lizzie. Lizzie looked at her now. She was saying nothing and her face was entirely blank, no expression betraying her thoughts.

◆ ◆ ◆

The sun played on the surface of the river, sending shards of sparkling light in all directions but when it disappeared behind a cloud, the water went dark, uninteresting, losing its magic. Brian Teal sat on a park bench with Sheila Brown beside him. His heart lifted. This was what life should be, a beautiful day spent in the company of a gorgeous girl. Sheila was very chatty, telling him all about her work, the staff there and some of the patients. She had plenty to say about the Matron on her ward.

"God she's a little Hitler. She wants everything done an hour ago. I mean how're you supposed to know what she wants done before she tells you? If you try to say anything, she says 'I expect you to use your initiative.' I feel like saying sometimes that I ain't got none. Not paid to think."

"But you like nursing don't you?"

"Yeah…if I'm honest I do, despite the old dragon. It makes me feel…you know…important…no I don't mean like I'm an important person…I mean it makes me feel I'm doing my bit. I can't go and fight but I can help out that way."

"Yeah, that's important."

"What about you then? I mean how come you didn't get called up?"

"Reserved occupation, see. There's got to be law and order at home. You wouldn't believe what some people get up to even when there's a war on."

"Like what?"

"Well last night, someone threw a petrol bomb – that's a bottle filled with petrol with a rag stuffed into the neck –

through a shop window in Maidenhead. Started a fire...gutted the shop but I think the people were okay apart from one."

"We had an old lady brought in last night, must have been about midnight, suffering from smoke inhalation from a fire. I bet that was the same place."

"Probably. Not aware of any other fires in Maidenhead last night."

"So why would someone bomb a shop?"

"The shop owners are Jews." Brain Teal stated it bluntly, expecting Sheila to understand.

"But that's terrible. That's the sort of thing that Hitler's thugs do. Why attack innocent people?"

Brian Teal sighed. "I don't know but you see what I mean. There's got to be Police when you have that sort of thing happening."

"Do you have to investigate it?"

This was an opportunity to impress. He spoke as casually as he could. "Of course. I was investigating this morning...discovered that two men had been hanging around the shop just before the fire started. We'll get them. No one evades the law for long."

"Let's walk a bit." They both stood and Sheila slipped her arm through Brian's. "Don't you get scared when you're dealing with criminals like that, I mean thugs who could attack innocent people? They must be monsters."

"Nah, not me. All in a day's work it is. You get used to it I suppose...like you probably get used to seeing blood."

"I suppose that's it but it's a shame that we have to get used to those things."

They fell silent and strolled along the towpath by the river. The ducks were mainly untroubled by their presence but occasionally one or two would waddle to the edge of the river and jump into the water with a squawk. A pair of swans swam slowly and majestically upstream, looking down at the lesser fowl with disdain, untouchable in their superior size and power. A cacophony of bird song assaulted the ears of those enjoying the fine May day, the trees alive with chattering starlings.

Brian Teal's arm slid around Sheila's shoulders. He felt a thrill when she did not remove it. He pulled her gently closer. "Shame we haven't got long today."

"I know but there'll be other days." She turned to him and smiled, her eyes glinting with playfulness.

Should he kiss her? He so wanted to put his lips against her lovely soft mouth but he didn't want to do anything that might alarm her and make her pull away from him like a frightened duck. He contented himself with the lovely proximity as they strolled along. A kiss on the cheek, that would be the thing, when he left her and maybe, just maybe, she would turn her head and their lips would touch.

CHAPTER 10

Inspector Hawkins panned his eyes around the room. The body lay on its back on the bed, a small red patch on the shirt around the knife. The top button of the shirt was undone; a tie had been discarded on the floor. Two small glasses, used, were on the small chest of drawers with a half empty bottle of port beside them. There had been a visitor. He stooped to look at the glasses more carefully. The smallest trace of lipstick smeared the rim of one glass. A woman then. One blackout curtain had been pulled aside and the window was slightly open.

He leaned over to examine the handle of the knife more carefully. It was quite ornate, silver, small. Some sort of ceremonial knife or perhaps a letter opener? Probably no chance of lifting fingerprints from it because of the intricate design in relief on the handle. He decided to wait for the doctor before pulling it out just in case the wound was still fresh, though judging by the blood on the shirt, it had stopped flowing some time ago.

His eye fell on the bedside cabinet. As well as the lamp, there was a book, 'The Greater Britain' by Oswald Mosley. Gingerly, Hawkins lifted the front cover using his handkerchief. His eye glanced down the publication information. First published in 1932. Hawkins stood up and his eyes narrowed. That was the period when Mosley was campaigning for the working classes and proposing fairly radical changes to the way the Country was run. It was before the very public support for the Nazis and anti-semitism. Interesting that the victim was reading it. He let the front cover drop.

Then he froze.

Behind the base of the lamp, not immediately visible,

was a packet of cigarettes. Du Maurier. The same brand as the two butts he had found in the street in Maidenhead. What connection was there between a trainee pilot, who appeared to be wealthy judging by his clothing, and two men attacking a Jewish shop? Was this man one of the attackers?

He turned his attention to the desk which had a drawer at one side and an opening beneath it. One photograph was propped on a stand: a group of young men in evening suits each wearing that supercilious expression of the very rich and under it the legend, 'The Bullingdon Club 1935'. A single blank sheet of paper lay on the desk with an opened envelope beside it. A copy of the bible, probably positioned in every room, was in the open section but nothing else. The drawer of the desk revealed only a few personal effects, a writing pad and three more unopened packets of Du Maurier cigarettes. Hawkins carefully pulled the letter from its envelope and ran his eye over the first page. It was chatty, upbeat, snippets of news from home. He glanced at the end: 'Your loving Mother and Father' and then a signature and kisses. But... there was no photograph of a loved one anywhere in the room.

Hawkins gingerly lifted the blank sheet of paper. It was the size that one would use to write a letter - no water mark just a slight crinkling of the paper. It had obviously been pulled from a pad as one end had traces of the glue; it had been folded once. He glanced into the waste-paper basket and retrieved a crumpled envelope. Straightening it out, he saw it was addressed in large, slightly childish handwriting to Melford at White Waltham. In contrast, the first page of the letter from the parents was embossed with the address and the second page matched the colour and texture of the first. Strange that the son did not use a similar quality notepaper. He checked the writing pad. It was not embossed but was of a superior quality and very different to the single sheet.

How would his parents react to the news of his death? Many parents had already received such news but they perhaps had the comfort of knowing their sons gave their lives fighting for a worthy cause. This man's parents would have no such comfort; they would have to face the fact that their son was hated enough by another to be killed.

The chest of drawers produced nothing of interest either, just clothes as one would expect but, as he turned, something caught his eye. It was a very small blob of green just under the bed. A button covered in green silk. From a waistcoat perhaps? He checked the wardrobe again. No buttons missing and nothing that would have a button like that. A button from a dress then.

A jacket was hanging on the back of the only chair in the room. Hawkins opened the left side and looked for the label. *Davies & Son, Savile Row* was emblazoned on the inside pocket. The lining of the jacket was a deep blue silk. Very definitely a man from a wealthy family. Using his handkerchief again, he slid his hand into the inside pocket, withdrew a bulging wallet and flicked it open. It was stuffed with cash, several of the notes of large denominations, confirming his wealth. In the wallet was a single photograph, the victim in graduate gown and mortar with an older couple, probably his parents.

There were also three membership cards, one for the Café de Paris in Coventry Street, one for a gentleman's club in Mayfair and the third for The British Union of Fascists. How did such an affiliation square with being a member of the ATA? Was Edward Melford a spy?

His cogitations were interrupted by a soft tap on the door. He turned to see a tall, well-dressed man. "Is it alright for me to enter?"

"Just a short way."

The visitor held out his hand. "Commander Trueman, Richard Trueman. I'm in charge of the ATA, run the base."

"Ah yes. Inspector Hawkins from Maidenhead Police. Glad to meet you though I could wish for a better situation."

"Indeed. This is a bad business. Shocking. I suppose it must have been an intruder."

Hawkins said nothing for a moment. "I've just about

finished here. The room must be kept out of bounds until the doctor has been and the body removed."

"Of course, Inspector."

"We will need to question everyone so perhaps we could go somewhere...less distressing and I could start with you, Sir."

Trueman led Hawkins along the corridor, down the stairs, past the lounge where all the residents were gathered in quiet expectation, to his office. When they were seated, Hawkins took out a notepad from his coat pocket and a pencil and sat, one knee over the other with the pencil hovering over the pad.

"I'm assuming that there will be no involvement of the RAF Police in this investigation, Sir?"

"That's correct, Inspector. The ATA is a civilian organisation and, unless RAF personnel are involved in this terrible event - possible because there is an RAF unit based here – you are the proper authority to investigate."

"Do you live on the base, Sir?"

"No I live in Windsor. I left here after the last briefing yesterday afternoon and went home. My wife and I were entertaining the other two instructors who are working with this group of recruits, that's Stephanie Garrett and Roger Carlisle. They don't live on the base either but often join the recruits for meals, hence their presence today for lunch."

"Tell me about the deceased. Was he popular... outward-going...reserved?" Hawkins noticed how Trueman shifted his position on the chair and cleared his throat. He was well used to tactics to create thinking time and immediately recognised a difficulty in answering his question.

"We discussed the recruits last night after dinner. I think we were agreed that Edward Melford could make a very good pilot though of course that's early days...flight training has only just started. You may not know that he comes...sorry came....from a very wealthy family. Father is General Melford and they have a country house near Cheltenham. Sorry, I've just thought, I need to contact his parents. Poor people will be devastated."

"All in good time, Sir. You were saying about the deceased."

"Yes, sorry Inspector, but the shock you know. As far as I can tell, he did not flaunt his wealth though he made no secret of it. He seemed…quite a generous young man, a cheerful, friendly disposition."

Hawkins picked up Trueman's hesitancy. "But?"

"There is a 'but'. When he brought his aircraft into land yesterday, he did not make a good landing – quite natural for a trainee pilot – but he was very angry and, before, he could be stopped, went into the hangar and blamed one of the ground crew. Said there was a fault. There was no fault it's just that the Tiger Moth has some characteristics which can catch out the inexperienced. So, beneath a very urbane, pleasant exterior, there does seem to lurk an anger."

"Any thoughts as to where that might stem from?"

"The reason he is not in one of the regular services is that one of his legs was affected by polio when he was a child. Perhaps, and I'm only speculating, perhaps there is a residual sense of being inferior or unjustly treated by nature. You know how these things can affect people."

Hawkins began writing notes. He said nothing for a couple of minutes then looked up. "How did he seem to get along with the other recruits?"

"As yet, I've not witnessed anything that suggests he does not get on with anyone. Seems to muck in…though I came under pressure from his father to ensure he had a single room. We only have a few of those. Perhaps likes his privacy…that may be related to his physical condition."

"I will need an accurate list of everyone who was on the base overnight and this morning. I think that will be all for now, Sir. I am happy for you to contact his parents but please say for the moment that we do not yet know how he died. We cannot release the body, obviously, until the Coroner gives the all clear.

That may be a week or so."

"I understand Inspector. I will telephone General Melford now. That's not a call I'm relishing."

◆ ◆ ◆

"Come on Brian, don't be shy. My Mum and Dad won't eat you."

"It's not that, Sheila. I just don't want to intrude into their Sunday afternoon. You know, they may be listening to the wireless."

"Not at this time of day they won't. Me Mum will be cleaning or cooking and me dad will either be pottering in the garden or reading a newspaper. He's always got his head stuck in a newspaper."

"Alright then but I won't stay long 'cos you've got to get ready for work."

Sheila took his hand firmly and, with his other hand on his bicycle handlebars, they walked away from the river through streets Brian didn't know. He would find his way out of the warren though he knew that. If not, he could always ask a policeman! Sheila opened a metal gate, the latch clanking, and, leaning his bike against the fence, he followed her along the path around the side of the house to the back door.

"Mum...I'm home... and look who I've brought to meet you."

There were footsteps in the hall and then a middle-aged woman wearing a scarf on her hair and carrying a duster and bottle of polish padded into the room. "Well now. Who've we got here?"

"This is Brian, Mum. We went for a nice walk along the river and I invited Brian in for a cuppa."

"Very pleased to meet you, Brain." She turned to her daughter. "Well you're a dark horse ain't ya? You never said you were meeting a boyfriend."

Sheila laughed. "Can't tell you everything can I, else what would you have to wonder about?"

"She doesn't tell me anything at all, Brian. I'll put the kettle on." Mrs Brown lifted the heavy kettle from the stove, filled it and lit the gas beneath it. "Now you two go and sit down through there. Not enough room for three of us in the kitchen."

Sheila smiled at Brian, the smile that won him every time. "Come on then."

They had not been sitting long when Mr Brown entered the sitting room. He was a tall man, dark hair slicked back from his forehead with pomade. He nodded a greeting and lowered himself into an armchair. "You walking out with our Sheila, are you?"

Brian had risen and had extended his hand but Mr Brown did not take it. "Well I suppose we are, Sir, yes." He glanced nervously at Sheila for confirmation.

"That's right and we're getting married next week."

Both Brian and Mr Brown looked at her sharply, Brian's mouth falling open."

"S'alright…I'm only joking."

"Not a joking matter, marriage. I mean look where it's got me."

"You don't know how lucky you are. Lovely wife who fusses over you and two wonderful children doing their bit."

"Humph." Mr Brown picked up a newspaper from the small table beside his armchair and shook it open.

"You're just a grumpy old man."

Mrs Brown came in with a tray. "Here's your teas." She handed them round and placed a cup and saucer on Mr Brown's side table. "He likes to have a squeeze of lemon in his tea but you can't get them nowadays."

Mr Brown had given his wife a look which Brian did not understand. He turned back to Brian and saw him watching him. "Ever tried it…lemon in yer tea?"

"No I haven't. I like my tea as it is."

"You should try it sometime. Lovely it is." With that, he lifted the paper and said nothing more.

Brian made small talk with Sheila and Mrs Brown though he found Mr Brown's brooding presence slightly disturbing. He seemed to give nothing away, Mr Brown, a closed book he was. He was relieved when his tea was finished and enough time had passed to say he had better go so Sheila could get ready for work.

She showed him to the door and he hesitated on the threshold. Should he kiss her or not? Would she be offended? What were the rules for early dates? He didn't know.

He felt himself being turned around to face her. She was smiling, a delicious impish smile. And then her arms were around his neck and she pulled him close. Her lips found his and his knees went weak. Suddenly it was over, she stepped back, waved and closed the door, leaving him standing on the step, mesmerised.

CHAPTER 11

Inspector Hawkins stood in the lounge with Commander Trueman beside him. Neither had to call the assembled group to order as everyone sat in watchful and expectant silence. He was a man of medium height and build, probably mid-forties Lizzie guessed, with that air of authority that men accustomed to giving orders acquire. His hair was brown, greying at the temples and thinning on top but it was his eyes that held one's attention. They were blue, bright blue, steady and penetrating. One would have to be a practised liar to fool him and he seemed to give nothing away.

He cleared his throat. "I'm sure you all know about the terrible event that has occurred here. I am also sure that you will not be surprised to learn that I will need to interview everyone. I'm afraid that means you cannot leave this building and I would prefer you to stay in this room, except of course if you need to use the facilities, until I have had an initial conversation with each of you. I understand that a meal will be served at six o'clock so of course you will move to the dining room for that."

He looked around the lounge, his eyes hovering on each person, looking no doubt for the slightest indication of anything suspicious. "I understand that one of you discovered the body and that a second person went into the room where the body lay. I would like to start with the person who discovered the body."

Graham Swinburne stood slowly. "That was me, Officer. Graham Swinburne."

"Thank you, Sir. Please come this way." Hawkins left the room and Swinburne trailed after him.

"Please try to be as helpful as you can to Inspector Hawkins. We need to get this cleared up as soon as possible.

I must leave you as I need to telephone Mr Melford's parents."
Commander Trueman's usual confident demeanour was gone.
He seemed to be stooping a little and his face was twisted with
anxiety.

"Not a pleasant duty to perform," Lizzie said to Patrick
Kenny who was sitting beside her.

"No, not pleasant at all."

"Why would anyone want to kill Edward Melford? He
may have been unpleasant but he wasn't bad enough to warrant
murder."

"I think only the murderer knows his motive. We can't
guess what issues there may be between individuals. Someone
with a grudge? Who knows?"

When Hawkins and Trueman had left, there had been a
relaxation in the lounge. Lizzie looked around the faces. Carlisle
and Garrett seemed concerned, leaning towards each other and
speaking quietly. Laura Hulett had the same hard expression
on her face that gave nothing away whereas Olivia looked
on the verge of tears, her eyes darting sideways but always
looking at the floor. Mark Sanders seemed concerned but not
unduly, as though his relatively longer life had prepared him
for such disasters. Kasia sat immobile with the same inscrutable
expression on her face. Patrick Kenny was too close to her to read
his expression.

"Why did you join the ATA Patrick?" she asked quietly.

He turned in surprise. "That's a bit like small talk isn't it?"

"Yes but we can't just sit here in silence."

"I joined probably for the same reason as you...to do
something for the War effort. Too old to join one of the regular
services but they were happy to have me here."

Lizzie nodded. "Are you still living in Liverpool?"

"No, I've lived in London for several years...until now that
is."

"How did you earn your living?"

"I was a pharmacist."

"Married?"

"You ask a lot of questions." He smiled

"I know…I'm interested in other people."

"Not married. Nearly was once but that was some time ago."

"May I ask wha…?"

"I think you just did. She was significantly younger than me but perhaps that's not the reason. I'm a Catholic, she wasn't. I wanted to marry in a Catholic church but she would have had to commit to raising any children in the Catholic faith. I think she took fright…" His face suddenly hardened and his eyes narrowed. "Actually I am sure someone convinced her it wasn't a good idea."

"That's so sad…I'm sorry."

He sighed. "Yep but it's to be expected."

"How do you mean?"

"It's like the weather. You get up and it's a beautiful morning but as the day ages, the clouds appear and the early promise is rarely fulfilled." He turned and smiled at her. "You see what age does to you."

"I hope I don't become so disillusioned."

"Oh I'm not disillusioned. I've just learnt not to let my expectations rise too high."

Lizzie fell silent and Patrick did not continue the conversation. She began to think what she would say when Inspector Hawkins interviewed her. Melford had upset people, not just one but several. Again she ran through the events she had witnessed. There was the incident with John Hale, the member of the ground crew, Melford's unpleasant remark about the young man who had asked Olivia to dance to which Kasia had responded with such anger, and that tiny detail she had noticed - the way the steward, Bloom, had looked when Melford had clicked his fingers. But none of those would provoke murder surely?

She closed her eyes to picture the scene that had confronted her when she had entered Melford's room, horrific though it was to re-live that moment. But the image that arose first was Graham Swinburne in shock. Somehow it seemed a little extreme. He had said last night he was involved in amateur dramatics. Could it be that his shock was an act, that he already knew Melford was dead?

And then the murder scene. What had her rapid glance around the room taken in? The curtain pulled aside and the window opened slightly. The body, something strange about it, as if it had been laid there carefully. And the blood on the shirt – why so little? The glasses, she remembered the glasses and the trace of lipstick she had noticed on one of them. And the green, silk button. The temptation to reach out and take it had been huge as she realised its significance. She looked at Olivia. Could it be that she had tried to defend herself against Melford? Was she upset by what she had done rather than what he had done? But Olivia was a refined, sensitive young woman. Could she really be a killer?

◆ ◆ ◆

Richard Trueman had had to wait while the butler fetched General Melford from his study. He liked to take a nap after Sunday lunch the butler had explained. What a rude awakening he would have.

A brusque voice barked down the phone. "What is it? Can't a chap enjoy some relaxation on a Sunday afternoon?"

"I am so sorry General Melford but I felt you should know what has happened straight away. I'm afraid you will need to prepare yourself for a shock. Something rather terrible has happened. Your son...Edward...I'm afraid he is..."

"Edward? He is what? Spit it out man."

"He is dead, Sir. I am so sorry."

"Dead? Dead? How can he be dead? Has he crashed a plane or what?"

"I'm afraid, Sir, that he was found dead in his room just

before lunch. I have the Police here but they are not as yet clear as to the cause of death."

"Police? Why the Police?"

"The death is unexpected, Sir, and they must check. We are waiting for a pathologist to arrive to ascertain the cause of death. I'm afraid until that has been established and the Coroner gives permission, the body cannot be released."

"Body? This is most strange, Trueman, and I don't like it one bit. What in God's name is going on down there?"

"I'm afraid I cannot say any more, Sir, until the Police and pathologist have determined the cause of death."

The conversation or perhaps more accurately the monologue from General Melford continued for some time. How was he going to tell Edward's mother? Who would inherit the estate now his only son was dead? What sort of organisation was the ATA that a young man died during training? And so on… Trueman held the handset away from his ear while the worst of the tirade was delivered. He was filled with alarm when Melford delivered his last words and slammed down the telephone.

"I'll be there as soon as I can get away."

Inspector Hawkins looked carefully at Graham Swinburne who sat in front of him. He seemed nervous, crossing and uncrossing his legs. "So Mr Swinburne, can we go over your movements once again to make sure my notes are accurate? You came back from the club in Mr Melford's car with Miss Olivia and Miss Laura Hulett at around midnight?"

"That's correct Inspector."

"You then went into the lounge and were joined by Mr Mark Sanders. You stayed there talking until 12.45 am and then went to bed. Do you share a room?"

"No…no. I'm in a double room but I don't at the

moment have a room mate. Mark Sanders and Patrick Kenny share a room and Eddie has…had a single room."

"Did you see anyone as you walked up to your bedroom?"

"No one at all. I left Sanders in the lounge and, as far as I know, Kenny was in their bedroom."

Inspector Hawkins looked out of the window for what seemed an age to Graham Swinburne who fidgeted on his chair, adjusting his position. Suddenly, Hawkins fixed his eyes on his interviewee. "You didn't like Mr Melford did you?"

"Me…I had no problem with Melford. I mean he had upset a few people but I had not had any issues with him."

"Whom had he upset?"

Well, there was an incident in the Café de Paris when he referred to a young man as a 'damned Jew'. That upset Miss Michalski as she is from a Jewish family apparently."

Inspector Hawkins raised an eyebrow and made a note. "And who else did he upset?"

"Well that mechanic – Hale – I think his name is. Had a go at him apparently after his landing went wrong."

"Would you describe Mr Melford as an unpleasant person then?"

"Well no, actually. That's the thing. He was in the main a very sociable man and generous. I mean yesterday evening, he suggested we all go to the Café de Paris and he had offered to pay for the ladies. He ordered champagne for us all when we were there and wouldn't accept anything for it. But…"

Inspector Hawkins looked up from his notebook. "Do go on."

"He seemed to have something of a dark streak to his nature as well as the light, fun side. Just occasionally I had caught him off guard and his face was quite brooding."

"And this morning, Sir. You say you rose and washed and were down for breakfast at about eight-thirty. Did you see anyone this morning…Mr Melford, or any of the others?"

"I think I may have seen Miss Michalski…I just caught

a fleeting glimpse of her as I came out of my room to use the facilities. She...if it was her...turned to go down the stairs. She seemed to be hurrying. But the curious thing is that she was not coming from the ladies' corridor. Had she been doing so, I would have seen her face clearly before she turned down the stairs but I saw her back. It was her hair that led me to believe that it was Kasia Michalski."

"What time would this have been?"

"About seven-thirty I would guess."

"Just a couple more questions for the time being, Mr Swinburne. When you went into Mr Melford's room to rouse him, did you notice anything, anything at all that struck you as odd, interesting or unexpected?"

Swinburne slowly shook his head from side to side. "To be honest, Inspector, I was so shocked, all I saw was the body on the bed, the knife protruding from his stomach and a small circle of blood on his shirt around it. I was so shocked I went straight out to raise the alarm."

"But you went in again with Miss Barnes did you not? Did you notice anything on the second visit?"

"I hardly stepped inside the room Inspector. I knew what I had seen. I tried to stop Miss Barnes from going in...didn't want her to be upset, you know how it is but she insisted. Plucky young woman is Lizzie Barnes."

"Did you touch anything in the room?"

"No...except the curtain. I drew back one of the blackout curtains. That was before I'd seen the body."

"Did you open the window?"

"No definitely not. It must have been open already."

"Thank you Mr Swinburne. I'll be talking to Miss Barnes next."

CHAPTER 12

"Thanks for calling me out on a Sunday afternoon. I didn't have anything else to do!" Doctor Jarvis shook the proffered hand of Inspector Hawkins who smiled at the heavy irony of his greeting.

"Wouldn't want you to be bored or worse having to tend the garden." Hawkins looked at the impeccably dressed, portly figure before him and suspected that his puffy white hands had never touched a garden implement in his life, had never touched anything in fact harder than his bow tie. He indicated the stairs. "Shall we?"

"Age before beauty, Inspector. Lead on."

Levity is often a feature of professionals working in very serious situations. Inspector Hawkins knew that Andrew Jarvis would give the victim's body and the scene his full attention, his sharp eye noticing tiny details that might escape even him. He supposed that some jocularity was a protection against the horrors that the pathologist must confront in his working life.

Melford's room had been locked and Hawkins had the key. He unlocked the door and pushed it open to reveal the scene. Jarvis stood in the doorway, his eyes scanning the floor in front of him systematically, as if a beam of light travelled across the boards and the heavily patterned carpet. He stepped forward and repeated the operation. Placing his bag on the floor, he opened it and took out a pair of tweezers. Squatting on his haunches, he picked something off the carpet not far from the edge. He held it up proudly for Hawkins to see. It was a long, black hair, bent in several places into curves.

"Is there anyone here with long, very dark, curly hair,

Inspector?"

"I've seen a young woman with that kind of hair but I've not interviewed her yet."

"She may have been in this room. Of course this hair may have been transferred to the clothing of the deceased and fallen off onto the floor here so it's not conclusive."

From his pocket, Inspector Hawkins took out a small wad of envelopes and offered one open to Jarvis who carefully dropped the hair inside. "Hope you've got enough of those. There may be lots more. Was our man a womaniser?"

"No one has said so as yet. I hope not, as there are four young women downstairs who might be suspects."

Jarvis continued his meticulous search of the floor. As he approached the writing desk, he dropped to his knees and examined a section of carpet with intense concentration. "Difficult to be certain but there are probably a couple of drops of blood on the carpet here but only a couple. Odd that – I would have expected more." Kneeling on the floor. his eye caught a delicate green button which nestled by the leg of the bed, out of sight to anyone standing. He lifted it with his tweezers and held it up.

"Ah another button. I found one earlier. Nothing missing from any of the clothes and no green waistcoat. I think they're from a dress."

"I agree Inspector."

Inspector Hawkins watched Jarvis stand again and examine the desk. "That letter is from his parents – family news, very chatty, nothing that sheds any light on his death. But that single sheet of blank paper puzzles me. There's a writing pad in the desk drawer but that sheet does not come from it...very different quality paper. And if he were about to reply to his parents, surely he would keep the paper attached to the pad as something to lean on until he had finished?"

"A blank piece of paper from someone else then. Perhaps some kind of message from the killer."

"Perhaps the killer intended to write something on it

but was disturbed."

Jarvis nodded and at last turned his attention to the body on the bed. He looked carefully at the blankets which appeared to have been pulled up the bed slightly, revealing the end of the mattress. "He wasn't stabbed whilst lying on the bed."

"That was my thought. Stabbed elsewhere in the room and then dragged onto the bed. The body is arranged almost neatly. Why would the killer do that? And perhaps I'm mistaken, but shouldn't there be much more blood?"

"Let's see how long the knife blade is." Jarvis took out his handkerchief and, wrapping it around the blade, gently pulled the knife from its resting place. He held it up for Hawkins to see; blood stained the metal. "About three inches long I'd say. Letter opener? It has penetrated most of the way but it may not have cut a major artery or vein. On the other hand…" Jarvis, bushy eyebrows raised, offered the knife to Hawkins who took out another evidence bag.

Doctor Jarvis bent over the wound looking at the blood stain. "Not much blood at all. Even if it didn't sever something large, one would expect more than that." His eyes travelled up the body, looking carefully for any signs of defensive wounds. Nothing. No scratches on the face, no bruises or cuts. He examined each arm in turn and when he reached the right hand, again took out the tweezers. He held up a long blond hair caught in a fingernail.

"What do you think Doctor?"

"I think our man might have been busy, Inspector. A woman with dark curly hair and a blonde. Was it a crime of passion? I can see it now. He's making love to a blonde woman and is interrupted by the woman he is supposed to be courting with dark curly hair. She is incensed, grabs the letter opener and plunges it into him." Jarvis smiled.

"It would be nice if murders were so easily solved." Hawkins bagged the blonde hair. "Just a few problems with that one. If he was aroused, there would be plenty of blood pumping around his system. And why would she bother to drag the body onto the bed? Would she be strong enough? The blonde woman would have screamed and raised the alarm."

"Alright Inspector. You win. I'll stick to the science and leave you to solve the mystery. The only thing I can say for sure is that he's dead!" he said with a grim smile before becoming businesslike. "I've ordered an ambulance to take the body to the mortuary. Should be here anytime now. I'll get stuck into him, so to speak, tomorrow morning and let you know as soon as possible what emerges from the autopsy."

"What about the lack of blood. What does that suggest?"

"Too many possibilities, Inspector, so I shouldn't say anything more at the moment."

Inspector Hawkins escorted Doctor Jarvis down the stairs and out of the building. As they parted, an ambulance drew up outside. Jarvis waited until the two crewmen had alighted. "He's upstairs chaps. Inspector Hawkins will show you where. He'll wait until you arrive!"

Lizzie sat bolt upright in the chair facing Inspector Hawkins across the desk. She had never been interviewed by a police officer before and the circumstances now filled her with anxiety even though she had nothing to fear. She hoped that she could offer some help but she dreaded having to give some of the information she held. She was sure that Olivia knew something about Melford's death and, God forbid, may even be responsible for it. But if, as she suspected, Melford had tried to rape Olivia – may even have succeeded though Olivia implied he had not – Lizzie's sympathies were definitely with her. She knew that her upbringing would not allow her to lie but would her own experiences in earlier life enable her to point the finger at another young woman who was defending herself from male sexual appetite?

Inspector Hawkins looked up from the folder he had been examining. "Right Miss Barnes. Let's start with your movements last night. Please be as precise as you can about times. Start from your return to the Base from the Café de Paris."

"We arrived back here at about eleven-thirty. I went up to our room and prepared for bed. Before getting into bed, I looked out of the window and noticed someone smoking a cigarette outside. I'm certain it was Mark Sanders. I saw Edward Melford's car pull in at about midnight, then I went to bed."

"You said 'our room' You share a room with…?"

"It's the four of us girls together, the sisters Laura and Olivia Hulett and Kasia Michalski."

"And did you women all arrive back in the first car?"

"No, Kasia and I travelled with Mark Sanders and Patrick Kenny while Laura and Olivia were with Graham Swinburne in Mr Melford's car."

"Did Miss Michalski go to bed at the same time as you?"

"Yes, except she went straight to bed and fell asleep very quickly. She was very tired."

"And the other two ladies, the sisters?"

"Laura came in about fifteen minutes I'd say after arriving back. I expect she used the bathroom. Olivia came in about fifteen minutes after that. I was still awake."

"Are you a light sleeper?"

"Sometimes…when I've had a day that has been fairly exciting…flying you know…find it hard to come down."

Inspector Hawkins smiled. "When looking out of the window, did you notice how Mr Melford seemed? Anything unusual?"

Lizzie felt herself blush slightly and looked away before turning her eyes back on Hawkins. "I think he'd had a bit to drink but he seemed in very good spirits. I think…I suspect he had amorous feelings for Olivia."

Hawkins looked up from his notes; his eyes narrowed. "What made you think that?"

"He took her hand and pulled her towards himself.

Olivia laughed it off but extricated herself. However, Mr Melford took her hand again and they went into the building together."

"What colour hair does Olivia Hulett have?"

"Blonde."

Hawkins nodded his head slowly. "When Olivia came into your room, did she say anything, how did she seem?"

Lizzie shuffled in her chair, struggling within herself at giving the information she knew she must give. "She was upset...very upset."

"What had happened to upset her?"

"She didn't say and in fact has said very little this morning either. She went into her sister's bed and they were whispering for a while but I couldn't hear what they were saying."

"Did any of the four of you leave the room during the night?"

"Yes. I went out at 12.40 am – I know it was that time as I checked my bedside clock – I just wanted to see whether something was going on."

"And was anything going on?"

"No. There was just Graham Swinburne and Mark Sanders having a conversation in the lounge. So I went back to bed."

"Did you go to Mr Melford's room?"

Lizzie was shocked. "No, absolutely not."

"And what about the others? Did any of them leave the room after you returned?"

"Well...I then went to sleep though I thought I sensed someone leave the room but I can't be sure. It may have been in a dream. You know that state when you're not sure if you're awake or asleep..."

"This morning...tell me about that."

"I was up early but Kasia and Laura were up before me. Kasia was in the lounge and Laura came in soon after me. Olivia joined us later; she still seemed quite upset, perhaps had not slept and the four of us walked to church with Graham

Swinburne. When we came back, Graham said he was going to get Edward up. As I was coming down from our room, I met him near the top of the stairs and he was in a state. I went with him to see what had happened."

"Did you notice anything about the scene, anything at all?"

"I have no experience of these things, Inspector, but I thought it was odd how he was lying on the bed. It didn't look right. If he had say fallen asleep in the bed last night before getting changed, I think he would not have been lying so straight and on his back. I had only seconds in the room but I did notice the way the bedclothes had been disturbed. I suppose he could have sat on the end of the bed and then dragged himself up, pulling the blankets out as he did so. But it didn't look right somehow. And the blood. I would have thought there would have been more of it…being stabbed in the stomach like that."

"Did you open the window?"

"No I didn't. The window was already open."

"You noticed a lot in a few seconds."

Lizzie felt a shiver of fear down her spine. Was the Inspector's last remark praise for her powers of observation or was it a dark suggestion that she had some involvement in the crime. She realised with dread that she was a suspect too, even though she knew she had had nothing to do with Melford's murder.

There was a tap on the door and Trueman stepped in. "There's a telephone call for you Inspector. Your wife. Do please use my office."

Lizzie made as if to get up but Hawkins held his hand in a stop signal. He left the room. A few minutes later he returned. "I'm afraid Miss Barnes we will have to resume this discussion tomorrow. I'm needed at home now."

CHAPTER 13

The hospital was quiet when Sheila arrived for work. She glanced at the big clock in the ward where she was based. Eight o'clock, the start of a twelve hour shift. Nights were great in that they were not often too busy but sometimes, in the early hours, time dragged and it was difficult not to yawn. Woe betide you if Matron caught you though. It gave Sheila a sense of real pride to wear her uniform, the white hat stiffly starched pinned to her hair which had to be gathered up neatly, and everything always freshly washed. Her Mum complained of course but she knew she didn't mind really...she was proud of her in fact.

She walked down the row of beds saying hello to any of the patients still awake and checking their charts to make sure they'd had their medicines. She would do the rounds a bit later to give the final medication before the patients tried to sleep. The old lady, Mrs Bloom, who had been brought in the previous night after the fire, was lying still, her breathing shallow and laboured. She seemed to be sleeping or perhaps too weak to open her eyes. Poor woman. It wasn't fair at her time of life...not fair at any time of life actually. What kind of monster could throw a petrol bomb into a building knowing there were people upstairs probably in their beds?

Some of the patients waved and gave a cheery 'hello' but others, like Mrs Bloom, were too ill to make that effort. There were no such reservations with Nancy O'Brien though. She was always up for some craic as she called it. She hoisted herself up on her elbows her red hair cascading onto her shoulders.

"God sure now look what the cat's brought in."

"Evening Nancy. How are you?"

"Still alive, that's the main thing as me ol' Ma used to

say. What have you been up to today? Out romancing no doubt." Sheila could not keep the smile from her face and she knew there was a slight flush on her cheek. "Ah God didn't I know it? Who is he then? Come on and tell me all."

"Matron does not like us talking to the patients except about their own health. You know that."

"But Matron is not here at the moment so you can tell me everything. " She patted the edge of the bed. "Now come on and sit you down here."

Sheila giggled but she didn't sit down; that would have been too much of a risk. Nancy was great fun but she would get you into trouble with her carrying on. She was older than herself and her red hair was unruly when, as now, it wasn't tied up. She was always smiling, laughing and grinning, her nose wrinkling under its scattering of freckles.

"I'll tell you but you're not to tell anyone else. Understood?"

Nancy made the sign of the cross. "I won't tell another soul, God help me if I do."

"His name is Brian. Nice chap. Lives in Maidenhead."

"You can do better than that. What's he do for a living and why's he not joined up...unless he's an old 'un. Is that it? Are you courting some old fella? You need to watch that type; he's only after getting inside your knickers and then he'll be off leaving you with something to remember him by."

"He's not old...he's a few years older than me that's all but he's in a reserved occupation."

"Reserved occupation is it?" Nancy's face broke into a wider smile than usual. "I know, he's a doctor isn't he? Is it that Doctor Webb, you know the one with the nice brown eyes?"

"No Nancy, he's not a doctor. He's a policeman."

"Oh Heaven save you, girl. There's no happiness to be had with a polissman. You can't have any fun with one of them."

"Don't be daft. He's a very nice young man."

"That's exactly what I'm saying. He's nice but I bet he's boring."

"Nurse Brown. What is going on here?"

"Nothing at all Matron. I was just asking Nurse Brown when I might be able to get out of hospital. Three kids at home you know. My husband'll starve them to death if I'm not back soon."

"That's a question for the doctor, not Nurse Brown. You know very well that having your appendix removed is a major operation and you will need to be in hospital for two weeks. One more week to go. And it's the first I've heard of three children."

"Another whole week. Mother of God, I'll die of boredom."

The atmosphere amongst the trainees had been subdued all afternoon. Supper in the mess was eaten in near silence and now they sat in the lounge, the wireless playing music softly in the background. The two instructors and Trueman had left after supper along with other staff who were not resident. As they had not been on the premises the previous night, they were not subject to the restriction Hawkins had placed on leaving the building.

Lizzie had noticed Oliva trying to slip away after supper to their room but Laura held her arm and steered her into the lounge whispering something urgently into her ear. They sat together on a settee, Laura flicking unenthusiastically through a magazine while Olivia's eyes seemed unfocused, vacant.

She could not help noticing Patrick Kenny. He was doing nothing but he appeared to be staring across the room at Laura. It was not the hazy-eyed look of the admirer; if anything, it suggested suspicion, even dislike. What was there between them? Did something happen last night? Perhaps Melford was not the only one to have had amorous designs on a lady. He sat with one leg crossed over the other, the lower leg of the latter swinging up and dropping back as if impatient for action.

Graham Swinburne was nestled in an armchair engrossed in a book. Frequently, he lifted his head, eyes closed for perhaps a minute and then returned to the book. Beside him, Kasia was reading the booklet of notes on aircraft. After some time, she heard Swinburne's voice. "I'm sorry to interrupt you Kasia, but I'm wondering if you could help me. You see, I'm trying to learn the lines for this play I'm supposed to be doing with the local dramatic society. I think I've got this scene sorted but it would be very helpful if you could give me the cues so I can check my lines."

Kasia nodded and reached out her hand for the book which Swinburne handed her. He leaned over towards her. "I'm Freddy Einsford-Hill, you see so if you can give me the line that comes before each of mine, that would be lovely."

Holding her finger in the book to mark the page, Kasia flipped the cover over. "How you say this?"

"Pygmalion. It's about a professor, Higgins, who finds a London flower girl – that's a girl selling flowers – and bets his friend that he could turn her into a lady by training her to speak and act properly. Pygmalion was a character in classical mythology who fell in love with one of his own sculptures. It's really about the arrogance of trying to make another human being be like oneself. Good stuff."

Kasia shrugged and gave Swinburne the first cue. He tried to keep his voice quiet but could not resist speaking his lines in character. Lizzie smiled. At another time it would have been comic and she would have volunteered to read another part but it seemed inappropriate in the present circumstances. She knew of the play but did not know it. Swinburne's very brief account of it rang true. How typical of a man to try to shape a woman to be what he wanted her to be.

Mark Sanders had gone outside for a cigarette – permitted by Hawkins provided he and any other smokers stayed close to the building - and now returned, dropping into an armchair near Lizzie with a sigh.

"If it's not too upsetting a question, Lizzie, what did Inspector Hawkins ask you?"

"The interview had not finished when he was called away by his wife; some issue at home. We have to resume tomorrow. I would rather have got done today but…"

"Swinburne said he started by asking about his movements last night."

"Yes…same for me. It's quite difficult to be precise about times though unless you happened to have looked at a clock ."

"Did he say what he thinks happened last night…I mean I know it's early days but he presumably has some theory?"

Lizzie turned to Mark Sanders in surprise. "No he didn't. I'm sure if he had an idea he would not tell me. I'm a suspect as are we all."

"Yes, yes of course." He was silent for several seconds. "I just can't understand what someone would have against Edward Melford. One would have to have a very powerful motive to murder someone. That mechanic perhaps…you know the one he had a go at."

"John Hale? He was certainly angry at the way Melford treated him but I can't believe that would have been enough to make him commit murder."

"One would hope not. Looking around all of us here, I can't believe anyone would kill him. I think it must have been an intruder, someone from outside. The window was open I'm told. But why Melford I wonder? Wrong place at the wrong time perhaps?"

"Perhaps." Lizzie looked across the room at Olivia, still looking at nothing as if lost in some nightmare. "I fear that…"

"You fear that what?"

Lizzie shook her head. "No, it's ridiculous. Forget I said it."

Mark Sanders was about to press her to complete her sentence but Lizzie stood up and crossed the lounge to sit next to Olivia. She was a troubled young woman who needed comforting.

◆ ◆ ◆

Sheila glanced at the clock. Nine thirty. Time to do the evening meds. Matron was in her office, the door ajar. She tapped and coughed quietly.

"No need to come in like a mouse Nurse Brown. What is it?"

"It's nine-thirty Matron. Shall I do the evening meds?"

Matron glanced at the clock on her office wall. "Yes please, Nurse. Make sure you write everything down on the patient charts. Must keep an accurate record." Matron stood and taking a bunch of keys that hung on a chain from her belt, unlocked the medicine cabinet. She handed Sheila a tray. "You should have everything you need there. And no chatting with the patients. They need to sleep."

"Yes Matron."

As she walked away from the office, Sheila mimicked Matron's words, silently shaping her mouth in the exaggerated way Matron had. What happened she wondered when nurses were promoted to senior posts such as sisters and matrons. Were they always bad-tempered or was it a characteristic they developed. If she ever took a senior role, she vowed to herself that she would never become like that. Nursing was about caring and making people feel better by chatting with them was part of the healing process.

The first patient she came to was Mrs Bennett. She lifted the clip board from the end of the bed and checked the medicines she had to administer. Just two tablets to help ease the pain. "Time for your meds, Mrs Bennett."

The elderly lady in the bed opened her eyes. "Thank you darling. I'm ready for a bit more. It does start to hurt you know." Mrs Bennett opened her hand so Sheila could drop the tablets into her palm. She popped both in her mouth at once and took a swig of water. The tablets went down with a gulp. She sank back on the pillow. "That's better. Thank you."

"Do you want me to re-arrange the pillows at all or do you need anything else?"

"No thank you, darling. That will be all now 'til I wake up. I'll probably need a bottle then – you know what I'm like. Your bladder shrinks you know when you turn fifty. Still lots of other things stop working too. No fun getting old…you make the most of your youth while you have it."

"I'll do my best. Night, night then. Just call if you need anything."

"Goodnight my lovely."

Sheila moved on to the next bed. It was Mrs Bloom. "Time for your meds Mrs Bloom."

The old lady did not open her eyes. Her breathing which had been slow and laboured was even worse and was accompanied by a rasping sound as the air was drawn in and expelled.

"Mrs Bloom, are you awake?"

There was no response and as Sheila looked at the sad figure in the bed, she heard a final coarse noise in the patient's throat. She lay still, no breathing at all. "Mrs Bloom, Mrs Bloom." Sheila felt tears prick her eyes but she remembered her training. She felt for a pulse…nothing, so she began to compress the chest and as loudly as she could shouted, "Matron, Matron, it's Mrs Bloom."

She heard the loud steps on the hard floor and Matron was at her side. Leaning over the body, Matron examined the patient's face carefully then she put her hand on Sheila's arm to stop the compressions.

"Well done for trying but it's no good. She's gone." With that, Matron pulled up the sheet to cover Mrs Bloom's face. Tears streamed down Sheila's face. "This is your first one I suppose. Not nice to lose a patient but you'll get used to it. Now dry your eyes and concentrate on the job in hand. That's the best way to deal with this."

CHAPTER 14

Inspector Hawkins bade a sombre "Good morning" to Sergeant Drake and PCs Teal and Green when he let the swing door swish closed behind him. "Any other problems over the weekend Sergeant?"

"Nothing, Sir. Been very quiet apart from the fire."

"That's because you don't know yet about the murder at White Waltham air base."

"Murder?" Brian Teal gulped and his eyes opened wide with surprise.

"Yes Constable, murder. I spent most of the afternoon there yesterday. It was one of the trainees with the Air Transport Auxiliary, a man of about twenty-five, I think, called Edward Melford. Stabbed in the stomach. The ATA is a civilian organisation so it comes under our remit. Doctor Jarvis examined the body and the scene and arranged for the victim to be taken away. He'll do an autopsy today. May have been an intruder – window was open – but no sign of anything on the ground outside and nothing to climb up to the room. Savage shrub growing underneath the window too...huge great thorns. So it looks like the culprit was one of the other trainees as they were the only people resident overnight. Not sure yet what the time of death was but probably happened Saturday night late or early yesterday morning."

"Blimey. That and the fire."

"Blimey indeed Constable. Interesting coincidence that both events took place on Saturday night. Anyway, Drake, I'm going to need you up there with me to interview everyone. I made a start yesterday and I've confined everyone to barracks but we need to get onto this quickly. Can't have a murderer roaming free at an air base."

"Yes, Sir. Glad to help out Sir."

"You Teal will need to do the follow up on the fire. Remember that you need to get back to Grenfell Road to interview the witness, find out if the two men waiting opposite the shop had accents, were they well-spoken that sort of thing and anything else he may have noticed. You also need to telephone Wethered's Brewery in Marlow and find out what places they supply in Maidenhead with bottles of their pale ale. Then check each place to see who they've been selling them to. It's a long shot but leave no stone unturned that's my motto."

"What about minding the station, Sir?" PC Green's youthful eagerness occasionally irritated Inspector Hawkins but he knew the Force needed that sort of enthusiasm.

"That's your job today Green. I know you're a bit inexperienced but it'll do you good to have some responsibility."

"Sir." PC Green stood a little taller and he squared his shoulders.

"Right Drake. Come into my office and I'll brief you fully, explain where I've got to."

Sergeant Drake followed Hawkins into his office and they sat either side of the desk. Hawkins took out his notebook and began to go through the sequence of timings for Saturday night that he had so far established. Drake nodded and made a few notes in his own book.

"Any suspect emerged so far, Sir?"

"Not really, but Doctor Jarvis found two very different strands of hair in the dead man's room, both long, one black and curly, the other blonde and straight. It suggests that our man had female company but not necessarily that night – might have been on a previous occasion. The victim, Edward Melford, seems to have upset a few people. Apparently he was usually good fun, generous, life and soul of the party but he had a darker side, occasionally quick to anger. We need to establish everyone's movements on Saturday night and on Sunday morning early and pick up any bad feeling there may have been between Melford and other trainees...or indeed anyone else at the ATA base. He upset one of the ground crew on Saturday afternoon."

"Right, Sir. So you just tell me who you want me to interview. I'll get the truth out of them."

"Yes, Sergeant, but we need to be subtle about this. If we go in guns blazing, it will just put our murderer on his guard."

"Quite so, Sir. I can..."

The sergeant's words were lost in the harsh jangling of the telephone. Hawkins reached forward and picked up the handset. He listened for a few seconds and then held the handset away from his mouth. "It's the hospital in Windsor." He listened again and his face darkened. He replaced the handset carefully on its cradle. "Mrs Bloom, the old lady who was taken to hospital after the fire, died last night. Jarvis will examine her today but I'm sure it will be damage to her lungs from the smoke. So we have a murder to solve and now a case of manslaughter."

Drake whistled softly through his teeth. "What is the World coming to?"

◆ ◆ ◆

Commander Trueman's face looked drawn, poor man. Lizzie sat in the briefing room with the other recruits and the two instructors while Trueman explained what was happening.

"Inspector Hawkins will be returning very shortly with his sergeant and he will need to continue conducting interviews with each of you. But I have agreed with him that it would be better for you to be doing something rather than sitting around waiting. Thus there will be two training sessions as usual. The first will involve Graham Swinburne, Laura Hulett, Mark Sanders and Patrick Kenny. The second will consist of Lizzie Barnes, Olivia Hulett, and Kasia Michalski."

He paused and scanned the group for any questions. There being none, he continued. "Our two more experienced pilots, namely Mark Sanders and Lizzie Barnes will have solo flights in a Tiger Moth this morning. You'll be given a circuit to navigate and be required to do some touchdowns." He smiled. "You will of course be tested on the circuit by being asked about key landmarks."

"Sir, is there any more news about Melford?" Graham Swinburne asked tentatively.

"No, there is nothing. As you know, the pathologist examined the body at the scene yesterday afternoon and will conduct an autopsy some time today. Hopefully that will tell the Police more. I expect each of you to be as helpful as possible to the Police...anything you saw or heard that might shed light on this terrible event, even if you don't see the immediate relevance. Right, those of you flying in the first session, please get flying gear on and meet at the hangars in ten minutes," he consulted his watch, "that will be at nine hundred hours exactly. Those of you in the second session will need to wait in the lounge until you are called by the Police officers."

The trainees trooped out of the briefing room and separated into the groups Trueman had defined. Lizzie, Olivia and Kasia walked together across to the main building where they were to wait.

"Why...why are they seeing us first?" It was Olivia, her face twisted with anxiety.

Lizzie put her arm around her. "I'm sure there's no significance in that Olivia. They have to divide us somehow. Inspector Hawkins started my interview yesterday and I'm sure I'll be called first to finish it off. I wonder they didn't group Laura with us – you know, all the girls together but perhaps they wanted to avoid doing that."

"I didn't...I..." Olivia's hand went to her face and she stopped suddenly.

Lizzie knew she was struggling again with her dark thoughts. She pulled her closer and hugged her until she let out a long breath. "Olivia, you mustn't upset yourself. I'm sure there is nothing to worry about. Let's just get into the lounge then we can talk about it."

Nothing further was said until all three were sitting in the lounge, huddled together. It was Kasia who spoke first.

"You will no doubt tell the Police about the row I had with Melford on Saturday night. I expect I'm the chief suspect," she said glumly.

Olivia looked at Kasia with surprise but it was Lizzie who answered. "People have disagreements all the time. They don't murder each other as a result."

Kasia shrugged. "I'm a foreigner. They will want to blame me, it's easier for them."

"I'm certain our Police do not operate in that way, Kasia. You mustn't judge our system by the way things operate in Germany or Poland for that matter."

"We'll see."

There was silence for a few moments. Olivia took a deep breath. "Can I ask you something in confidence?"

Kasia nodded but Lizzie said, "Be careful Olivia. If you tell us something we feel the Police should know, we have to tell them."

Olivia looked into Lizzie's eyes. What did she read there? Honesty, loyalty, pragmatism? Lizzie was not sure but Olivia felt able to continue.

"Do you think I should tell the Police that Edward became...was amorous towards me last night?"

"If they ask, Olivia, you must tell them. If you did nothing wrong, you have nothing to fear."

"But...but they will think I killed him to stop him..."

"If that were the case, Olivia, you would be able to plead self-defence. No woman should have to put up with the unwanted attentions of any man. She has a right to defend herself." Lizzie stood up and walked to the window to calm herself. After a few seconds , she returned to her seat.

"You feel very strongly about that I think."

Kasia's eyes were searching but Lizzie had resumed her usual mask. Always seem confident, never let any crack show, was her motto and she cursed herself silently for letting the mask slip a little.

"I'm not like you, Lizzie," Olivia said. "I know everyone thinks I'm carefree and confident because that's how I appear but I'm not. That's why Laura looks out for me. I cover up with gaiety but much of the time I feel...vulnerable."

"I know what you mean but you have to fight that, you have to believe in yourself. You...we...have as much right to happiness as any man and we have the right to make decisions about what we do with our lives and how far we let a man...you know..."

Again there was silence before Olivia spoke again, softly, an admission. "I was in his room on Saturday night but I did not stab him. I'd like to have done but I would never have the courage to do that." A tear squeezed from each of her eyes and rolled slowly down her cheeks. Lizzie and Kasia, sitting either side of her, put loving arms around her.

◆ ◆ ◆

"Sorry to disturb you again, Sir, but I need to ask you a few more questions about the two men you saw on Saturday night waiting outside the shop down the road."

"You'd better come in Constable."

PC Teal was led by Mr Foster into the sitting room, furnished with a comfortable if slightly faded three piece suite. The moquette fabric was worn and darkened with use on the arms and springs creaked as he sat down. He noticed the picture on the wall, a view of Windsor Castle painted as if it had just been built, the walls pristine and a long, pointed flag waving almost horizontally from a post on top of the tower.

"The Inspector wanted me to come back to see you again, Sir, to try to get some more information about the two men. In particular, he was wondering what sort of accents they had."

"Accents?"

"Yes, Sir."

"How d'you mean? Like if they were local or foreign?"

"That sort of thing, Sir, and if they were well spoken... you know upper class, middle class, working men."

"One of them was local and a working man I think. Perhaps I detected something foreign, Irish maybe, in the other one's accent but I couldn't be sure."

"Well that's helpful, Sir. Do you remember anything else?"

"There was one thing. The taller of the two men was wearing brogues...couldn't be sure what colour because there was so little light but I would make a guess that they were brown. Could be wrong of course."

"That's very helpful, Sir." PC Teal wrote 'brown brogues' in his notebook.

"Course there could be lots of men who wear brogues and even brown brogues. Not exactly rare but it probably means he was a bit proud of his appearance...you know liked to look smart, that sort of thing."

PC Teal noted the slight derision in Mr Foster's voice and reflected that his host could never be accused of that; he wore a rather shapeless cardigan, buttoned up and trousers that looked as though they might collapse at any moment. Still, not his place to judge.

"Well that is very useful information, Sir. I'll report that to the inspector. No, don't get up...I can see myself out."

But Mr Foster did rise from his chair, slowly, holding his lower back. "I gather the old lady, Mrs Bloom, was taken to hospital. Do you know how she is, Constable?"

"Yes, Sir. I'm afraid she died last night from her injuries."

Mr Foster's mouth opened and he stared wide-eyed at Teal.

"Goodbye, Sir and thank you again."

CHAPTER 15

The three young women looked nervously at Inspector Hawkins who, notebook in hand, faced them in the lounge. "Good morning, ladies. I think you all know who I am – Inspector Hawkins of Maidenhead Police – and this is Sergeant Drake." Three pairs of eyes examined Drake; he was middle-aged, a figure that had perhaps once been solid but now boasted a generous amount of flesh. His face was slightly puffy beneath the greying hair and he stood, feet apart, wearing an assumed authority like an invisible cloak.

Hawkins continued. "We will interview each of you and, to speed the process, Sergeant Drake and I will initially conduct the interviews separately. Miss Barnes, our discussion was interrupted yesterday so I will start with you whilst Sergeant Drake will interview Miss Olivia Hulett. I would be grateful if you would stay in this room Miss Michalski. Not sure how long it will take but we'll try not to keep you waiting."

When Lizzie and Hawkins were seated, he wasted no time on niceties. "I think Miss Barnes, we had covered your movements on Saturday night and Sunday morning. I had commented just before we were interrupted that you have acute powers of observation but I would like to ask you again whether you had ever been in Mr Melford's room before you discovered his body?"

"No Inspector I had not. I am not in the habit of going into men's bedrooms."

Inspector Hawkins looked up sharply from his notebook, surprised by the force of the response. "I'd like to ask you now about your opinions of Mr Melford and anything you may have observed about the way others related to him. Did he have any enemies and, before you answer, I do know already about the incident on Saturday afternoon with the mechanic?"

"My opinions…they're mixed. At times, he seemed to be a very generous, fun-loving man but one who had grown up with many advantages in life…I mean a background of wealth and some privilege. He never made an issue of his limp but perhaps that affected him more than he let on. There must have been frustrations for him. But…I saw a darker side to his character. It wasn't just the incident with John Hale the ground crewman." Lizzie stopped, again wrestling with herself. What she knew she should say could incriminate Kasia. She knew that what she had said about Olivia being so upset on Saturday night must have put her in the frame. But, honesty had been drummed into her from early childhood and this was serious. If Olivia or Kasia had stabbed Melford, they must face justice.

"When we were in the club, there was an incident. Nothing very dramatic but I think I should mention it. A young man with I think Jewish features – his face, his hair - asked Olivia to dance. She declined, very graciously, but he was persistent. Edward told him quite forcefully to go away though I must stress there was no threat of physical violence. But when the young man left, Melford used the expression 'damned Jew'."

Again Hawkins looked up quickly. "And how did that go down?"

"Kasia – Miss Michalski – is Jewish, from Poland and she reacted very angrily, challenging him to explain why he had said 'damned'. He tried to brush it off but it soured the atmosphere and left Kasia quite upset for some time."

"I can imagine it did. Were there any other examples of anti-semitism from Mr Melford?"

"Not that I witnessed. One of the others, Graham Swinburne, seems to think Edward was sympathetic to the cause of Oswald Mosley. He didn't seem to me the type to be so unpleasant but, as I said, I think there was a darker side to his character."

Inspector Hawkins made a few more notes. "Well

thank you Miss Barnes for being so straight with me. Sometimes people omit things trying to protect friends and so on. Far better to tell us everything so we can get to the bottom of it."

Conflict burned in Lizzie's mind. She knew she should mention the button she had seen but to do so would incriminate Olivia further. Honesty won. "I'm sorry, Inspector. I should have mentioned this yesterday but I saw...." She paused and took a slow breath. "I also noticed a small button on the floor... I recognised it. I think it must have become snagged in Mr Melford's jacket when he was dancing."

"Who is the owner of the button?"

"Olivia...Miss Hulett."

"Did Mr Melford dance with all the young ladies in your party?"

"Yes...I think..." Lizzie ran through the events of the club. "No. Actually he did not dance with Kasia...Miss Michalski."

"Is there anything else you think I should know?"

Lizzie hesitated before replying, a hesitation that Hawkins did not miss. "I think this is probably nothing at all... it's such a tiny detail...but I'll tell you anyway. Before we had dinner on Saturday night, the four of us girls were at a table in the bar having a drink when Edward joined us. He wanted to order wine for the table but instead of going to the bar to speak to the steward, he clicked his fingers and summoned him over. I could see that the steward resented it...being treated as a servant and in such a...dismissive manner."

"Did the steward say anything about it, do anything?"

"No, but his facial expression was very clear. He did smile at Kasia before he left though. It seemed somehow pointed...you know...I'll smile at the lady but not at you if you treat me like that."

"What's the steward's name?" Lizzie noticed the smile on the Inspector's face as he asked, as if he were humouring her. She felt slightly put down: he obviously considered the information she had just supplied to be trivial.

"Mr Bloom," Lizzie said as she stood to leave.

Hawkins' mouth opened and the smile rapidly disappeared.

◆ ◆ ◆

PC Teal was back in the station. He sat at Sergeant Drake's desk, the telephone handset held to his ear with one hand and a pen in the other.

"So you're sure you only supply the two places in Maidenhead and one in Windsor with that type of bottled beer. How come? I mean surely there are more places who would want it?"

She sounded nice, the young woman – it sounded like a young woman – on the other end of the line. Miss Brazier she had said and when pressed added Susan. "There's just those. We supply barrels to quite a few places but it's only the ones with off-licences that take the bottles."

"Ah I see. And how many bottles do you tend to supply to each?"

"Not many of the pale ale, maybe a dozen a week. The bitter is more popular in a bottle."

"Well thank you very much for your help. I'll know who to speak to if I need more information."

"That's my pleasure Officer. I hope it gives you what you need."

When Teal replaced the handset, he looked at the information in front of him. It certainly made the job possible. He would do the Maidenhead places immediately and then cycle over to Windsor in the afternoon. "Now I wonder if someone might be at home and out of bed?" he said to himself.

"What was that Brian?"

"Oh nothing. I've got to go and check a couple of places in Maidenhead about this beer and this afternoon, I'll have to go to Windsor. It's very important…might lead to an arrest for that fire. I suppose you'd like to be doing detective work. It'll come, mate, just got to do the basics first. You'll be alright won't you Derek, guarding the fort?"

"Born to it mate. I can handle anything."

"Is that so? I'll have a word with the Sergeant then and have you out on a Saturday night in the centre of town when the pubs are turning out. You'll be fine with that won't you?"

"Like I said. I can handle anything."

Brian Teal laughed and shook his head.

◆ ◆ ◆

"Please sit down, Miss.." he consulted his notebook…"Miss Hulett."

Olivia sat abruptly in the indicated chair, crossed her legs and leaned forward, her brow deeply furrowed.

Faced with a beautiful young woman, Drake felt his resolve weaken. He knew he could not allow himself to be swayed by her lovely face. He must treat her as the suspect she was, not let himself be seduced into leniency. "Now then, Miss, I need first to go over your movements on Saturday night. Please start from the time you came back here from the club."

"We arrived just about mid-night. I know that because a church clock struck twelve times before we went inside the building."

"And, Miss Hulett, what were you wearing on Saturday night?"

"I was wearing a satin dress…green."

"Thank you. Do go on."

"We all came in and chatted for a while and then I went up to bed."

Drake looked at her, his eyes narrowing in what he hoped was an intimidating manner. He knew where she had been. "You say you were chatting. To whom exactly were you chatting?"

"There was Edward Melford and my sister for a bit and Graham Swinburne."

"Were Miss Laura and Mr Swinburne still with you and Mr Melford when you went to bed?"

"I...I'm not sure...I think..." Olivia's face began to crumple. She knew there was a risk she would start crying and she did not want to do that, did not want to be the weak, pathetic girl.

"Exactly where were you chatting? In the lounge or... elsewhere?"

"In the lounge." She pulled a handkerchief from her sleeve and held it to her face.

"Are you sure about that? You see, I don't think you're telling me everything. I think you went somewhere else, you and Mr Melford."

"No...no...I'm sure we stayed..."

Drake had the scent in his nostrils and was enjoying the moment. "You went to Mr Melford's room didn't you?"

"No, no I didn't, I told you we were in the..."

"Lounge...yes you said. The problem is I don't believe you and the reason I don't believe you..." Drake leaned forward over the table and his voice dropped to a hiss, "is because we found a long blonde hair in his room. That hair was yours. No one else has long blonde hair. Miss Barnes is fair but not blonde."

Olivia stared at him in horror. "I wasn't there."

"So let me imagine the scene. Mr Melford invites you to his room. In his mind is what is in the mind of many a young man with a beautiful young woman. He's thinking that he will get you into bed. You've had a few drinks, your guard is down and he starts coming on to you. Perhaps you wanted to go some way down that road but he wanted to go all the way. You tell him to stop but that only seems to fuel his desire." Drake could feel the words flowing as they did in the stories he sometimes read in his wife's magazine. "Did he touch you...you know... inappropriately?"

"No…yes…he…"

"Well which is it? Yes or no?"

A sob broke free and Olivia's shoulders heaved as the scene on Saturday night played in her mind. "I don't know…I don't know what happened but I left the room and went to bed."

"So you admit, you were in his room and he was coming on to you.?"

Olivia nodded, sobbing now.

Drake decided to change tack. "I can understand how difficult that must be for a woman when a man won't take 'no' for an answer. Very distressing. He would have been stronger than you of course and you must have been terrified that he was going to force himself on you. It would be quite understandable to defend yourself any way you could." He slid a green button across the table. "Yours I presume…no doubt pulled off by Mr Melford."

Olivia sat hunched on the chair, shaking silently, her handkerchief still to her face. She said nothing.

"So let's get it finished. You saw the knife lying on the writing desk where it had been used to open a letter. In desperation, you picked it up and as he came for you again, you held it in front of you and pushed it into his stomach. Or was it that he ran onto it, so desperate was he to get his hands on you?"

Olivia still said nothing.

"Either way, you stabbed him didn't you?" Drake's voice began to rise as he sensed victory. "You pushed that knife into his gut. Why don't you just admit it? Plead self-defence if you will but…" Drake was shouting, "you killed Edward Melford!"

Suddenly Olivia was on her feet. "I did not kill anyone, I didn't touch any knife. Why are you trying to blame it on me?" A strange mixture of fear and anger filled her; she turned and fled from the room. Drake watched in surprise and some alarm as the door banged closed behind her. What was he supposed to do now?

CHAPTER 16

Inspector Hawkins walked with Lizzie back to the lounge and invited Kasia to follow him. There was no chance to say anything to Kasia, no chance to warn her that she had told Hawkins about the row with Melford in the club. She felt a twinge of anxiety; it seemed like a betrayal but she reassured herself with the strong conviction that Kasia could never kill anyone.

The day was fine again and she looked longingly out of the window at the other trainees being put through their paces. Today was something of a test but she was very confident; she had after all flown a Tiger Moth solo many times. It was the aircraft she trained in initially. She smiled fondly to herself at the memory of her grandmother, Margaret, always a rock, never questioning or prying, providing support with no words just her presence. There had been dark times when Lizzie needed that. She had never told her grandmother about the things that troubled her young life, had never told her parents, but she had always felt her grandmother's unequivocal love in a way she had not with her own parents.

It was Granny Margaret's legacy that had opened the skies for her, given her a freedom she had only dreamed of. It was enough to pay for the course of lessons that earned her a solo pilot's licence but, more importantly, it gave her self-confidence, a way of proving to herself that she was worth something after all that had happened. Her older brother, Ralph had joined the RAF and was now a fighter pilot, flying Spitfires. That was probably what alarmed her parents when she announced her intention to learn to fly two years ago. They still could not understand why she wanted this job with the ATA, wanted her to meet some nice chap – a banker, someone rich and steady – and settle down to a life of domestic drudgery.

That was not for her. Her mother's life was an endless round of social gatherings and committees, the Church, the WI, the golf club. That would be a living hell and offered no inducement against the wonder of soaring up into and above the clouds. The roar of the engine when you opened up the throttle and gathered speed down the airfield, that magical sensation as the aircraft lifted from the ground as if you were a bird.

A Moth approached the airfield and dropped low enough just to touch the wheels down before the engine revved and it lifted again to rise into the hazy blue sky brushed with delicate white cloud. She would be up there soon, flying her circuit and hoping that she managed to find the landmarks.

A door slammed somewhere just outside the lounge and Olivia rushed into the room, clutching a handkerchief to her face, her eyes wild.

Lizzie flung her arms around her and held her tight. "Olivia, darling, whatever's the matter?"

It took a great deal of consolation before Olivia's sobs had subsided enough to respond. "That man, that Sergeant Duck, whatever his name is, he accused me of killing Edward. I knew it. I knew they would try to blame me but I didn't do it…I didn't Lizzie. You must believe me."

Lizzie knew then that Olivia was telling the truth. No actor, however good, could say what she had just said in the way she had said it if the opposite were true. She spoke softly, close to Olivia's ear. "I do believe you Olivia. Now calm yourself and we'll discuss how to manage this."

Lizzie felt Olivia's body relax and she breathed deeply. "He was shouting at me, blaming me for killing Edward."

"Let's sit down." Lizzie guided her to a settee and they sat side by side. "What I suggest we do, is go through the events of Saturday night – I know it will distress you to think about them – but we must get everything clear then you can make a simple statement to the Sergeant or Inspector Hawkins and, if it's allowed, I'll be with you."

Olivia turned to face Lizzie, relief and gratitude exuding from her eyes. "Will you Lizzie? Thank you. I get so nervous and I can't think when people have a go at me."

"Let's start with you arriving back here on Saturday night. Take your time but tell me exactly what happened."

"Edward had drunk quite a lot – you know that – and he had whispered things to me when we were dancing. I took no notice...put it down to the drink. When we tumbled out of the car, we were all in good spirits, he took my hand and pulled me towards him – out in the car park that was."

"Yes...I happened to be looking out of our window and saw that."

"I pulled away, made a joke of it, but let him take my hand and lead me inside. All four of us chatted for a few minutes in the foyer and then Graham went into the lounge and Laura went up to bed. Edward said he had some port in his room and invited me up. I know I was foolish to go but I thought, if I humoured him a bit, that would be enough. You know how it is with men...you have to manage them."

"I do indeed."

"In his room, he poured us some port and we sat on the bed. He put his arm around me and tried to kiss me. I didn't mind a peck on the cheek but I wouldn't let him kiss me on the lips. He started getting a bit insistent so, to get away, I stood up, took both glasses – they were empty by then – and put them back by the bottle. I was about to say that I should go when he stood up between me and the door. Next thing his hands were all over me, feeling my...you know... private parts and pulling at the top of my dress. He pulled so hard, some buttons came off. Then he was...." There was a choking sob and Lizzie pulled Olivia closer.

"He pulled up my dress and his hand went underneath tugging at the top of my stockings. I couldn't shout, I was so surprised but I managed to push him away, twisting as I did so. I just managed to pull myself from his grasp and rushed out of the door."

Olivia was silent for a few moments and Lizzie struggled to contain the maelstrom of emotions she herself was feeling, all that anger and humiliation she had buried for years.

When Olivia spoke again, her voice was pleading. "That's the truth, Lizzie. I did not stab Edward Melford."

◆ ◆ ◆

PC Teal pedalled slowly through the town to the Red Lion. It was, you might say, a working man's pub, quite rough and ready, the floor wooden boards and the tables plain, square, uninteresting. It was not the sort of pub he would take Sheila to. No, she was classy and a woman such as her needed to be in more comfortable surroundings...a log fire, not burning at this time of year of course, in a big inglenook chimney and soft armchairs...actually a nice big sofa, one of those with a very high back so people couldn't see what you were doing.

One day perhaps. This was a great opportunity for him, doing detective work. If it went well, perhaps he could ask Hawkins to do more. He could fancy himself as Hercule Poirot, solving crimes with his prodigious brain, though he was not sure he did have a prodigious brain.

There were a couple of old men in the bar sipping pints but no sign of the landlord. One of the old men spoke. "You'll be a'ter George, the Landlord will yer? What's he been up to now?"

"Waterin' down the beer I should think judging by the taste of this." His fellow took a long draught from his beer, swallowed and grimaced. "I sometimes wonder why we drink in 'ere Albert."

"It's the company!" Both old men cackled, spluttering and wheezing.

"Excuse me!" shouted Teal, leaning over the bar and directing his voice through the open door at the back. "Can I have a word please. It's PC Teal from Maidenhead Police."

A few seconds later, a small, wiry man in his fifties shuffled through into the bar. Wisps of thinning hair covered his pate and a few strands strayed onto his forehead. "What can I do for you? We're all above board 'ere. Nothing against the law."

"I'm sure that's the case, Sir. I'm investigating an important matter involving the death of a lady recently. My investigations at the moment concern bottled beer."

The landlord looked at him blankly. "Bottled beer?"

"That's right, Sir. I'm told by Wethered's Brewery in Marlow that they supply you with bottles of their Pale Ale."

"They do, yes. What of it?"

"I wonder, Sir, if you have regular customers who buy that?"

"We do have a couple of men who like to take a few bottles home with them."

Teal's pulse quickened. "And could you give me their names, Sir, and if possible their addresses?"

"No I can't. Neither of them are like proper regulars in the pub...not like these two.." he nodded at the two old men who were all ears, "they just come in maybe once a week for the bottles so I don't know their names nor nuffin' about them."

"That's a pity. I wonder if you could do me a favour. When they next come in, could you please find out names and addresses. You can telephone the station and leave a message for me...PC Teal."

The landlord shuffled from foot to foot. "Well, I dunno...people like their privacy...don't come in 'ere to be shopped to the Police."

"I just need to ask them a couple of questions. It would be very helpful. Thank you." Brian Teal knew George would not supply any information and he headed for the door. Before he reached it he turned. "Perhaps you could tell me, Sir, if either of these two men are tall."

"Tall? Nah, neither of 'em is tall. Both quite short arses I'd say."

This detective lark was not so easy then, Brain Teal

thought, as he swung his leg over his bike.

◆ ◆ ◆

"I have gained a good knowledge of people's movements on Saturday night and Sunday morning before the body was discovered but I'd like you to confirm that you returned from the Café de Paris in the car owned by Mr Sanders at about eleven-thirty and went straight to your room. Miss Barnes said you fell asleep very quickly."

"That's correct, Officer."

"Did you leave your room during the night?"

"No."

"What time did you get up in the morning?"

"I think it was about seven o'clock."

"What did you do then?"

"I sat in the lounge and read a manual about aircraft."

"Did anyone see you or did you see anyone?"

"No to both questions…not until Laura and then Lizzie came into the lounge."

Hawkins paused, his eyes narrowing and fixed on Kasia. "We have a witness who says at about seven-thirty you were going down the stairs but he saw your back suggesting that you had come from the men's corridor not the women's."

"I went from our room straight down the stairs. It can't have been me."

Hawkins changed tack; he found that often took people off guard. "Could you please tell me about the disagreement between you and Mr Melford at the club."

Kasia shrugged. "Nothing to tell. He used an expression which I disliked and I told him so."

"I think you are Jewish are you not? From Poland?"

"That is correct Inspector. My family left Poland last September."

"Not an easy time for you and your family. Have you experienced any anti-Jewish behaviour or attitudes since coming to this country?"

Kasia laughed. "Of course. There's plenty of that. It's not just the likes of Melford you know."

Inspector Hawkins nodded. "I imagine you feel a great deal of anger towards people who are derogatory about Jews."

"Yes…but not enough to kill someone for it. I am not like the Germans…we do not kill people just because we disagree with them or dislike them."

Hawkins paused. "Do you know Mr Bloom, the steward?"

"Of course I know who he is. I don't *know* him…I'd not met him before coming here."

"Did you ever go into Mr Melford's room…perhaps a romantic assignation?"

Kasia looked stunned. "Of course not. If I wanted to visit a gentleman's room, it would not have been Melford."

"Are you sure about that?"

"Of course. Why do you ask?"

"It's just that in Mr Melford's room, we found a long, dark, curly hair that I would guess came from your head."

Before Kasia could reply, there was a knock on the door which opened and Sergeant Drake poked his head around it. "Sorry, Sir, could I have a word please?"

CHAPTER 17

Sergeant Drake was not happy. It felt like a criticism. It was obvious that blonde was guilty…all the evidence pointed to her…the blonde hair caught in Melford's fingernail and she had admitted being in his room. He had the distinct impression that the Inspector thought he had failed in some way. Ok he had been a bit pushy with her but you can't let up on a possible murder suspect because she does that girlie thing of bursting into tears. It was a distraction, a deliberate ruse to get him off her back. And now the Inspector would take over, claim all the glory of finding the killer.

The mess was empty so he went through the swing door into the kitchen where all was bustle, pots and pans being crashed around, steam filling the air in great puffs when a lid was lifted. He had to bellow to be heard. "Where can I find Mr Bloom?"

A chef walked slowly towards him wiping his hands on a cloth. "Mr Bloom? You'll find him at home probably or at the funeral parlour. He ain't at work today on account of his mother."

"His mother?" Slowly Sergeant Drake made the connection. "Of course, she was the lady that died in the fire."

"That's right." The chef stared at Drake who seemed transfixed. "Anything else I can do for you?"

"Did you have any dealings with Mr Melford, the trainee who was killed on Saturday?"

"Not dealings. He came in the kitchen last…must have been Friday…with a bit of paper."

"A bit of paper? What did he want?"

"No idea. Mr Bloom dealt with him. Anything else?"

"No, no. Thanks for that."

"Rightio. Must get on then." The chef turned and went back to the vast bank of ovens.

Drake went to find Hawkins. He would have to interrupt once more but that was better than putting his foot in it again. But he didn't need to interrupt as Miss Michalski was leaving the office, a look on her face that could have been anger or distress. He stepped inside.

"Mr Bloom is not at work today, Sir. His mother was the one who died in that fire on Saturday night so I expect he's at home, making arrangements for the funeral and so on. Probably best to leave him today isn't it?"

"We can't afford to leave it Sergeant so take the car, go to Grenfell Road and track him down. But…" Hawkins glared at him, " for God's sake take it easy…softly, softly, Drake, gets further than going in guns blazing. The man is grieving and we must respect that. Main thing we need to know is what time he arrived at work on Sunday morning and what he did."

"Yes Sir. Softly, softly it is. How did you get on with the Polish woman?"

"She must be considered as much of a suspect as the blonde you interviewed. She could not account for the hair in Melford's room - didn't deny it was hers mind – said it must have attached itself to his clothing when they were dancing and then fallen off. But Miss Barnes said she didn't dance with Melford. I'll let her stew for a bit then see her again."

Drake would normally have been chastened by the Inspector's cautionary words about his approach to interviewing Bloom but the chance of driving the Inspector's car was a rare one and very welcome. Perhaps he should take it for a little spin first…but maybe not!

He wound the window down as soon as he had set off, enjoying the breeze that danced into the car and played around his face. Wonderful! By the time he had driven the few miles to Maidenhead, he was feeling refreshed, important, magnanimous. The interview with Mr Bloom would be nice and easy; after all he couldn't be a suspect as he was not there over Saturday night. Must be rough though, losing your mother in that way. Drake wondered how Teal was getting on with the bottled beer and the witness on Grenfell Road.

After turning into Grenfell Road, he brought the car to a halt just beyond the shop. Mr Bloom lived next to it. It was a sorry sight, the interior blackened and workmen now boarding it up. There certainly were some right bastards about...should be off in the army, that would sort them out.

The houses in this stretch of the road were all right on the street. Standing erect, he used the large brass knocker on the door and stood back a little. Some thirty seconds later, he heard a latch being removed on the inside and a key grate in the lock. The door was opened a very small amount and he could see the brass chain that prevented it opening further.

"I'd like to speak to Mr Bloom please, is he in?"

"I am Bloom. Have you found the culprit?"

"I'm Sergeant Drake from Maidenhead Police. I'd like to ask you a few questions, Sir. May I come in?"

The chain was removed and the door opened revealing Mr Bloom. He was in his early forties, about six feet tall with a slim figure, slightly stooped. He looked as though he had a wiry strength, one of those men who at first glance looked frail but in fact were as powerful as someone more thick set. His nose was aquiline, giving him the appearance of an eagle or a bird of prey and this was emphasised by sharp eyes that darted from one thing to the next.

"So Officer, what is the news?"

"Well, Sir...I realise that you are very recently bereaved but sadly we are having to investigate another matter...a death...at White Waltham air base. I think you work there."

"I do yes. This is that Melford man. I was at work yesterday but now my mother..."

"Yes, yes of course Sir. Please accept the condolences of myself and the other officers at the station. A terrible thing to have happened."

Bloom stared at Drake but said nothing; it looked as though he were assessing whether Drake's sympathy was genuine.

"It would be helpful to know, Sir, what time you arrived at work on Sunday morning."

"It was about six-thirty. I rose at six as usual and left soon after...I have breakfast at the base not at home. I cycled so it would take about twenty minutes."

"And what did you do when you arrived at work, Sir?"

Bloom looked quizzically at Drake. "What do you think I did? I started work, preparing the mess for breakfast, making sure the kitchen staff had everything in hand. Breakfast is served from eight o'clock and it takes a while to get things ready."

"Of course, Sir. And did you see or hear anything out of the ordinary...anyone lurking around as you arrived for example, anyone walking about the building."

"No. Apart from the kitchen staff, the first person I saw was one of the trainees...Miss Barnes I think...who came into the mess to ask when breakfast would be served."

"So nothing unusual. How well did you know Mr Melford?"

"Not at all. He was just another of the recruits."

"You had not had any dealings...any trouble with him?"

Bloom's eyes hardened. "No."

"I understand he came into the kitchen on Friday."

Bloom thought for a moment. "Yes, now you mention it he did. Wanted to know what was for lunch I think."

"Anything else?"

"No."

"Ah...it's just that one of the other trainees said there was an incident on Saturday evening when Mr Melford clicked his fingers for service. She thought that might have made you angry."

"I have no recollection of such a thing." Bloom spoke with barely contained hostility. "Are you suggesting that because that man was disdainful, I murdered him? My mother is lying dead because someone fire-bombed my brother-in-law's shop and you are wasting your time asking me such trivial questions. How dare you Sergeant, how dare you? Leave my house now." Bloom's arm shot out, pointing to the door.

"Now steady on, Sir. I'm just doing my job. We have to ask these questions and we are investigating the attack on the shop. One of our constables is at this very moment pursuing a lead we have."

"Huh! I don't suppose it will come to anything." Bloom's voice was as hard as steel and laden with irony. "Goodbye Sergeant. Call again when you can tell me who murdered my mother."

◆ ◆ ◆

"It is completely unacceptable that your Sergeant treated Olivia in the way he did." Lizzie stood feet slightly apart, hands on hips and glared at Inspector Hawkins. She had learned that attack is often the best form of defence.

"This is a murder investigation, Miss Barnes, and whilst I understand that you are concerned about your friend being upset, we have to ask difficult questions. You must realise that people lie to conceal the truth and we do not know at this stage who is lying and who is not. We will discover that though, make no mistake about it."

"Your sergeant accused Miss Hulett of murder. That is a very serious allegation to make when you have no proof. The fact that she may have been in Mr Melford's room does not mean she killed him."

"No but we must find out exactly what happened in that room on Saturday night however embarrassing it may be for some. Sergeant Drake has had to go and interview someone else so I will now complete the interview with Miss Hulett. We cannot have people walking out of our interviews."

There was a gasp from Olivia who was sitting, huddled

on the sofa. Lizzie turned and noticed her hand shaking. "Olivia will tell you what happened – she's already told me – but I insist that I be with her in the room as she is now very distraught."

"Are you a lawyer?"

"No but I am a friend and she is entitled to that surely."

"It's not usual and she is not entitled to it as you say but I am happy for you to be there provided you do not interrupt."

Lizzie nodded and perched on the edge of the sofa beside Olivia. "Come on sweetheart. I'll be with you. Just take your time and tell the Inspector what you told me."

Olivia allowed herself to be led, trembling, into the office behind Hawkins. When they were seated he spoke to her in a kindly manner. "Now Miss Hulett, Sergeant Drake tells me you had admitted being in Mr Melford's room but you denied stabbing him. It would be helpful if you could tell me exactly what happened. I realise it is distressing for you to recall these events but take your time. It is important that we establish exactly what happened."

Slowly, coaxed and occasionally prompted by Lizzie, Olivia went through the events of that night in Melford's room. Twice she faltered and Hawkins waited, his facial expression one of concern not condemnation. Lizzie was impressed how he gradually enabled Olivia to relax and tell her story. She became more confident that Hawkins would believe Olivia as her account progressed.

When she had finished with her leaving Melford's room, Hawkins very gently said, "As you went back to your own room, Miss Hulett, did you see anyone else. I realise you were in a distressed state and just wanted to get back to your own room but please think hard."

Olivia thought for a moment, no doubt tracing that agonising journey back to safety. She shook her head. "No…I saw nobody…but as you say, I was not really aware of anything other than getting away."

"When you were in his room, did you notice anything? Did you see the knife for example? Was the window open?"

"I didn't notice anything. I was concentrating on keeping Edward...on making sure he didn't..." She looked up at last at Inspector Hawkins. "I don't remember seeing a knife or anything. Obviously, I saw the bottle of port and the glasses which we drank from. I'm sure you saw my lipstick on the rim of one glass."

"This is a difficult question, Olivia. When Mr Melford was becoming most insistent, were you frightened for your safety...I mean was he angry that you were resisting, did he use violence against you?"

"Yes of course I was frightened. He seemed determined to...you know...and he ripped open the front of my dress, pulling off some buttons. Had I stayed, I know he would have...he would have...."

"Yes, I understand Olivia. I'm gaining the impression that Mr Melford was something of a Jekyll and Hyde character... he could be charming and generous but harboured a nastier side. Would you agree?"

Olivia looked at Hawkins. "Absolutely. He was no gentleman as I originally thought. He was determined to get what he wanted whatever the cost to me."

CHAPTER 18

The sound of a car pulling into the station forecourt caused Brian Teal to look up from the desk where he had just started to write a note for Inspector Hawkins up-dating him on progress that morning. It was the Inspector's car so he crumpled the piece of paper and threw it in the bin. But it was Sergeant Drake who entered the station, looking important, swaggering slightly.

"Hello Sarge. Nicked the Inspector's car have you? Maybe you bumped him off to get it. 'Vaulting ambition'. That's Shakespeare that is…Macbeth…it's the only bit I remember from school."

"Don't be ridiculous Teal. Inspector Hawkins asked me to take the car to do an important interview. I'll be going back to White Waltham shortly to carry on interviews there. Thought I'd drop in here first, make sure you're not sitting around idle. Where have you got to?"

"Well I went back to Grenfell Road and spoke with Mr Foster again. He said both men had accents that were probably working men, not posh or anything like that but one might have been Irish. He did say that the taller one wore brogues which he thought might be brown but he couldn't be sure of the colour 'cos it was quite dark."

"Not a lot of help then?"

"No Sarge. Same issue with the two pubs in Maidenhead who sell the Wethered's Pale Ale. They have regular customers for it but don't know names or where they live. There's a place in Windsor that Wethered's also supplies so I'll cycle over there this afternoon and see if I have any luck."

"This is going to be a hard one to crack but we've got

to try now there's a death. Just interviewed the woman's son. He works out at White Waltham…a steward. Not very co-operative but I suppose that's understandable." He looked at PC Green who was leaning against the front counter. "Anything come up this morning Green?"

"Nah, Sir. Dead boring it was."

"Boredom, Constable, is sometimes better than excitement."

"Not in my book, Sarge."

"There will be times in your career, Green, when you long for boredom."

PC Green smiled. "The only thing I had was some old biddy came in complaining about vandals chucking red paint over her garden fence on Saturday night. Hardly the crime of the century is it?"

"Red paint…Saturday night? Where does she live Green?"

"Uhh…hang on Sarge…I'll check the log. I wrote it all down." PC Green consulted the log book. "Here we go. Mrs Lester…came in at 10.18 am…pot of red paint and a brush thrown over the fence. Hit her shed and the paint went all over her prize rose bush. She said she wouldn't have minded if it were in Autumn as the colours would match the season but she'll never get it off the leaves."

" Address, Green, her address?"

"Oh yeah…um…114, Grenfell Road. She said it's on the corner with High Town Road. Quite a posh bird she was."

"Did she see who it was?"

"Not really. Said she was going to bed when she heard the crash of the pot hitting the shed…mind you she didn't know then what it was…looked out the window and all she saw was two blokes getting into a van and driving off."

"Time?"

"Er…" Green consulted his watch. "…just gone mid-day Sarge."

"No you idiot, Green. What time on Saturday night did

this happen?"

"Oh...er...I think she said just gone eleven...at night that is."

Sergeant Drake looked at PC Teal and they both nodded. "That's our bombers I bet," said Brian Teal. "In a van. That's interesting. Sounds like they're well organised."

"And well resourced. You need to pay this lady a visit this afternoon Teal before you go to Windsor. See if you can get anything more out of her, make and colour of van for example."

"Will do, Sarge."

"Is that important Sarge? I thought it was a bit of Saturday night vandalism."

"Your boring morning, Green, might just prove to be the clue we need to discover who fire-bombed the shop on Saturday night and caused the death of old Mrs Bloom. Not so bad now is it...boring?"

Lunch was a desultory affair, eaten in near silence. Lizzie sat beside Olivia whose anxiety had eased now that she had been able to tell Hawkins what had happened in Melford's room on Saturday night. Lizzie felt that Hawkins believed her account. He must have realised that Olivia was fragile, a porcelain doll, easily broken, and not someone who could grab a knife and push it into someone whatever the provocation.

All the recruits were at the same long table as previous meals but the four young women sat at one end. Kasia seemed out of sorts, eyes fixed on her plate and taking mouthfuls of food in a mechanical manner.

"How did the interview go with Hawkins, Kasia?" Lizzie asked as gently as she could.

Kasia looked up. "As I expected. He tried to blame Melford's murder on me. It's because I'm a Jew. Easier to blame the foreigner because no one cares about them."

"That's not true, Kasia. He must realise that you and your family have suffered and anyway what evidence could he possibly have?"

"He said they found a long, black curly hair in Melford's room. I'm the only one here with hair like that."

"But that's ridiculous. Did you go into Melford's room at all?"

"Of course not. It must have got attached to his clothes somehow...I don't know how as I have not been close to him."

"But that's entirely flimsy. You cannot be charged with murder just because they found a hair in his room. I mean, it might have come from one of the housekeeping staff when they were cleaning. Anyway, the window in Melford's room was open – I saw it myself when we found the body. It probably means there was an intruder."

"Perhaps."

"I suppose I'll have the drilling this afternoon. It's disgraceful the way that Sergeant accused Olivia of the murder. My sister could never do such a thing."

"I suppose they're trying to get something that will lead to the killer. They seem rather lost at the moment and suspect everyone. He didn't accuse me of anything but he seemed to think that I went into Melford's room. Not sure if it's a reflection on Melford's desire for women or their view of us being loose that they assume all of us have been in his room." Lizzie laid her cutlery carefully on her plate. "Someone must have significant history with Melford to kill him. None of the things he did to upset any of us would prompt murder."

The conversation died and, after lunch, all the recruits walked into the lounge to await the start of the afternoon session. At least I'll be flying, Lizzie thought with relief, as sitting around doing nothing was not in her nature.

Mark Sanders picked up a paper from the table and began to read whilst still standing. He opened the first page and held the newspaper in front of him. The other recruits sat down;

no one spoke. Lizzie could see the banner – The Daily Express.

"Listen to this," Sanders announced. "There's an article here that says some of the refugees from Germany and Austria who have entered the Netherlands are actually German agents who have been planted to assist the German invasion. The writer...er it's a Hilde Marchant - that name sounds German doesn't it? – says that no refugees from those countries can be trusted. She calls them Fifth Columnists, you know like in the Spanish Civil War."

Lizzie glanced at Kasia and was aware that other eyes were on her too.

"She says the Germans will do the same in this country and we shouldn't trust any refugees from Germany and Austria. She's calling for internment of all aliens."

Kasia was suddenly on her feet, her eyes blazing, her voice cracking. "That's typical of this country. Just blame the foreigners for everything. How dare she suggest all aliens as she calls us are spies and enemy agents?" Her voice dropped in volume. "I know what you're all thinking. You think I killed Melford don't you? The Police certainly do. Blame the foreigner, that's the easiest thing to do. Doesn't matter if it's right or not. We were promised safety and a welcome in this country but all we get is suspicion and blame. Haven't we been through enough?"

She dropped onto the settee and burst into tears. Lizzie, sitting next to her, did the only thing she could think of - flung her arms around her and held her tight. Kasia tried at first to shake her off but then sobbed on her shoulder.

There was an embarrassed silence for several seconds before Patrick Kenny spoke. "Although I've spent nearly all my life in this country, I was born in Ireland so I guess that makes me an alien too. They may just as well blame me for Melford's death as Kasia. We just have to make sure we help Hawkins to find the real killer."

This produced a chorus of support for Kasia and eventually, she lifted her head, blinking away the tears. "Thank you," she whispered, "thank you for your support. But you can see why I do not feel welcome here when people are putting forward such ridiculous views. That article will lead to all sorts of problems for us refugees because people will believe it...will want to believe it."

"You're amongst friends here, Kasia, and if you've done nothing wrong as I'm sure you haven't, you have nothing to fear from our justice system. Hawkins is no fool and he'll want harder evidence than what he mentioned to you."

Once again, PC Teal thanked God that the weather was still fine as he cycled back to Grenfell Road. He found the house easily on the corner of Grenfell Road and High Town Road. Interesting how the nature of the houses changed at that point. Whereas further down Grenfell Road they had been terraced, although not tiny, on High Town Road, they were large, detached with big gardens. Number 114 faced Grenfell Road but it had a fence along the side of the garden stretching some way down High Town Road. Brian Teal could see the roof of the shed that the pot of paint had hit. He walked back to the front and rang the door bell.

An elderly lady, short and slim, smartly dressed in a skirt and top with a cardigan answered the door. She wore a string of pearls around her neck and had pearl earrings. Teal was not much of an expert on jewellery but felt he should take an interest now that he was courting.

"Afternoon Madam. Is it Mrs Lester?"

"Yes indeed. Are you here about the pot of paint."

"I am Madam. May I come in?"

"Of course." Teal noticed how she looked down at his shoes but must have judged them clean enough. She led him into a large and very comfortable sitting room, the furniture not modern but covered in a rich red fabric that matched the curtains. Two settees faced each other across a large coffee table which was centred on the fireplace surrounded by marble. Mrs Lester gestured to one settee and she sat opposite him.

"Er, thank you Madam. Could I just check the details you gave to my colleague this morning please. If I have this right, the incident occurred soon after eleven o'clock on Saturday night. You heard something hit your shed, looked out of the window and saw two men getting into a van."

"That's correct Constable. But of course I didn't know what had hit the shed until next morning. If you need to see the pot of paint and the brush, I've got them in a bag in the scullery... thought I'd better preserve the evidence."

"Thank you Madam. I would like to take those with me...as you say, evidence. Can you tell me anything about the two men you saw?"

"Very little I'm afraid. The van was parked near the end of our garden on High Town Road and, even if it had been closer, it was too dark to see much. One was taller than the other and they both wore hats so I didn't really get a look at them. I thought it strange though. Vandalism is normally the preserve of the youth but those two didn't have the look of young people about them and boys would not have access to a vehicle."

"Can you tell me anything about the van...the make, size or colour."

"I'm afraid I'm no good on cars, Constable. All I can say is that it was fairly small and looked black. I didn't see if there was any name on the side and to be honest it happened so quickly I didn't have time."

"Well thank you Madam. That has been very helpful."

"I'm afraid it's not much to go on but do you suppose you'll be able to catch them?"

"I certainly hope so Madam. From what you've told us, it sounds like they are the men who fire-bombed the shop along the road."

"Oh my goodness." Mrs Lester's hand went to her mouth.

Brian Teal liked to make an impression.

CHAPTER 19

Soon after Kasia's outburst, Inspector Hawkins entered the lounge. "I would like to start this afternoon by interviewing Miss Laura Hulett. Sergeant Drake will return to the air base shortly and will interview Mr Kenny." Hawkins raised his arm towards the door.

"Miss Hulett..."

Laura sat in the chair indicated by Hawkins and laid her crossed hands on her lap. She did not smile and seemed very calm. Was that the composure of an innocent or was he confronting someone who knew how to present a face? "Now Miss Hulett, I have gained a good knowledge of most people's movements on Saturday night and Sunday morning so I don't propose to go over ground I am clear about. Have you at any time been inside Mr Melford's room?"

"No."

"Did you know Mr Melford before joining the ATA a week ago."

"No. I saw his name on the list they sent us a few weeks ago. That was the first I had heard of him."

"Have you had any cause to dislike Mr Melford...has he done anything that made you angry?"

"No."

"Miss Hulett, I find that difficult to believe. You witnessed I think the incident at the club between Melford and Miss Michalski, surely that gave rise to some feelings about him?"

"I don't agree with anti-semitism but you asked me if he had made me angry. I was not angry about it."

"And what about your sister, Olivia. She has given me

an account of what happened in Melford's room on Saturday night. She was very upset about it. Surely that must have made you angry."

Laura shrugged. "Perhaps a bit but I don't go round killing people because they've upset my sister."

"Is Olivia someone who's prone to uncontrolled behaviour, sudden bursts of anger?"

"No she isn't. My sister has a very gentle nature. She has a vulnerability which makes her prey for some."

"And therefore you are very protective of her...perfectly understandable that."

"I am protective but not in a violent way."

"Did you leave your room on Saturday night after Olivia had returned so that would have been after," Hawkins consulted his notes, "twelve thirty?"

"No."

"I think you're lying to me, Miss Hulett. You see, your answers are as brief as possible and you seem to be holding yourself together in case you reveal something you don't want to reveal. I think you dislike Melford anyway but hated him for what he tried to do to your sister."

"I disliked him for that, I disapproved of him, but I certainly would not be capable of murdering anyone."

"You disapproved of him. Interesting word to use. Why?"

"He was one of those rich young men who think they can have anything they want. He could be charming certainly but in reality he was anything but charming. He blamed his failures on others..."

"The incident with John Hale, the member of the ground crew, you mean?"

"Yes and the way he treated others. It was his duplicity I disliked, presenting himself as a nice young man, soft and gentle to attract women, but being a self-centred, spoilt brat."

Hawkins raised his eyebrows. "What did he do to attract young women?"

"Oh being very charming, splashing his money about... he could turn on that smile, his eyes focusing on the object of his desire, making her feel as though she was the most special woman in the World. It's an old tactic but sadly still works."

"As it did with your sister presumably?"

"Yes to some extent but she was more concerned about keeping him at bay without making him angry. A young woman can't afford to make a man like that angry...he has contacts, influence which he would use, as well as the risk of physical violence...as indeed proved to be the case with Olivia."

"Did he hit her? Olivia did not say so."

"No but he did try to...you know..."

"Yes. And why do you call him 'unpleasant' besides of course what he allegedly did to your sister?"

"Instinct, the way he acted and of course the photo of him with the Bullingdon Club at Oxford. Everyone knows what they're like...take what they want, do what they want and don't care about who they hurt."

The eyes of Inspector Hawkins narrowed like a tiger focusing on its prey. "How do you know he was a member of the Bullingdon Club?"

Laura suddenly stopped, looked confused and blushed. She looked out of the window. "I...I think Olivia must have mentioned it."

Hawkins waited a few seconds watching Laura writhing in front of him. "Or Miss Hulett, you were in his room and saw the photograph."

◆ ◆ ◆

PC Teal flew along the road from Maidenhead to Windsor. His heart was light. Soon, if luck was on his side, he would be able to see Sheila again. But first he had to find The Prince Harry pub to see if they could tell him who had been buying bottles of Wethered's Pale Ale. It would be a waste of time, he was sure of that, but it had to be done. 'Leave no stone unturned' the Inspector was fond of saying. Something may crawl out.

He had checked the map back at the Station and found the pub by the old Corn Exchange or Guildhall or whatever it was…a magnificent building with columns that held up the first floor and which sat opposite the Castle Hotel. He pedalled along Arthur Street. There would be a bit of a wiggle around the station and then he would come out opposite the West end of the Castle. A right turn onto the High Street and a short way up to get there. And the great thing was that it was not very far to Sheila's house. His heart quickened a little as he thought of her and he had to brake suddenly when an old woman stepped off the pavement in front of him.

The pub was certainly a bit more up-market than the two he had visited in Maidenhead. He strolled to the bar and was greeted by a young woman who smiled a welcome.

"Afternoon officer. What can we do for you?"

"I need to ask the Landlord a few questions…don't worry, nothing wrong here, just need to find out if he knows someone."

"I'll just fetch him."

While she was gone, PC Teal looked around the saloon bar he was in. Comfortable armchairs and sofas, low ceiling, pictures on the walls of what looked like actors. Nice place to have a drink or maybe even a meal, though it might be a bit expensive. Certainly a good place to bring Sheila one evening.

The barmaid returned with an older woman behind her. "I'm afraid, Mr Dewhurst is out at the moment but this is Mrs Dewhurst the Landlady."

The older woman smiled at him as he gave his name. "I swear police officers get younger by the day. How can I help you Constable?"

Brian Teal stood erect, his head almost touching the beam on the ceiling. "I'm investigating a very serious matter, Madam, that took place on Saturday night in Maidenhead. We are trying to track down the perpetrator of a serious crime and one lead we are following is that he may have bought bottles, or at least one bottle, of Wethered's Pale Ale from you. Wethered have given us the names of all the establishments that they supply with that particular item and you are the only one in Windsor. Do you have regular customers for off-licence sales of the Pale Ale."

"We do have a few regulars, Constable, but we don't sell a lot of it."

"Can you give me the names of any of them?"

"I'm afraid not. Some of them drink here but most who buy bottles just come in for those and leave."

"Perhaps you can tell me something about those that do that."

"Well there's an old man, a bit dodgy on his feet, buys only a couple of bottles a week. There's a woman comes in, lives nearby I think, who buys some for her husband - he can't get out. There's a chap who comes in occasionally and buys a few bottles. He's a nice enough bloke but he strikes me as someone who's got ideas above his station if you know what I mean."

"Not really Madam. Ideas above his station?"

"Yeah you know the sort. We get quite a few in here... imagine they're something a bit special because they drink in a better establishment than your average working man."

"Can you tell me anything about him? Tall, short, slim and so on."

"Oh he's quite tall, taller than you, Constable, has to duck his head a little to avoid that beam."

"And is it the way he speaks that makes you think he sees himself as better than he is?"

"Not really the way he speaks. I know you'll think this is daft but I always notice this...women do...he wears expensive shoes...brown brogues. I suspect they cost rather more than a working man would normally be able to spend. I think he wants to appear more well-to-do than he actually is."

PC Teal caught the word 'brogues'. "Brown brogues, you

say. Are you sure about that?"

"Course I am. Like I said, I always notice things like that."

"Can you tell me where he lives?"

"No idea Officer. Sorry. He sometimes comes in for a drink of an evening and meets another chap...an Irish bloke. They just sit over there in the corner and talk. Nothing unusual about that."

"I know the chaps you mean." It was the barmaid. "They was in here on Saturday for a while and a few weeks ago some posh bloke came in and joined them for a while. Now *he* did speak fancy, very la-di-da."

"That's very interesting Miss. You've both been a great help, Madam. If they come in again, could you please try to get a name at least and let us know – just call Maidenhead Police Station. Thank you very much." PC Teal left the pub and retrieved his bicycle. It must be the same man. Someone who probably lived in Windsor, hence the car to get to Maidenhead. But it was still a needle in a haystack. He glanced at his watch. Only three o'clock. He needed to kill an hour before going round to Sheila's. He'd go and walk by the river again and imagine she was with him.

"You take that aircraft there, Lizzie." Commander Trueman's too busy to be instructing this afternoon and so we'll only be needing the two planes. You may as well take the one he was to use." He pointed to a Moth sitting on the apron.

"Wasn't that the one Melford flew on Saturday afternoon, the one he thought had a faulty rudder?"

"Yes, but Hale checked it again when Melford complained and he is certain there's no problem."

That was enough for lizzie who was eager to take to

the air. After kitting up, John Hale swung the propeller and the engine fired into life. She let it turn over to warm up while she did her pre-flight checks and, at a thumbs up from Hale, taxied out to the end of the runway.

This is what she wanted to be doing. The engine was turning over, a lovely smooth drone and she watched the tower for the flag to go. There it was. She opened the throttles and felt the thrill as the engine roared into life. Slowly the aircraft crept along the grass and gradually gathered speed until she was being bumped and jostled. One had to crane over sideways to see what was ahead until enough speed had been reached to lift the tail from the ground. A few seconds later, she pulled back the joystick and the Moth lifted as smoothly as a swan rising from the surface of a lake.

Lizzie's heart lifted too. The aircraft rose slowly, leaving the airfield behind, the buildings diminishing with every second. It was a glorious day for flying, only high cloud brushed across the vast dome of blue and the lightest of winds. It wouldn't last of course. Bad weather would come sooner or later but she was determined to make the most of the fine days until then.

She had been given a route by Roger Carlisle and a list of places. At each point, she was required to identify a suitable landmark such as a church tower, an isolated tree, a factory building. The first leg was easy. Fly north west and pick up the River Thames, then follow that to Henley. The old bridge that crossed the river should be a useful landmark. It took only a few minutes to reach the Thames where she leaned the plane to port and followed a long sweeping bend around to Henley. There was the bridge with the church beside it and the town spread around the north bank, sleepy in the pale May sunlight.

The second waypoint was Basildon Park, a large country house. It was on the River Thames too, West of Henley, but it was clear from the map that the river took a meandering course to get there so she decided to head off across country and find the river again later. She tilted the plane to port and, with her left foot, turned the rudder the same way to help the turn. At first, the aircraft turned as normal, but then she felt the nose pulling to starboard. What was happening?

Lizzie straightened the plane and twisted her head to look backwards. She had to free her safety harness and twist her body to see properly but when she moved the foot control, the rudder did not move. She tried the starboard pedal but again no movement.

There was a problem. Perhaps Melford had been right all along. Would she be able to get back to base and land safely? There was no option but to try.

CHAPTER 20

"I'm sorry to keep you waiting, Sir, but I had an important interview to conduct regarding another matter." Sergeant Drake gestured to a chair and Patrick Kenny sat in it, slight amusement playing in his eyes at the officer's self-importance.

"That's no problem Officer; I'm not doing anything else this afternoon apparently."

"Now, Sir, could you please talk me through your movements on Saturday night and the Sunday morning."

"Saturday night, we went to the club in London. I went in Mark Sanders' car with Miss Barnes and Miss Michalski. We retuned at about eleven-thirty and went our separate ways inside the building. I went to our room...I share with Mark Sanders, but he stayed up. I think he went outside for a cigarette but I'm not sure what he did after that. I read for a bit then went to sleep."

"And Sunday morning?"

"Got up at about seven-thirty, washed, dressed and came downstairs for breakfast at just gone eight o'clock."

"You didn't go to Church with Mr Swinburne and the ladies I understand."

"No. I borrowed a bicycle and went to church in Maidenhead."

"Which church would that have been, Sir?"

"St Joseph's Catholic Church...it's on Cookham Road. I'm a Catholic you see which is why I didn't go with the others."

"I see, Sir. Presumably someone could vouch for your presence there?"

"Yes, Sergeant, dozens of people. When you have hair

136

my colour, you tend not to be missed in a crowd."

"Of course, Sir. And did you come straight back to the base after the service?"

"No. I cycled over to Windsor to see my sister in hospital. She's just had her appendix out."

"Right, Sir. Her name would be…?"

"Nancy O'Brien. She married an Irish fellow and came over to this country only two years ago. I came over when I was six and lived with an aunt and uncle in Liverpool which is why I speak as I do but she has an Irish accent still."

Sergeant Drake carefully wrote down what Patrick Kenny had told him. "We can of course verify your visit there, Sir."

"Easily I would have thought."

"Now, Sir, how did you get on with Mr Melford?"

"I didn't have much to do with him. He was not the sort of man I would befriend…different class, different background and probably different views."

"Did you dislike him?"

"Yes…but not enough to kill him. I had no particular gripe with him, just didn't like some of his attitudes."

"His attitudes, Sir?"

"Towards Jews – I'm sure you've been told about the incident with Miss Michalski." Drake nodded. "And actually towards other people. He was arrogant, believed himself to be better than others because he was rich. I'm afraid it tends to be the way with public schoolboys. I'm sure you've also been told about the incident with John Hale, the member of the ground crew on Saturday afternoon."

"Yes, Sir. We know about that. May I ask you why you came over to this country at such a young age but your sister did not?"

Patrick Kenny thought for a moment. "You have to understand the nature of Ireland, Sergeant. It's a poor country full of poor people but families tend to be large. I'm the third child, the third son in fact, in our family. The first two were useful to help on the small farm my parents had but those of us who came later were just more mouths to feed. Girls are easier to manage as they can help out in the home and, if possible, do domestic work for people who are richer. My aunt and uncle were in a better position in Liverpool and agreed to take me in to help my parents."

"I'm sorry to hear that, Sir."

"It's nothing unusual, Sergeant. Ireland and its people are still suffering from the years of exploitation and mistreatment visited on them by successive British governments."

Sergeant Drake looked up from his notebook at the bitterness in Kenny's voice. "But you are happy to help out with the War...unlike some of your compatriots."

"Hitler must be defeated, Sergeant, before he terrorises the whole World. I am happy to play a part in doing that."

Drake said nothing for several seconds. "Is there anything else you can tell me, Sir, about Mr Melford's death?"

"You haven't asked me whether I saw anyone on Saturday night."

"I assumed you would have mentioned that, Sir, when giving your account of your movements."

"Sanders came to bed and went to sleep very quickly. He has a tendency to snore so it woke me. It was about one-thirty in the morning when I heard knocking on a door – not our door. It seemed quite insistent. I slipped out of bed and poked my head into the corridor."

Kenny stopped and seemed to be debating with himself whether he should continue.

"And what did you see, Sir?"

"Laura Hulett was standing in her dressing gown knocking on Melford's door. I asked her what on earth she was doing at that time of night but she said nothing. 'Trying to break up another relationship are you?' I said. 'That was not my doing,' she hissed. 'You poisoned her against me and you know it,' I replied. She said nothing but walked away along the corridor as if going back to her room. I called her something unpleasant under my breath and went back to my bed."

"What on earth was that about?"

"I was due to be married to a younger woman...when I was living in London. A friend of hers persuaded her to dump me I think because I am quite a bit older than her though she gave some excuse about me being a Catholic. I loved her and my happiness was destroyed. That's why I joined the ATA. The friend who poisoned her against me was Laura Hulett."

Inspector Hawkins had explained to Commander Trueman that he needed to make a couple of important telephone calls. 'Our facilities are yours, Inspector' Trueman had replied. The operator had seemed surprised when he had asked to be put through to the British Union of Fascists. He held the handset and gazed sightlessly out of the window as he turned over in his mind everything he had been told. There was no obvious solution to this case nor indeed the death of Mrs Bloom in that fire. He sighed. It was a bad World.

"You're through," the operator sang.

"Good afternoon. My name is Inspector Hawkins from Maidenhead Police. I am investigating two very serious matters and wonder if you can help me with some information. Firstly, can you please confirm that one of your members is a Mr Edward Melford?"

The voice at the end of the line was East End of London through and through. "I'm afraid we never discuss our members, mate."

"That may be so but you need to answer my questions honestly and promptly. Do you have a member called Edward Melford?"

"Like I said, Guv. We don't discuss our members."

Hawkins fought to keep his temper. "Failure to answer my questions constitutes obstructing an officer of the law in the conduct of his legitimate business. Now you can either answer my questions or I will apply for a search warrant and turn your offices upside down to find out what I need to know."

"You better speak to someone else if you're going to start threatening us."

The line went silent but Hawkins could just make out a muffled conversation somewhere nearby though he could not hear anything said.

A very different voice came on the line, male, well spoken, public school educated he guessed. "My name is Oliver Forsyth, London Region Co-ordinator. Now officer, what can I do for you?"

"Firstly confirm that Edward Melford was one of your members."

"I can confirm that Officer."

"I need to know how active a member he was. Did he organise events, did he lobby politicians, what was his role in your organisation?"

"You are using the past tense, Inspector. Why so?"

"Because Mr Forsyth, Edward Melford was murdered on Saturday night and I need to find his killer. It may be that if he was involved in...shall we say certain activities, he may have aroused serious antagonism."

"Murdered? My God. You think it may have something to do with his role in The BUF?"

"I have to explore that possibility, Sir."

"Well he was involved in recruiting members in part of the London region and he may have organised some activities... protests that sort of thing."

"Anything else. Attacking Jews for example?"

"We have our views about Jewish people, Officer, but we do not go round attacking them or promoting violence."

"You would say that wouldn't you? What part of the London region did he organise?"

"The South-west so an area South of the River Thames and West of the A23 - the road that runs from London to Brighton."

"How far out of London did his area reach?"

"He managed Berkshire, Hampshire and Surrey. This is terrible news Inspector. Who on Earth would want to kill him. He was very likeable, generous, good company.."

"But he disliked Jews and made no secret of it. I also need to know the names and addresses of any members you have in the Maidenhead and Windsor area. Perhaps best to give me the names of all your members in Berkshire."

"Now that is asking too much, Inspector. What use will those names be in discovering Melford's killer?"

"They may prove useful but I am also investigating a fire, started deliberately in a shop owned by a Jewish family; an old lady died as a result of that fire. So I'll have those names."

"The BUF, contrary to popular opinion, does not engage in those sorts of activities."

Hawkins was losing patience. "Oh no of course not. You help old ladies across the road and provide food parcels for Jewish families in need."

"No need to be sarcastic Inspector."

"Just give me the names or I'll procure a search warrant."

"It will take me some time to get that information together and, of course, I will need some verification of who you are…can't give out information to any Tom, Dick or Harry."

"If I don't get that information tomorrow, you'll find out soon enough who I am."

◆ ◆ ◆

Lizzie's memory of her training was hazy on the procedures in the event of rudder failure but she was confident she could still fly the plane. The problem would be landing it as

141

she would not be able to control yawing on the landing approach nor when the wheels touched the ground. The rudder was definitely not working; of that she was absolutely clear. She was tempted to try to complete the assignment but knew the right thing to do was to get the aircraft back to base and land it in one piece. She just hoped that nothing else was wrong. If the ailerons failed, she would be in real trouble.

She tilted the aircraft hard to port and found the nose wanting to go to starboard. 'Adverse yaw' that was what it was called. Something about the lift generated when the aircraft tilted pulling the nose in the opposite direction of the intended turn. She kept the plane tilted and willed it round. It came, protesting all the time until she was able to straighten up and hope she was in the right direction for White Waltham.

It was not far and she should be able to find the airfield but it did take a few more adjustments before she was able to identify the spire of White Waltham church which she and the others had attended what seemed an age ago. She had to take a wide sweep to bring the aircraft round to face West. Her first attempt to line up with the runway was not successful. The aircraft yawed badly each time she tried to correct her heading and she had to pull up and go round again. Her anxiety level was rising. She had seen figures on the ground watching and when she looked back, the fire truck was moving into position on the apron.

She managed to gain a good line on the runway at the second attempt and she prayed to herself that nothing else would go wrong. "Now come on girl. You can do it." As the aircraft dropped over the edge of the airfield, a small gust of wind put her off course. She struggled with the controls, tilting the aircraft one way then the other as if trying to control a wild horse.

"I'm going down this time whatever!" she shouted to the air and pushed the stick forward. She braced herself for the landing, knowing she was going to veer off the runway and probably break the undercarriage. "Here goes," she yelled.

CHAPTER 21

As Hawkins replaced the handset, there was a tap on the door and Drake put his head around it. "Got a minute, Sir? I've just finished with Mr Kenny – there's something you should know."

"Come in Drake. What have you got?"

"It was a bit odd, Sir. Kenny didn't say anything about this when I asked him first about his movements on Saturday night. He said he'd gone to bed...that was all. But just before we finished, he said that he had heard knocking at a door - not his door – at about one thirty. He looked out to investigate and saw Miss Hulett, Miss Laura Hulett that is, banging on Melford's door. He said something to her and she walked off but here's the interesting thing. He said that he was due to marry a younger woman when he was living in London but Laura Hulett had persuaded the lady to dump him."

"Very interesting Drake. How did he seem when he was telling you?"

"Seemed a bit uncertain at first...you know...as to whether to say anything. He must realise it's incriminating."

"Yes, but is it true I wonder? If he has an axe to grind with her, maybe he's made it up to cause her trouble. What do you think?"

"Perhaps...but there's lots of other ways of causing her trouble aren't there? Seems a bit far to go when the possible consequences are being tried for murder."

Hawkins nodded. "You're probably right Drake."

"I think I need to check a couple of things he told me. Said he went to church on Sunday morning and then went to the hospital in Windsor to see his sister whose had an operation. I'll get over there tomorrow morning and check. Bit suspicious of the Irish."

"No love lost between the Welsh and the Irish then?"

Drake smiled. "It's not that, Sir. Just didn't trust him."

Hawkins sighed. "Probably best to trust no one. This case and the fire on Saturday are going to prove a nightmare. We're getting nowhere. I've just been on the telephone with someone from the British Union of Fascists. Didn't want to tell me anything at first but he said he would give me details of all members in this area. I suspect we'll have to chase him for it. I threatened to obtain a search warrant, said I'd turn their offices over if he doesn't give me the information I want."

"Quite right, Sir. Course we won't know if he's telling us about everyone."

"True Drake, true. I need to speak with our Miss Hulett again but she's on flying training now so I'll need to wait until she finishes. I'll try to get through to Jarvis, see where he's got to with the post mortem. Can you interview Sanders please?"

"Pleasure, Sir. He seems to be the only one without something to hide or some axe to grind."

"Yes. Miss Barnes doesn't seem to be directly involved but she is very protective of the other women so may be partial. Thank you Sergeant. See what you can get from Sanders."

"Very good, Sir."

The door closed behind Sergeant Drake and Hawkins could hear his footsteps striding along the corridor. He lifted the handset once more and asked to be put through to Doctor Jarvis at Windsor hospital. Again he ran over the evidence they had gleaned so far; there was very little that was concrete but Laura Hulett's failure to mention something so significant as knocking on Melford's door and the fact that she had denied being in his room when she so obviously had pointed the finger of suspicion in her direction.

Doctor Jarvis came on the telephone. "Afternoon Inspector. You'll be wanting me to solve the mystery for you won't you?"

Hawkins let the good-natured jibe pass. "What have you got?"

"Let's start with the old lady as that's straightforward. There were no visible injuries to her body but her lungs were in quite a state. I suspect they were before the fire but the smoke caused significant further damage. She just could not take enough oxygen into her system to keep going, poor thing."

"So the fire did kill her?"

"Oh yes, certainly, though proving that the person who threw the fire bomb intended that will be extremely difficult."

"Of course. It will be manslaughter if we ever find out who's responsible. What about Melford?"

"Ah now that is much more tricky. I've made a start but... the knife as you know was not long and it did not penetrate far. He had a degree of fat around his tummy already – obviously liked the good life – and that protected him to some extent. No major arteries were cut and no organs but at the moment, we have to assume that's what did for him. I'm just not sure precisely how. He was in his cups as they say and the shock may have caused heart failure. Lots of alcohol in his system would probably have exacerbated things."

"Can you give me a time of death?"

"Not with any certainty I'm afraid. You see when he was found, he was described as cold but that would be inevitable. We can calculate time of death by the loss of temperature – we know it's about two and a half degrees Fahrenheit per hour but that slows as the body reaches the ambient temperature of the room. Of course a lower ambient temperature produces quicker cooling and the window was open. Though it wasn't a cold night, it was certainly cooler outside than in."

"You're not giving me much to go on."

"I realise that Inspector but that's the way things are in my profession. Rigor mortis had set in when I examined him at the scene but that does not give a precise time as it can take up to forty-eight hours to be completed. Stomach contents show a high level of digestion so he hadn't eaten for some time

– probably when they had dinner at about seven o'clock. So he could have died late Saturday night or even Sunday morning earlyish."

"Can you tell me anything that is definite?"

"I can tell you that his heart was okay as you'd expect in a young man, which does negate my theory about shock causing heart failure. There was some damage to his lungs caused by smoking – a build-up of tar – but not enough to cause death. Similarly, his liver was not the most healthy I've seen – some build-up of fatty deposits, caused I'm sure by drinking – but again not enough to put him at risk of death."

"So really, we've got nothing?"

"I didn't say that Inspector. I've sent blood samples to the lab for testing. I am sure they will find plenty of alcohol but there may be something else there. Of course it is difficult to test for everything...much easier to test for a specific substance. That means it's over to you Inspector."

"Thank you Doctor Jarvis. Contact me as soon as you have the results from the laboratory."

"Will do."

Hawkins replaced the handset slowly, a profound disappointment filling him. It sounded as though the knife may not have killed Melford but presumably the assailants' intention had been to do so. That was all they had at the moment. Enough to charge Miss Hulett? Not sure but he needed to put pressure on her.

Lizzie gripped the joystick and braced herself. This was not going to be pretty. She felt the main wheels bump on the ground and the aircraft lift off again only to come down moments later. She knew she would have no control over the direction of the Moth as soon as it was on the ground and the best she could do would be to lift the flaps to slow it as soon as possible.

The Moth seemed to race over the grass and she could do nothing to stop it veering off the runway. It continued to turn, bouncing on the rougher ground. Would the undercarriage take the strain? If it collapsed now, the aircraft would slide across the airfield, possibly catch and pitch forward, over turning and smashing itself to pieces and her with it.

And then it happened.

The Starboard wheel must have collapsed as the Moth tilted alarmingly to that side and the wing scraped the grass. The drag caused the aircraft to slew back to starboard violently and the port wheel collapsed. She ducked and put one hand in front of her face as the tips of the propeller flew off when they smashed on the ground. Gradually, sliding on its belly, the aircraft came to a stop. Lizzie could hear the clattering of the bell on the fire truck but somehow it did not register. She gripped the joystick and sat frozen in her seat, half expecting the ordeal to continue.

Gradually, she came to her senses. She had got the aircraft back and largely in one piece and she herself was still alive. The fear and extreme activity of the last few minutes suddenly turned to euphoria. She had done it! She had brought the aircraft home. She unclipped her harness and stood up shakily.

The fire truck screeched to a halt beside the aircraft and the men leapt out dragging hoses ready to douse any flames. An ambulance, bell also ringing, stopped on the other side and two men jumped down. One rushed to the rear of the vehicle, opened a door and pulled out a stretcher. Lizzie took off her goggles and flying helmet. She let drop the small door at the side of the cockpit and stepped down. At least it was not so far to go!

"Miss, Miss. Are you alright?"

"Yes thank you. Just a bit shaken. It's okay, you won't need that."

The ambulance man holding the stretcher looked at it

and then at her. He seemed disappointed. "Are you sure, Miss? Might be best to lay down for a bit until we get you checked over."

"It's the aircraft needs checking over, not me." She turned and walked towards the hangars where a reception committee seemed to have formed. Most waited but Olivia Hulett ran towards her.

"Lizzie, Lizzie...are you alright?"

"I'm fine thanks Olivia. Aircraft's a bit of a mess."

"What happened?"

"Let's get to the others so I only have to say it once."

The two young women walked side by side, Olivia's arm around Lizzie's shoulders. Lizzie wanted to shake it off but she didn't want to offend Olivia who she knew was trying to repay the kindness she had shown her. It was a good sign that Olivia had pulled herself away from introspection, even for a short while. As they approached the apron, Roger Carlisle and Commander Trueman stepped forward, their faces a mixture of horror and relief.

"What happened, Lizzie?" Roger Carlisle asked.

"Rudder packed up. Seemed fine at first but then it would do nothing. I managed to get by using the ailerons but I knew the landing could be tricky." She turned towards Trueman. "Sorry about the aircraft, Sir, but I couldn't do anything at all once I was on the ground."

"Don't worry about that."

"Perhaps Melford was right Sir. This was the aircraft he used on Saturday...you know when he had difficulty landing."

"No, there was nothing wrong with the rudder. That was just inexperience."

"I had Hale check the aircraft thoroughly after the flight on Saturday. It's not been used since so something must have broken. I will watch Hale as he checks it again." Carlisle spoke with determination.

"You say it seemed fine at first but then packed up?"

"Yes, Sir. I think something must have broken or the control lines detached."

John Hale was out with other members of the ground crew jacking the aircraft up to slide a bogey under it. They had it secured quickly and began to tow it back to the hangar. Cables dragged along the ground at either side of the plane. The group on the apron followed it into the hangar, like a group of mourners following a coffin. As soon as they had brought the plane to a standstill, Carlisle stepped forward and spoke with Hale.

Hale examined the full length of the cables on the port side and showed Carlisle the ends. They both walked to the other side of the aircraft and did the same. They looked solemn as they re-joined the group of watchers.

"The cables on both sides have failed." Carlisle said. "But John believes they were cut."

John Hale looked nervous. "They were cut almost all the way through but in both cases one strand had been left intact. The cables have multi-strands for strength. I have never known one fail before like that. Had they done so, one or two strands might break but the rest of the cable would hold. These have been cut through so that no one would notice until pressure was applied to the rudder. And when you use the rudder, there is a huge amount of air pressure on it. One strand in a cable would not be able to take that."

Trueman was horrified. "So you are saying it was deliberate?"

"Yes, Sir. Certainly looks that way."

CHAPTER 22

There seemed to be some disturbance out on the airfield, so Drake positioned Mark Sanders facing into the room. Didn't want him distracted by whatever might be going on outside. "Now, Sir. Please go through your movements on Saturday night from the point when you returned to the airbase."

"We arrived back here at about eleven-thirty I think. I had a little walk outside to clear my head you know and then I smoked a cigarette until the other car, Melford's car that is, arrived. That was about mid-night. Shortly afterwards, I went inside to the lounge and sat with Graham Swinburne for a while chatting about this and that. We went upstairs to our different rooms at about twelve-forty-five I guess."

"Did you go up together?"

"Pretty well…I may have been thirty seconds behind him."

Mark Sanders seemed at ease, confident and Sergeant Drake's view that he was straight and uninvolved was confirmed. "And Sunday morning, Sir?"

"I rose at about quarter past eight I think, washed, dressed and went down to breakfast. Some of the others had already finished and left the mess by then. After breakfast, I went for a walk around the airfield."

"Any particular reason for that, Sir?"

"No, except again to get some fresh air."

"And when you say 'around the airfield' exactly where did you go?"

"I walked around the perimeter." Sanders crossed his legs. "I have an interest in Botany, you see Sergeant, more particularly wild flowers and there are often some gems growing at the edge of places like air bases. They come up amongst the long grass."

"I see, Sir. And what time did you arrive back at the main building?"

"Not sure exactly but I think it was about mid-day. I was walking slowly looking for plants so it took a while."

"Now did you see anyone else or anything that struck you as odd either on Saturday night or Sunday morning?"

Sanders thought for a while and shook his head slowly. "No...can't think of anything."

"I'd like to ask you about Mr Melford. Did you know him before joining the ATA? Did you form any opinion of him during the week you've been here? Are you aware of any enemies he might have...that sort of thing?"

Again Mark Sanders shook his head slowly from side to side. "No I didn't know him beforehand and I'm not aware of any enemies. He did upset a few people but I don't think they would have become enemies...certainly not enough to kill him."

"Well, thank you, Sir. If you think of anything else that may be useful, do please let us know."

"Of course, Officer."

The two men rose and Sanders held out his hand. Sergeant Drake shook it and looked him in the eye.

Brian Teal leant his bike against the fence and strolled as nonchalantly as he could the few steps to the front door. He had to confess he was a little nervous. Sheila was not expecting him and may not be pleased to see him. He raised his hand and lifted the brass knocker but did not let it drop. What if he wasn't the only one? Maybe she had other male friends and one might be visiting?

He tried to dismiss the thought from his mind. If that were the case, he reasoned, he would say he was just passing – which was true sort of – and be on his way before he became too embarrassed. But he knew it was not that simple. His heart was already engaged and he would be bitterly disappointed if it turned out that she was just playing with him.

He took a deep breath and let the knocker fall. He knocked a second time to suggest confidence and squared his shoulders. He heard rapid footsteps in the hall and the door which obviously tended to stick, was yanked open.

"Brian…I didn't expect to see you today." Sheila stepped out of the doorway and put her arms around his neck. She pulled him closer and kissed him on the mouth. "What a lovely surprise…" She looked at his uniform. "But shouldn't you be at work?"

"I am. Had to check something out in Windsor so thought I'd call see if you were up and about."

"I've just got up. Come in and have a cuppa."

Brian's heart had lifted at her welcome and he stepped inside brimming with confidence. She obviously liked him. Mrs Brown was in the kitchen and she seemed pleased to see him as well.

"Look what the wind's blown in Mum."

"Oh hello Brian. Nice of you to drop in. D'you fancy a cup of tea?"

"That would be lovely Mrs Brown, thank you. I've had to cycle over from Maidenhead. I'm investigating an incident that happened there…you know Sheila, the fire which killed the old lady."

"Yeah, poor old thing. So what's it got to do with Windsor? It was in Maidenhead you said."

"Well obviously I can't tell you much 'cos the case isn't solved yet but I had to check something with the staff at The Prince Harry pub on the High Street."

"I know that place…never been in there though. It's a bit posher than your average pub isn't it, being on the High Street and all?"

When the tea was steeped and poured Mrs Brown shooed them into the sitting room as she said they made the kitchen look untidy. They sat together on the settee. Brian wanted to put his arm around Sheila and hold her but somehow it felt wrong in his uniform. They chatted about nothing in particular or rather Sheila chatted and Brian watched her eyes which seemed always to be smiling. She was animated, waving her hands around and occasionally tossing her head to free her face from her hair which was not yet tied up for work. She was lovely.

At last Sheila jumped up. "You'll have to go, Brian... sorry, but I must have something to eat and change."

Bran Teal glanced at the clock on the mantelpiece. Nearly five o'clock. Goodness how the time had flown. "Yes of course. I need to get back to the station. Report in." His eye moved back to the clock for something had triggered a memory. Beside the clock was a packet of cigarettes, an expensive brand. Was that the sort that the Inspector had found outside the shop? He dismissed the idea. What of it? Just a coincidence if they were but...

"Whose cigarettes are those then?" he asked as casually as he could.

Sheila glanced at the mantelpiece. "They're me dad's. Doesn't usually smoke those - they're too expensive but I think someone gave them to him."

"Oh right. Nice. Well I'll be on my way." He moved into the hall and called into the kitchen. "Thanks for the tea Mrs Brown. That was lovely."

"That's a pleasure Brian. I'm afraid I've not done any baking yet – usually do that on Tuesday – otherwise you would have had a cake or a scone or something."

"That's a shame but maybe next..."

"What makes you think there'll be a next time PC Brian Teal?" Sheila's voice was playful and her eyes danced."

"Oh well, I'll just cycle off and go back to my miserable, lonely existence then," he said as he walked backwards down the garden path with Sheila following.

"You can come over on Saturday though can't you?"

He smiled and put his arms around her waist. "I'd come every day if I could." He kissed her slowly, gently on the lips and she responded.

Then she pulled away. "Now get on that bike of yours before you make me late."

"Yes Miss." He grinned, swung his leg over his bike and looked back to the door. She was standing in the doorway, smiling and he blew her a kiss.

◆ ◆ ◆

"But, Sir. I've already told you. I checked that plane on Saturday afternoon after Mr Melford had complained. There was nothing wrong with the rudder and nothing wrong with the cables. I operated the pedals several times checked the tension on the cables, even ran my hand along them to make sure there were no breaks."

Richard Trueman, Stephanie Garrett and Roger Carlisle stood around John Hale who was seated in Trueman's office. Carlisle and Garret stood behind him and Trueman in front. Carlisle and Garrett nodded to each other and then to Trueman.

"We believe you John but you understand the seriousness of the situation. It is reasonable to suppose that you had a grudge against Mr Melford after the way he treated you. The fact that it was the rudder suggests it was a calculated plan to embarrass him. Obviously, he would have had one of us with him and we would have been able to bring the plane down, though we would have had the same problem as Lizzie Barnes when it hit the ground. You can understand the Police needing to interview you."

Hale's head was cast down, his eyes on the floor. "I've always worked to the best of my ability, Sir. I've gone the extra mile to make sure the aircraft are in perfect condition. There has never been an issue before." Suddenly he lifted his head. "It

EAGER FOR THE AIR
EAGER FOR THE AIR

could have been Melford himself, Sir. He might have gone into the hangar after I left and sabotaged the aircraft to discredit me."

"He wouldn't sabotage the aircraft he knew he would be flying though would he?"

"Perhaps he was intending to pretend sickness this morning, Sir, so he wouldn't be flying."

"There might be all sorts of possibilities John but the fact remains that it is your job to ensure every plane is airworthy and that Moth was not. It's a great tribute to Lizzie Barnes that she managed to return to base and land without smashing it completely."

The conversation was interrupted by a knock at the door which immediately opened. Inspector Hawkins strode in. "I understand Mr Trueman you have another suspect."

"That is putting it too strongly, Inspector. John Hale here, our senior aircraft engineer, is adamant that the plane Lizzie Barnes flew this afternoon was thoroughly checked by himself on Saturday after Mr Melford complained. He is certain that there were no faults with it and especially the rudder mechanism which he checked especially thoroughly." Commander Trueman prided himself on his fairness. He would not condemn John Hale, who, had always been absolutely reliable and above suspicion until now.

"Perhaps I might ask Mr Hale a few questions, Sir."

"Of course Inspector."

"I'm happy for you to be part of the interview, Commander Trueman, but I see no need for us to detain Flight Lieutenant Carlisle nor Miss Garrett."

"Of course, Inspector. We must be getting along. We need to debrief the crew from this afternoon's session." Stephanie Garrett could not resist one last shot. "It is very fortunate that it was Lizzie Barnes flying that aircraft. It's not just her experience but she has a very calm head on her shoulders."

John Hale looked at her. "Yes Ma'am. It is fortunate. There is someone very dangerous at the base but that person is

155

not me." His anger was evident in the tight control of his voice, a low, bitter sound.

When the door had closed on Carlisle and Garrett, Inspector Hawkins drew up a chair beside Trueman's desk and gestured to Trueman to sit in his own. "Now Mr Hale. How long have you worked here?"

"Well for the ATA about six months, pretty well from the start."

"Have there ever been any issues with the maintenance of any of the aircraft?"

"Well obviously things go wrong with them occasionally but we always make sure they are completely airworthy before they are used. We don't take chances...no need to."

Hawkins nodded. "What time did you leave the base on Saturday afternoon or evening?"

"It was about six o'clock, Sir. I wanted to make sure that Melford's aircraft...the one he had flown...was thoroughly checked over so I did it myself. The other engineers had gone by the time I had finished."

"So no one was on hand to verify your checks?"

"Well no Sir. I saw no reason to keep anyone else. After all, it was Saturday."

"Quite so. And when you left, where did you go?"
"Home."
"Were you at home all evening and night?"
"Yes, Sir."
"Can anyone verify that?"
"My wife. We had a meal and then listened to the wireless. Went to bed at about ten thirty."
"Were you on the base on Sunday?"
"No. Sunday's me day off...I stay well away...though of course if there was a need..." His eyes flicked to Trueman.

"I may have to speak with you again Mr Hale. But for now, Commander Trueman, I think Mr Hale can go. If, of course, we discover that you did sabotage the aircraft, you will be charged with attempted murder, even though no one was hurt."

"Attempted murder?" John Hale's face dropped and he stared at Hawkins.

"John, I suggest you go home now but come to work as normal in the morning," Trueman said.

Hale rose slowly. "Sir." He turned and left the office, closing the door quietly behind him.

"I am sure he had nothing to do with it, Commander Trueman. And in fact, I intend now to interview one of your recruits on suspicion of murder."

It was Trueman's turn to look horrified.

CHAPTER 23

The post-training de-briefing had been short. Stephanie Garrett and Roger Carlisle sensed that the trainees were not able to concentrate, so concerned were they about what had happened to Lizzie. The two instructors had adopted a very measured approach, stating that mechanical failures were an occupational hazard and that a calm presence of mind was needed for this job. The trainees were subdued, especially when Roger Carlisle pointed out that pilots in the RAF engaged in combat missions were having to deal with attack from enemy aircraft and ground artillery which caused damage to their aircraft. He was trying to make them feel better but it back-fired.

It was thus in a sombre mood that the trainees returned to the main building to change for dinner. The four young women trooped up the stairs to their room, Olivia being particularly solicitous of Lizzie, something which Lizzie would have preferred to be without.

"I could never have dealt with that Lizzie. I wouldn't have known what to do."

"Not at the moment...you've only been training for a week. But I've been flying for the best part of two years now. You'll be fine when you've had more experience."

"It's frightening though that there is someone who is prepared to sabotage an aircraft and perhaps kill its occupants," said Kasia. "I did not like Melford, but to go to those lengths to embarrass him, maybe kill him is...disturbing."

"I think we should try to put it out of mind for Lizzie's sake." Laura was a little curt. "Doesn't do any good to dwell on these things."

The four of them changed out of flying clothes and into

dresses. Olivia was not so particular about her make-up as she had been on Saturday and was ready in the same time as the others. "Shall we go down? I must admit, I don't feel like eating."

"You must eat, Olivia. You'll just make yourself ill. With the training we're doing every day, you must keep your energy up. Now come along. Lizzie's fine - aren't you Lizzie? - so let's not think about it."

"I am fine...a bit jittery when I first landed but it's all in a day's work. I'm sure we'll face more difficult challenges when we're fully trained and in service." She linked arms with Olivia and they squeezed together as they stumbled along the corridor. At least this brought a little light to Olivia's eyes.

The other trainees were in the lounge, sipping drinks, along with a few operational pilots who looked at the four young women with interest. There was a young man in a steward's jacket serving at the bar and, when they had obtained drinks, they sat at the table they had occupied on Saturday evening. They had just settled themselves when Commander Trueman accompanied by Inspector Hawkins appeared. They stood by the door and Trueman coughed loudly.

"I'm sorry to disturb your evening, ladies and gentlemen but Inspector Hawkins needs to ask a few questions of a couple of you to clarify things. Inspector."

"I need to speak with Miss Michalski first. Would you come this way please Miss?"

Kasia looked at the others, a deep frown creasing her forehead. "Me. Why me?" she said but she rose slowly and walked towards Hawkins. He smiled at her, turned and left the lounge with Kasia behind him.

"Just needs to clarify a few things probably," Lizzie said lightly, glancing at Olivia's alarmed face. "Nothing to worry about."

They did their best to make conversation but all of them kept glancing at the door, waiting for Kasia's return. It was at least five minutes before she came back. Kasia's concern had been replaced by anger. "Damn cheek. You know he said that I must have been in Melford's room. They found a hair they believe came from my head on his carpet. I had said, it perhaps had attached to his clothes at some point in the evening and had fallen off in his room. He said they have a witness who said I did not dance with Melford so how could a hair from my head have attached to his clothes."

"Oh dear...I'm afraid he did ask me if you danced with Melford. I couldn't remember you doing so." Lizzie was beginning to feel that she was incriminating everyone.

"How do they know it is my hair? It may have been from someone who used that room previously. It may have come from a cleaner. I told him he was being ridiculous. It's just as I said. They want to blame me because I am a foreigner, a German agent waiting for an invasion to attack you British like it said in that newspaper article."

"But he seemed satisfied with your explanation?" offered Laura. "I mean he hasn't accused you of murder has he?"

"No...not yet."

They sensed the presence of Hawkins hovering in the doorway. "And now Miss Olivia Hulett, please."

Olivia gasped. "Me?" She pointed at herself and her face went pale. "But I've told you everything I know. There's nothing..."

"If you would be so good Miss. I'll not keep you any time at all."

Again they tried to continue conversation as if everything was normal but it was impossible. Who would Hawkins want next? What was he asking? Laura in particular looked anxious, her mouth twisting and working as if she were chewing. She stood when, after only a few minutes, Olivia came back in the room, looking relieved.

"What did he want to know?"

"Well it was really odd. He asked me if I had noticed a photograph on the writing desk in Melford's room. I hadn't noticed it all. I was too busy trying to fend him off. Then Hawkins just said, 'Thank you Miss' and let me go."

"Bizarre. I think there was a photograph....a group of young men in dinner suits." Strange Lizzie thought how she must have seen it but it didn't register until now.

Alarm spread over Laura's face but Hawkins was suddenly in the room again. "Miss Laura Hulett please. She stood up and faced him. "I suggest you finish your drink, Miss Hulett. This may take a little longer."

He glided out through the doorway and Laura picked up her glass. She drained it in one, placed it carefully on the table and smiled grimly at the others. "See you sometime."

It was Olivia's turn to be alarmed. Lizzie laid a hand on her arm. "Don't be anxious Olivia. I'm sure he has things to clear up with everyone."

"But...but Laura wouldn't do anything...." Olivia bent her head and her hand went to her mouth. Lizzie knew she was trying not to cry. A doubt suddenly burst into her mind. Had Olivia been truthful in her account of what had happened in Melford's room? Was she in fact responsible for his death and was now in agony because her sister would be blamed?

Someone turned on the wireless and Lizzie glanced at her watch. Just a few minutes before six o'clock. The clipped voice of the BBC announcer gave a weather forecast. It would remain fine for at least another two days.

The bell of Big Ben struck the hour and as the last dong faded, the voice resumed, "This is the BBC broadcasting from London. Now the news for today, Monday 13th May 1940. Our new Prime Minister, Mr Winston Churchill, made his first speech to the House of Commons today. In it, he spoke of his determination to win the war against Germany. We are able to bring you an extract from the speech."

A different voice, sombre, rich, impressive came over the airwaves. It was the voice of an experienced orator yet conveyed a sincerity, an honesty that could not fail to gain attention and admiration.

"We are in the preliminary stage of one of the greatest battles in history.... that we are in action at many points - in

Norway and in Holland - that we have to be prepared in the Mediterranean, that the air battle is continuous and that many preparations have to be made here at home.

I would say to the House as I said to those who have joined this government: I have nothing to offer but blood, toil, tears and sweat. We have before us an ordeal of the most grievous kind. We have before us many, many long months of struggle and of suffering.

You ask, what is our policy? I will say: It is to wage war, by sea, land and air, with all our might and with all the strength that God can give us; to wage war against a monstrous tyranny, never surpassed in the dark and lamentable catalogue of human crime. That is our policy. You ask, what is our aim? I can answer in one word: Victory. Victory at all costs -Victory in spite of all terror - Victory, however long and hard the road may be, for without victory there is no survival."

There was silence in the room, the faces of everyone registering the importance of his words, the clear statement that this was not going to be easy, not going to be quick. When that news item had finished, Graham Swinburne stood up straight. "I propose a toast to our new Prime Minister...to Winston Churchill." Glasses were raised, clinked and everyone drank.

The speech had done nothing to dispel the sombre mood though it had filled each and every one of them with a new determination to play their part fully in Britain's war on Hitler. 'The monstrous tyranny' which Churchill had mentioned was an accurate description of the horrors perpetrated by the German Third Reich. They were engaged in fighting an attack on freedom, on democracy, on decency.

◆ ◆ ◆

Inspector Hawkins opened the door of the interview

room and pointed to the chair where Laura should sit. "Please sit down...I'll just be a minute." He left the door to the room ajar and stepped back so that he could watch her but she could not see him. She had been hostile when he told her he would question her at the Station, insisting that she be provided with a meal. In the car, she had been silent, a silence which she wanted him to believe maintained her hostility but which he suspected was to prevent herself betraying any fears and doubts.

Now she looked around the room, the starkness of the two-tone walls. Her eyes settled on the picture of the King. His Majesty was not smiling in fact he looked rather severe. The portrait had been chosen deliberately to convey to suspects the seriousness of their position. Laura sat down, but upright on the chair, her knees drawn together and her hands in her lap. He noticed how restless those hands were though the rest of her body seemed to convey calm. She was controlling her appearance very well and Hawkins guessed there was turmoil in her mind. His ploy of bringing her to the station might work if he could break through that stone wall of her face.

When he had seen enough, he walked in with a folder of his notes and sat opposite her, the table in between. I have a few questions to ask, Miss Hulett, a couple of points to clarify that's all but it would be better for you if you answer honestly at the first time of asking. I will get to the truth...in fact I think I'm almost there. You told me that you had never been inside Mr Melford's room yet you knew about the picture of him with The Bullingdon Club. You said your sister Olivia must have told you about it but, when I asked her just before seeing you, she had no recollection of it at all."

Laura looked a little flustered. She would not look him in the eye. "It must have been someone else then...Lizzie... perhaps he even mentioned it himself."

"Miss Barnes did not mention that picture. She was only in the room for a few seconds. And no one else has mentioned it either." Hawkins paused and in a kindly voice said, "Why don't you just admit you were in his room Laura?"

"Because I wasn't, I wasn't. I have not been in his room."

She was agitated, desperate. Hawkins paused, allowing her mind to grasp that she was not being at all convincing. "I have a witness who said you were knocking on Melford's door late on Saturday or rather in the early hours of Sunday."

"That's just Patrick Kenny. He's got something against me....just trying to get me in trouble."

"How do you know it was Patrick Kenny... unless you were there as he said?"

Laura froze. Hawkins saw a realisation in her eyes. "I'm not saying anything more."

"Well Miss Hulett, I am not releasing you until I have satisfactory answers to my questions. I hope you enjoy your night in our cell." Hawkins stood but she did not flinch. As he walked out of the room he reflected on how a night in a cold cell might free her tongue. He was now certain he had Melford's murderer.

CHAPTER 24

Lizzie did not sleep well. She had spent the evening trying to re-assure Olivia that Laura would be brought back soon. But soon never came and they retired for the night feeling utterly despondent. Olivia lay in bed sobbing quietly under the covers, her body shaking, so Lizzie slipped on her dressing gown and lay down on the bed beside her. She held her like a parent holds an upset child and gently shushed her to sleep. It took a long time, however, to ease her fears and Lizzie then found sleep hard to find when she eventually lay on her own bed.

Despite the lack of sleep, perhaps because of it, she was up early and stepped softly downstairs. Mark Sanders was in the foyer, looking out at the rising day. "Morning Mark. How are you today?"

"I'm ok. I guess like everyone else, I didn't sleep well. How about you?"

"Olivia was very upset...took a long time to calm her down and get her to sleep. I left her in bed. Kasia too. We're all horrified that Laura was taken to the Police Station and has clearly had to spend the night there. What is Hawkins thinking? He surely can't believe she killed Melford. I mean a woman would not have the strength would she?"

Sanders shrugged. "I'm afraid it's beyond me, Lizzie. I've no idea how they can begin to find out who killed him. I still think it was an intruder. The window was open apparently."

"I can understand how an intruder could let himself down from the window to make an escape but he would have had to use a ladder to get in that way. There's nothing to climb up...no downpipe from the gutter, no convenient climbing plant."

"I suppose so." Sanders hovered for a moment and then said, "I'm going to have a walk before breakfast…just around the airfield. Saw some wild flowers on Sunday and I want to see if the buds have opened. That's my passion…wild flowers. Would you care to accompany me?"

"I'd love to. Some fresh air may wake me up."

The morning was fresh, the fine weather of the past few days continuing. Lizzie breathed in deeply, the cool air already reviving her dampened spirits. A group of starlings were chattering away sitting on the ridge of the main building's roof. The slightest breeze wafted scents across to them from the shrubs growing around the building and gently lifted some strands of Lizzie's hair which she had not yet tied.

They strolled beside each other and Sanders led the way across to the hedge that grew along nearly the entire circumference of the airfield, obscuring the lower part of the fence behind it. His gaze never wavered from the long grass. "Now somewhere along here there were a couple of Snakeshead Fritillaries. Ah here…see? They are fairly rare. They're still flowering but the flowers will drop soon. They're essentially a spring plant. Such delicate flower heads though. You can see why they are so named."

"They do look like snakes' heads don't they?"

Sanders didn't answer but stepped forward eagerly scanning the grassy margin, his eyes full of an excitement that Lizzie found endearing. "I think you're not a professional botanist are you? Why not?"

"I'm an engineer. Oh that's interesting too but I chose that for university because everyone said there would be few career opportunities for a Botanist. They were right of course. And in some ways I'm glad that I went for engineering as a career because I have Botany as my passion unsullied by the tedious elements of work."

"It's really important to have a strong interest outside work. I'm afraid my passion is flying…don't do anything else so

I'll have to find something if and when the ATA winds up."

"That'll probably be a while yet. Look there." Sanders pointed to a straggling plant with small lilac flowers, the petals of which were narrow and seemed to stick out in all directions. "D'you know what that is?"

"Sorry, no. I'm afraid I'm no good with wild plant names. My mother tried to teach me lots of names of our garden plants and I remember quite a few of those but she gave up on the wild flowers. I just couldn't remember them...I suppose I wasn't interested enough."

"Shame that, but each to his...or rather her own."

They continued strolling along the edge of the airfield with Mark Sanders pointing out numerous plants and explaining what time of year they flowered and what properties they had. He was a mine of information and certainly knew his stuff. Always keen to engage with people at a deeper level, Lizzie thought about Mark's family, his father dead and his mother needing his support.

"Do you have siblings Mark?"

He looked around in surprise. "Yes. A brother. He's in the navy and away at sea at the moment. He's not very senior... you need to come from the right family to become an officer. That's one good thing about the ATA – family background is not an issue, it's all done on merit."

"Yes, I like that about the ATA. I think it comes from Trueman. He's a man who judges people on their worth not their wealth." Sanders said nothing and returned his gaze to the airfield margin. "You said your father is dead."

He looked around again. "Yes."

"How long ago did he die?"

"It was nine years ago in February."

"That's sad. So he probably was not very old."

"No. He wasn't – mid-fifties."

"How did he die?" Mark Sanders looked troubled by the question. "I'm sorry, please don't answer if it's distressing."

He looked away. "No, it's fine. Heart attack."

Lizzie had a strong sense that he did not want to talk about it. Probably had not yet come to terms with it. Sudden death is perhaps harder to deal with. She felt she needed to change the subject. She was about to suggest they return for breakfast when she noticed a plant pushing up well above the top of the grass. Its leaves were oval shaped, pointed at the tip and grew at intervals on alternate sides of the stem not from the same point. It looked as though buds had formed but no flowers had appeared. "What's that one called Mark?"

"Um…er…I don't know."

The hesitancy in his voice caused Lizzie to look at his face. He seemed confused, embarrassed perhaps at not knowing a plant. He did not meet her eyes.

"Must be very rare if you don't know it."

"Looks as though it might be a perennial…you know, a plant that grows up every year."

"Oh well. Never mind. Perhaps there'll be a book on those shelves in the lounge that will tell us. Bit hard to identify perhaps when it's not in flower."

"True, it's much easier when the flowers are out. Anyway, shall we go back and get some breakfast? The fresh air has woken my appetite."

Sergeant Drake and PC Teal were called by Inspector Hawkins into his office as soon as he arrived at the Station. Hawkins flopped into his swivel chair behind his desk and sighed deeply while Drake and Teal sat in front of the desk. The clock on the side wall was reading five past eight and ticked loudly as if to remind them that time was rolling on and they had solved neither case.

Hawkins looked and felt weary. "Right gentlemen. Let's take stock. Firstly the fire. What have you got to report PC Teal?"

"Well, Sir, we know that one of the two men who were on Grenfell Road that night was tall and may have been wearing brogues. Both of them smoked expensive Du Maurier cigarettes and we believe they left – and presumably arrived - by a small van though we don't have anything to identify the vehicle. The pub in Windsor called The Prince Harry has sold bottles of Wethered's Pale Ale to a tall man who wears brogues and who sometimes meets an Irish man for a drink. One Saturday, they met a posh bloke in there."

Hawkins nodded. "Not a lot to go on is there?"

"I'm afraid not, Sir, but we have got somewhere. I asked the landlady at the pub to let us know if the two men came in again and to see if she could get a name."

"Well done Teal. You've done what you can. I telephoned the British Union of Fascists yesterday. Hopefully someone will get back to us today and give us the names of their members in the Maidenhead and Windsor area. If they don't, we'll go up there with a search warrant."

"So we still don't know who these men are?"

"That's right Sergeant but we'll get them. They are bound to have left some trace. Now the murder at White Waltham. We have any number of suspects so let's go through the evidence. Olivia Hulett was in Melford's room on Saturday night where he attempted to force himself on her. Picking up the knife and stabbing him would have been an act of self-defence but she denies touching it."

"She's the one, Sir. I mean look at the way she just walked out of the interview with me, turned on the waterworks like some women do."

"As I say, Sergeant, she is a suspect but there was something about the way she gave me her account of Saturday night that was credible. I believed her...could be wrong of course but I don't think she did it."

"What about that Polish woman then, Sir? She was seen going down the stairs by Swinburne, I think you said, and it looked as if she had just come from Melford's room?"

"That was Sunday morning; of course she said Swinburne was mistaken. We don't have a precise time of death so Melford could have been stabbed on Sunday morning. And we found a hair in the room that looks like one of hers. She had that dispute with Melford at the club about Jews. She certainly did not like Melford's views but she was very open about that."

"What do you think about the mechanic, Sir, John Hale?"

"He may have tampered with the aircraft after the flight on Saturday but that didn't kill Melford because that plane was not used until Monday afternoon. He was off the base on Saturday night and all day Sunday. Had he got into Melford's room, someone would have seen him surely? We could charge him with attempted murder but no one was actually hurt. He said that Melford could have sabotaged the aircraft to prove that he, Hale that is, had been negligent."

Teal's eyes lit up. "D'you think this Melford chap was a German agent, Sir. He sounds like a Nazi sympathiser with his view about Jews. Nasty bloke by the sound of things."

"Anything seems possible in this case, Constable. He certainly seems to have been someone who antagonised people. Several of them spoke about him being charming on the surface but having a darker side."

"There was something odd, Sir, when I spoke with Bloom, you know the steward at the base. Melford had been in the kitchen on Friday but the chef said Bloom dealt with him. Now Bloom didn't mention anything about that at first. He said Melford was asking what was for lunch but what if there is a connection? Bloom's a Jew and Melford obviously dislikes them."

"We need to keep him in mind, Sergeant, but he had very limited opportunity on Sunday morning to kill Melford and we have no evidence he was anywhere near Melford's room."

"True, Sir. And we've got nothing on Swinburne, Sanders or the Barnes woman. I'll be going to the hospital in Windsor shortly to check that man Kenny's account of his movements on Sunday morning."

" I don't think it's Kenny, Drake. I'm pretty sure we've got the killer in one of our cells. I'm going to put pressure on her today and I think she'll crack."

"All the same, Sir. I'd like to check out this Kenny. Something about him makes me suspicious."

Hawkins smiled indulgently at Drake and then turned to Teal. "This is the age-old rivalry between the Welsh and the Irish, Constable."

"Not a bit of it, Sir. But there's something not quite right."

"That's fine Sergeant. You go and check him out. I'm going to interview Miss Hulett again soon…just let her sweat a bit longer…then I'll get out to White Waltham."

CHAPTER 25

Lizzie cajoled Olivia out of bed and made her come down for breakfast. She only nibbled some toast but did drink a full mug of tea. She was lost in her own misery, hunched in her seat, eyes bleary from troubled sleep though, Lizzie was pleased to see, she was no longer crying. Such a different person to the vivacious young woman who had captivated everyone until that fateful Saturday night.

"I don't think I can do any training today, Lizzie. I won't be able to concentrate."

"I'll have a word with Stephanie Garrett. I'm sure she'll understand." Lizzie glanced at her watch. "There's plenty of time yet. It's only eight fifteen and we won't start until nine thirty I'm sure. I wonder if they'll abandon training today...I mean everyone is very upset."

When Lizzie realised she would not be able to persuade Olivia to eat any more, she suggested they go outside for a walk in the morning air. Her walk with Sanders had certainly lifted her own spirits and she was sure it would make Olivia more hopeful about Laura. Olivia did not exactly agree but she let herself be taken out, arm in arm, with Lizzie. They walked a circuit which went around the hangars and back behind the main building. Lizzie tried to distract Olivia by pointing things out: birds, the expanses of blue sky and the shapes of clouds. Though apparently a purposeless ramble, the route she had chosen was deliberate; she wanted to check outside Melford's window to see if there were any signs of an intruder.

"The shrubs are looking so lovely aren't they? You feel everything is bursting into life."

"I'm sorry Lizzie but I can't feel that at the moment. All

I feel is a terrible sense of impending doom. Why did they take Laura to the Police Station?"

"I don't know Olivia. They could have questioned her here but there must be something. Did she say anything to you about Saturday night or Sunday morning?"

"No."

"They must suspect her of something but," Lizzie added hastily, "I'm sure there will have been a misunderstanding. Laura does not come across as obviously angry or the type of person who would be prone to violence."

Olivia was quiet for some moments. "She does...I don't know if I should say this but I think I can trust you, Lizzie... she does have a very controlled appearance. She locks things up inside her, never shows what she's feeling but, occasionally, it does burst out...you know if she's really angry about something. And she's so determined and hard in a way. We're very different."

"Yes that's obvious. I think I sense what you mean but the word 'hard' worries me."

"What I mean is that she decides what she wants or what she's going to do and she carries it out whatever the cost to herself. She's fearless I think."

"She should make a good pilot then."

"She will definitely..." Olivia gulped, "...if she isn't..."

"Now Olivia. You need to be strong. Take a leaf out of Laura's book. You must tell yourself that it's a mistake. Laura will be released later today, I'm sure of it." Lizzie knew that she herself was determined like Laura and she now voiced the thought that had been growing in her mind. "Olivia, you and I need to work out who did kill Melford. We're not going to let Laura take the blame."

Olivia looked at Lizzie in amazement. "How on earth are we going to do that?"

"I don't know but we need to think things through." They were now strolling along the front of the building and Lizzie flicked her eyes to the upper floor to work out which was the window in Melford's room. Her mind was racing thinking how she must try to talk with everyone and piece together the evidence as Hawkins had been doing. But now they were approaching Melford's window. The sun was warm on their faces and shone on the mass of fresh, yellow flowers of a forsythia.

Lizzie looked up at the window. If anyone had jumped from the room, they would have been cut or at least their clothes torn on the pyracantha bush adjacent to the forsythia. She scanned the soil looking for any sign of indentations made by a ladder.

Nothing. An intruder could probably be ruled out.

But something caught her eye on the ground between the forsythia and the pyracantha, a glint of blue, something which had reflected the sun. She took a step backwards and bent over, peering between the bushes. There it was, a small blue bottle. "Well what have we here?"

Olivia bent over beside her and saw the bottle. She reached forward but Lizzie's hand shot out and grabbed her arm. "No...we mustn't touch it. I'll use my handkerchief and that pyracantha has thorns as sharp as rapiers."

Lizzie lifted the bottle carefully and held it up for both of them to see. It was some four inches tall, had a cork stopper and the thick glass was ribbed on both sides. "You see that ribbing? That tells us this contained something poisonous. My father has bottles of weedkiller ribbed like this but bigger. They put toxic substances in bottles like this so that you know as soon as you pick them up that they contain a poison...even if you're blind."

"What's it doing here?"

Lizzie glanced up. "That's the men's corridor up there and I'm certain that Melford's room is directly above us – that window there." She pointed with her arm outstretched. "We can easily remember where the bottle was – right next to the forsythia bush, here in fact where there is a slight indentation in the soil. We need to get this to Hawkins. It may not be related at all to Melford's murder but on the other hand, it might be."

◆ ◆ ◆

Sergeant Drake looked enviously at the Inspector's large, black Wolseley as he mounted his bicycle. It was not right at his age to be cycling around the countryside. Still, he consoled himself, Windsor was not far and it was another fine day. He had thought of telephoning the hospital but he wanted to meet Kenny's sister, get the measure of her, see if his instinct was alerted.

It was a pleasant ride through Maidenhead, out on the Windsor road and so to Windsor. The road went past the horse-racing track and some riders were out exercising their mounts, standing high on the stirrups, allowing the horse to flow beneath them like waves. Strange the way some people made a living but probably much less stressful than his own job...no rowdy drunks to manage on a Saturday night, no sly burglars to apprehend, no evasive murder suspects to interview.

The King Edward VII Hospital was an imposing building a short distance up from the High Street with large Georgian windows and a very impressive monument on the forecourt. It spoke of grandeur and even Sergeant Drake, normally very confident if not bumptious, felt its presence like a superior being. He leant his bicycle carefully against the front wall, making sure the white paint of the wall was not scratched. Taking his helmet from his saddle bag, he mounted the steps to the grand entrance.

A rather attractive woman probably in her thirties was sitting at the reception desk holding a telephone handset. He stood in front of the desk, smiling patiently until the receptionist had finished the call.

"Good morning, Constable. What can I do for you?"

"It's Sergeant actually, Sergeant Drake" he said, dropping his shoulders and pushing out his chest.

"Oh I do beg your pardon, Sergeant." Her face was still smiling but the warmth had left her eyes. "How can I help?"

"I've been told that a man visited one of your patients on Sunday morning. I need to check that is true. The patient is a lady called Nancy O'Brien...I don't know which ward she's in."

"Let me just check. Likely to be the main women's ward." The receptionist flicked through a box containing filing cards. "No one called O'Brien in our current patients." Suddenly her hand went to her mouth. "Oh I'm being so stupid. Mrs O'Brien was discharged this morning." She flicked through a different box. "Yes here she is. She was on Laburnum Ward. I'm afraid we don't keep a record of visitors at Reception but if you pop up to the ward the Sister or one of the nurses will be able to tell you." The warmth returned to her smile.

"Thank you Miss." Sergeant Drake graced her with a big smile in return and strode away, his heels ringing impressively on the stone floor. He found the ward easily but on entering he was soon accosted.

"Visiting time today is not until this afternoon." A small, sharp-featured woman he took to be the Sister, confronted him.

"Would you be in charge of this ward?"

"Yes I am."

"Well Madam, I'm here on Police business. I need to speak to any nurse who was on duty on Sunday morning, about eleven o'clock. I'm investigating a murder you see and I need to check what I've been told by one of the sus...one of the people I've had to interview."

"I was on duty on Sunday morning, Officer. Which patient was the person visiting?"

"A Mrs Nancy O'Brien who was apparently discharged this morning. Her visitor was her brother, a man with red hair so, if he was here, you wouldn't have missed him."

Sister smiled. "You're right there Sergeant. Once seen, never forgotten. He did visit yes...stayed about an hour. We allow visitors on Sunday morning. For some, it's the only time they can get in…work you know."

"Of course. I would like to speak with Mrs O'Brien so I'd like her address please."

"Come with me." She led him into a small, very tidy office and pulled open the drawer of a filing cabinet. Her fingers marched across the top of the files. "Neville…ah O'Brien. Here we are." She lifted the file from the drawer and opened it. "35 Albany Road. That's not far from here. You go straight down St Leonard's Road – the hospital sits on that - and keep looking at the road names on your right. There's lots of turnings but you shouldn't miss it."

"Thank you Sister. Very helpful."

She looked tired, strained, drawn, thought Hawkins, sitting hunched forward on the chair almost hugging herself for comfort. He did not enjoy making people uneasy but sometimes it was necessary. A little pressure and that hard exterior would crack.

"I trust you had a restful night Miss Hulett." She stared at him, hostility radiating from her silent figure. "We will resume the interview I started yesterday but I need to point out that if you refuse to answer my questions and say nothing, I will keep you here until you do. Her eyes did not flinch. "So how do you explain the fact that you were seen outside Melford's room but you said nothing about it and that you were aware of Mr Melford's picture of the Bullingdon Club even though you claim not to have been in his room?"

Laura said nothing so Hawkins leaned forward over the desk, his voice low, threatening. "When this comes to trial, Miss Hulett, and you are facing a judge and jury, the full intimidating presence of the court with the public in the gallery, you will not be so calm. And when the truth finally comes out, there will be no mercy for you if you persist in hindering my investigation."

Laura sat motionless returning the stare.

Suddenly Hawkins was on his feet and shouting. "This is ridiculous. I know you went back after speaking to Mr Kenny and you went into Melford's room didn't you?"

"No. Kenny dislikes me...he made that up."

"Why would he do that? Why would he lie to a Police officer?"

"You need to ask him that."

"Sergeant Drake has already done that and he explained without any hesitation the animosity between you. If he'd made it up, he wouldn't have been so honest about that would he?"

Laura stared at the table but Hawkins could see she was shaking. Her face was set hard but the tightness of the mouth suggested she was trying to hold back tears ...or perhaps some critical information. A doubt, stealthy as a cat, crept into his mind. Was he on the right track? Was it her or one of the others?

"Say something for God's sake and let's get this over."

Laura shot to her feet. Her eyes were wild, her voice cracking as she shouted, "Alright, alright. I was in his room. Are you satisfied now?"

"And you stabbed him with that small, silver knife because of what he had done or tried to do to your sister, didn't you?"

"Yes, I picked up the knife and I stabbed him. I killed him." She glared at Hawkins across the desk, her eyes full of a fiery hatred.

CHAPTER 26

Albany Road was quiet, terraced houses on both sides standing solid and impassive, the image of respectability. When he had turned into it, Sergeant Drake could see all the way down to the end. There was just one vehicle parked a short way down on the right hand side, a van. Cycling closer, he saw the van was black and had the legend 'Butler's Grocery' on the side panel. It was standing outside number thirty-five.

He propped his bicycle against the wall and knocked on the door, a good, loud, burst of knocks making a satisfying echo in the hall within. About a minute later, the door was swung open and a man, probably late thirties or early forties, stood facing him. He was of medium height and stocky build, a round face with a ruddy complexion topped with short black hair.

"Yes? What is it?" The voice was gruff, the accent unmistakeably Irish.

"Morning, Sir. Am I at the residence of Mrs Nancy O'Brien?"

"You are. What do you want?"

"And would you be Mr O'Brien?"

"I am. Michael O'Brien. What of it?"

"Probably better if I could come in, Sir. Might take a bit of explaining."

O'Brien opened the door and slowly stepped to one side to let him in, watching him closely all the time. He led the way through a door into a sitting room which was sparsely furnished and had a rug in the centre of the linoleum floor.

"Polissman to see you Nancy."

Drake held out his hand to stop her rising from her chair. "No need to get up, Madam. I won't keep you long. I understand you've just come out of hospital."

"That's right...this morning."

"Do you know a Mr Patrick Kenny?"

"I do, yes...he's my brother."

"Can you confirm that your brother visited you in hospital on Sunday morning."

She looked increasingly concerned. "He did, yes. Has he done something wrong?"

"Not as far as I know, Madam. He is based at White Waltham air base at the moment," she nodded, "and I'm afraid there has been a murder there. We simply have to check everyone's movements on Saturday night and Sunday morning."

"A murder? But surely you can't think that Patrick would…."

"No, no of course not Madam. Just checking everyone's movements to make sure their stories are correct. That's all I need to know." ·

Sergeant Drake was aware of O'Brien hovering in the room as if guarding his wife. He turned to him and in his most pleasant manner said, "Not working this morning, Sir?"

"No. I had to collect Nancy from the hospital. The boss said I could have the morning off...as long as I needed."

"The van outside, Sir...is that yours?"

"It's not mine...like I don't own it...but I drive it. I work as a delivery driver for the Grocery."

"Do you have use of the van at other times?"

O'Brien shifted his weight from one foot to the other and back again. "I can do...on occasions I have."

"You do jobs for other people using it perhaps?"

"I've done a few favours...one or two...for friends like."

Drake started to turn away and a thought struck him. "Were you using it on Saturday night Sir?"

"No...Saturday night...no. Not at all."

"Where were you on Saturday night? Your wife was in hospital so you would have been on your own."

O'Brien's eyes did not meet Drake's but flitted around the

room, not even looking at his wife. "Just went for a drink…in the town."

"Which pub would that have been in, Sir?"

"It's one on the High Street. The Prince Harry it's called."

"Thank you, Sir." Drake began to walk towards the doorway into the hall. He turned, "Thank you Mrs O'Brien. I'm sorry to have troubled you…hope you have a speedy recovery." He decided to fly a kite. Looking at Mchael O'Brien, he said, "The only reason I asked about the van, Mr O'Brien, is that it was seen in Maidenhead on Saturday night at about eleven."

There was the slightest narrowing of O'Brien's eyes. "Must have been someone else using it, Officer. I was in the pub as I told you."

"Who has keys to the van besides yourself?"

"There's a set kept in the shop. There may be another set that Mr Butler has I wouldn't know."

Drake smiled. "Thank you for your help, Sir." He opened the door and went into the street. Definitely something suspicious there. He'd talk with the Inspector and investigate more fully.

Hawkins held Laura's stare for several seconds. "Perhaps we should sit down and talk through exactly what happened in Mr Melford's room on Saturday night." He spoke as if they were meeting about something inconsequential, introducing the calm after the storm.

Both of them sat slowly and Laura, now pale and trembling, spoke quietly, all her anger and bluster gone. "As you say, I waited until Patrick Kenny had gone back into his room. I was angry with him for blaming me about his fiancée, my friend, when it wasn't my fault. I suppose that fuelled my anger against Edward Melford." She looked up at Hawkins, her eyes watery and appealing. "My sister, Olivia, is talented, lovely, full of life, a joy to be with. Everyone finds her so. When she came back from Melford's room, she was like a rag doll that has been torn, battered, abused. How can anyone do that to someone who is... was so lovely?"

"I'm afraid Miss Hulett, there are such people in the World."

She nodded. I am a couple of years older than Olivia and I've always looked out for her...at school...everywhere since early childhood. I felt I had let her down. I should have intervened when we came back from the Café de Paris but... she is a grown woman now and must make her own decisions. When Kenny was out of sight, I went back to Melford's room. I listened but could hear nothing so I thought he was perhaps already asleep, although there was a crack of light at the bottom of the door. I opened it quietly and went in, letting it close behind me. He was standing at the end of the bed...he didn't seem to be doing anything but he looked very drunk. He was swaying and breathing very strangely."

"How do you mean strangely?"

"His breath was noisy but not regular...occasionally he sounded as though he was wheezing, sometimes as though he was gasping. All I wanted to do was remonstrate with him, tell him how much he had upset Olivia. I started off...said how dare he treat my sister like that...but he just looked at me strangely. I had walked right into the room and his face twisted in a horrible snarl. He was flushed, his eyes large and staring. He started to move towards me and stupidly I moved backwards. He kept coming and I felt myself pressed against the writing desk." Laura stopped, her face twisting in agony at the memory.

"Take your time Laura. I know this is distressing for you." Hawkins could see the fight to regain her self-control. Here was someone who was not used to letting her guard down. He began to feel sorry for her.

"I put my hands either side of me on the writing desk to keep my balance but he kept coming towards me. He was muttering something…not completely sure what because his speech was very slurred but I think he said something to the effect that he hadn't been able to have my sister so he'd have me instead. He came right close to me and I pushed against the writing table behind me. Something fell over. I shoved him away. He swayed drunkenly for a moment and came at me again. I was terrified. I was thinking 'Is this it? Is this where he rapes me?' I slid one of my hands across the table not able to see of course what was on it…I didn't know what I hoped to find but I wanted something to threaten him with. My hand closed on something cold and slim and I grabbed it. Only then did I realise it was a knife."

"Think very carefully, Laura. This part is very important." His eyes were glued to her face watching every flicker, every fleeting expression, trying to judge the accuracy of her testimony.

"I held it in front of me, said something like, 'Get away from me' but he kept coming. His last two steps though seemed almost uncontrolled…he sort of staggered towards me, lurched I suppose…and he fell against me. It was only when I pushed him away I realised the knife had gone into him." Again her eyes, wide with appeal, sought his. "I didn't mean to stab him…I didn't mean to kill him."

And then she broke, like a fine porcelain vase, shattering into pieces.

Hawkins waited until her sobs had subsided. "And you pulled him onto the bed?"

"I didn't know what to do but it didn't feel right to let him fall on the floor. He was heavy but I'm quite strong. He was leaning against me though my hands held him away. I moved him, still standing, to the bed…it was only a couple of feet… and he slumped down on it. I had to get onto the bed behind him to drag him fully onto it. I made sure he was lying straight, on his back, so that it looked as though he had been sleeping. It seemed right to leave him so he looked peaceful. I checked my own clothes but no blood had stained my dress. There seemed to be very little blood. Then I made sure the writing desk was tidy, picked up the picture and set it upright. That's when I saw it was of The Bullingdon Club."

"Did you open the window?"

"No...I didn't see if it was open or not...I don't remember."

Inspector Hawkins let a silence fall between them as if to respect the departed. He spoke gently. "Is there anything else you want to say, Laura?"

She shook her head. "I'm sorry. I didn't mean to kill him...just wanted to tell him what he had done to Olivia."

"As far as you know, did he...did he rape Olivia?"

Again she shook her head. "No, I don't think he succeeded but only because she struggled and got away. He would have done...that was his intention."

"You will need to write a statement, Laura. PC Green will bring you paper and a pen. Just write down what you have told me and then sign it."

She looked at him, her lip trembling but then she seemed again to take control of herself. "Will I hang?"

"That's a decision for a judge but I think you have a strong case for arguing self-defence. You may be charged with manslaughter rather than murder. I will leave you to write your statement. Thank you for being honest at last. It is so much easier."

Inspector Hawkins left the interview room and closed the door quietly behind him. He felt none of the elation he would normally feel at solving a case. Instead, he felt weary, as though he had been through an ordeal. And there was something else... that doubt niggling at the back of his mind. Had he got the true story or was there something else? Was Melford the potential rapist Laura painted him to be? He needed to check his past and the Bullingdon Club connection. By all accounts Melford was someone who believed he had a right to everything including, it seems, the sexual favours of young women. He decided he would go to Oxford that very day.

When he walked into the front office, PC Green waved a note in the air. "Telephone call from White Waltham, Sir. Doesn't sound important to me but the chap seemed to think you should be told."

"Told what Green?"

"Someone's found a glass bottle in a flower bed, Sir. God knows why they think that's important."

"Just give me the detail, Green."

"Yes, Sir. It's a small, blue bottle with ribs on each side. It was found beneath Mel someone's window."

Hawkins stopped. "PC Teal. I've got to go to Oxford. You need to get out to White Waltham and collect that bottle. Get any information you can – who found it, what time it was found and exactly where. Then take the bottle in an evidence bag – don't touch it yourself – to Doctor Jarvis at Windsor Hospital. Ask him to have the contents analysed, assuming there is something in it still."

"Right, Sir. Will do." PC Teal was delighted to be out of the Station again and heading for Windsor.

"Green, please take Miss Hulett a paper and pen to write her statement and give her a cup of tea. She's had a very distressing morning so be nice to her."

"Of course, Sir. I'm always nice to people…especially young women." He grinned but Hawkins ignored him.

CHAPTER 27

Lizzie sat with Olivia and Kasia in the lounge. They had been excused training by Trueman after presenting him with the bottle. Lizzie had demanded that at least Olivia but preferably the three of them should be allowed to visit Laura at the Police Station.

"That's not my decision, Lizzie. I'll need to ask Inspector Hawkins. I suspect the answer will be negative as, if she is a suspect, they won't want any outside influence on her."

"Surely they must allow family to visit...on humanitarian grounds?"

"As I said, it's not my decision."

Now they sat quietly in the lounge. Olivia would occasionally shake and Kasia or Lizzie would hold her close to give her comfort. "It's my fault," she said on one of these bouts of sorrow. "If I hadn't gone to Melford's room, Laura wouldn't be in trouble. They must think she went and killed Melford because of what he tried to do to me. Unless..." she choked on her words.

"Unless what, Olivia?" Lizzie squeezed her hand and continued gently. "It's better to voice your fears than let them fester unheard."

"Unless they are putting pressure on her to find out if I did it. Perhaps Hawkins doesn't believe me."

"I'm sure he believed you Olivia. Try not to think like that."

When Olivia had subsided into her own tormented mind again, Lizzie decided to scour the bookshelves. The books were not very well organised but eventually she found what she was looking for, an illustrated guide to British wild flowers. She sat down and began to flick through the pages. She knew it was a hopeless task but maybe she would see that plant that Sanders had been unable to identify. It would please her a good deal to be able to provide the name of it to such an expert.

The book had only black and white illustrations, mainly of the flowers and in some cases the berries so identifying the plant would not be easy. The stems of the plant they had seen had been quite long and thin and those leaves growing alternately on the stem rather than sprouting on both sides from the same point like most plants should help her find it.

Her investigation was interrupted by Commander Trueman who entered the lounge with a police officer. "Ladies, this is PC Teal from Maidenhead Police. He has come to collect the bottle you found this morning, Lizzie. He would like to be shown where it was found exactly."

All three of them went outside with the constable even though Kasia had not been with Lizzie and Olivia when they had found the bottle. Lizzie led the way straight to the spot. "This is where it was lying, Officer." She pointed to the spot.

"How can you be so sure it was exactly there, Miss?"

"Because I made a note of the spot right beside the forsythia. If you look carefully, you can see the slight indentation made by the bottle. It was clearly dropped from some height, an upstairs window I'd suggest. Now if you look up, you'll see that there is a window in each room along the building. The window directly above this is in Mr Melford's room – the man who was murdered. His window had been opened by someone on Saturday night. I suggest to you that the murderer gave whatever was in the bottle to Melford and then dropped it out of the window."

"Steady on Miss. We can't leap to conclusions like that. I'm to take the bottle to Windsor Hospital where the pathologist will arrange for it to be tested in the lab. What was in the bottle might have been quite harmless."

"It is a poison bottle, Constable. You wouldn't put something harmless in it."

"Let's take it one step at a time shall we? Thank you for your help ladies."

"When will my sister be released?" Olivia's hands were clasped tightly together.

"Who is your sister, Miss?"

"Laura Hulett."

"Ah. Right. I'm afraid I can't answer that but I can tell you that she has confessed to the murder of Edward Melford."

Olivia let out an anguished wail and sank to her knees.

St Augustine's College, Oxford was not one of the most prestigious nor best known of the Oxford University colleges but boasted the same fine old buildings of honey-coloured stone. Inspector Hawkins parked nearby and entered under the archway. He could see the quadrangle with its beautifully tended grass inside and a few members of the college strolling around in academic gowns. He turned to the right to the Porter's Lodge.

"Good morning Sir." The gentleman behind the screen was in his fifties and could be described as well fed. He was impeccably dressed in a suit and tie and wore the traditional bowler hat on his head.

"Inspector Hawkins from Maidenhead Police. I have an appointment with the Master at eleven."

The porter consulted his book. "Ah yes, Sir. Very good. I'll have someone show you to his rooms."

"I'm here to discuss a former student, Edward Melford. Did you know him?" Hawkins detected the slightest change in the man's eyes, betraying not only knowledge but something else. Was it fear or dislike? Warm recollections were certainly not passing through his mind.

"It's not my place to discuss members of the College, Sir. You'll need to speak to the Master." The porter glanced in both directions. No one was near. Lowering his voice, he added, "You may wish to ask the Master if you can see the Donations Ledger...look at May nineteen thirty-five."

He then turned away, business-like, as if he had said nothing and called someone from the inner room of the lodge. A moment later, a lanky young man, similarly dressed, appeared and escorted Hawkins through a labyrinth of corridors and stairs to the Master's rooms. He stopped outside a solid oak door with a brass name plate on it. 'Dr Pemberton-Smythe Master.' The Assistant Porter knocked and an instruction to enter was given.

The young man escorting Hawkins opened the door and took one step inside. "Inspector Hawkins from Maidenhead Constabulary to see you Master."

"Thank you Purdey. That will be all."

The Master was tall, slim, probably late fifties with an urbane manner. His smile spoke of superiority as did his languid, upper class accent. He offered a seat in a comfortable armchair and coffee which Hawkins declined. The room was beautiful, oak panelling on the walls and striking paintings in various places. A large desk with books spread on it rather dominated.

The Master swept the sides of his gown in front of him, eased himself onto another armchair close to Hawkins and laid one elegant leg over the other. "Now Inspector, what can I do for you?"

"I'm investigating the murder of one of your former students, Edward Melford."

"Melford...murder...good grief! Whatever happened?"

"We are still investigating, Sir. You obviously remember Melford. What can you tell me about him? I am especially keen to know if he was someone who had enemies."

"Enemies? No, Inspector. I don't recall any enemies. He was not the most academic of students but he was good company, well-liked and engaged fully in the life of the College. I can't imagine why anyone would want to murder him."

"That's invariably the case with murder, Sir, until one starts turning over stones. Did he have lady friends whilst at College?"

"I really don't know, Inspector. That's not the sort of thing that is brought to my attention."

"No...misdemeanours then Sir?"

"Well I'm sure there may have been an occasional late entry to College at night but nothing serious that comes to mind. Do you have any...information?"

"Why do you ask?"

"I'm just wondering why you raise it that's all."

"I have to ask, Sir. It's often something in the past that is the root cause of a murder." Hawkins noticed the Master's weak smile and that he avoided his own eyes. "I'd like to look at the Donations Ledger, Sir."

"The Donations Ledger? Whatever for Inspector? Why would there be a connection?"

"Humour me Sir."

"That's most irregular, Inspector. Our donors like to be guaranteed discretion. I can't release that information without prior permission."

"That's a shame, Sir." Hawkins began to stand. "It just delays things a bit. I'll apply for a warrant then..."

"Well, Inspector. I suppose I might show it to an officer of the law, provided of course you can assure me that the information will not be made public."

"Of course."

"I'll need to have it brought from the Bursar." The Master's self-assured poise melted away. He walked to another door and had a word with someone in the adjoining office. When he returned, he forced a smile and said, "It will be a few minutes, Inspector. Can you tell me how Melford was killed?"

"I'm afraid not, Sir. We do have a suspect in custody but we need to verify certain facts." The Master said nothing but seemed restless as they waited for the ledger to be brought. "I believe Melford was a member of the Bullingdon Club."

The Master coughed. "Was he? I'm afraid I wouldn't know about that. The Bullingdon Club is not a College, nor indeed, a University Society."

At last there was a tap on the door and a grey-haired, stooped man came in with a large leather bound book. "The Donations Ledger, Master."

"Thank you Jenks." The Bursar dipped his head in a sort of bow and disappeared. "Here you are Inspector. I hope it is of some help."

Hawkins made a show of flicking through the pages from the front of the ledger, glancing at dates, names and amounts. When he reached the pages for 1935, he studied the list carefully. There were some ten donations made in late May 1935 all of substantial amounts.

The name General Melford leapt out from the page.

"You had several donations in May 1935 Master, of significant amounts of money. That is very different to the pattern in previous years. What happened then to give rise to all of these at the same time?"

The Master waved a languid hand in the air. "Oh I expect we had an appeal. We do that from time to time."

Hawkins took out his notepad and a pen and made a list of the donors underlining General Melford and the amount he had given. "Melford's father was very generous."

"Yes...yes...many of our parents are. Grateful, you see, for the education we provide."

Hawkins said nothing for a few seconds until he saw from the corner of his eye, the Master shift uncomfortably in his chair. He lifted his head suddenly from the ledger and looked directly at the Master's face. "I think there is something you are not telling me, Dr Pemberton-Smythe."

A fleeting look of alarm passed like a ghost over the Master's face. "No, no. I have nothing else to say. And now, Inspector, unless you have any other questions, I really must get on. I'm researching the Restoration playwrights at the moment. It's a period that is often overlooked as being superficial but it is important to understand all periods of literature." He stood and offered his hand.

Hawkins gave him the ledger. "Thank you Master. If there's anything else, I'll be back. I can see myself out." As he negotiated the old wooden staircase and found his way back to the Quad, he felt an anger boiling inside him. He knew the Master was hiding something and he hated the arrogance of that kind of man. Like Melford, the Master was someone who believed that the law did not apply to him and his kind. We shall see, he thought, we shall see.

At the Porter's lodge, he thanked the Porter and signed out in the visitors' book. As he was doing so, the Porter who was standing at the window, glanced right and left as he had done before and silently pushed a piece of paper towards him. He looked at it. On it was a name, 'Grace Upton' and under it was written, 'Ask Oxford City Police."

Hawkins took the paper and slipped it into his pocket. His eyes met the Porter's who returned his gaze unflinchingly. "Thank you...thank you very much. I'll do that."

CHAPTER 28

Brian Teal turned his bicycle back towards Maidenhead with a heavy feeling of disappointment in his breast. He knew of course before he had set off for Windsor that he would not be able to see Sheila at that time of day; she would be tucked up in bed asleep. He imagined her lovely hair spread on the pillow and the gentle rise and fall of her chest as she lay peacefully breathing. Not for the first time, he pictured himself waking beside her, seeing the morning sun glinting off a lock of hair, turning it gold.

He sighed and pressed harder on the pedals. He couldn't wait until Saturday, he knew that much, so he would cycle over after work tomorrow or perhaps even later today. The thought of seeing her again sooner than they had arranged filled him with a new energy and in no time at all he was flying along the road, the wind in his hair and wanting to shout joyous things to the swans on the river.

The bike careered into the Station forecourt and he swung his leg over the saddle well before it had come to a stop. He wheeled it to the back of the building and put it in the rack. Sergeant Drake was in the outer office with PC Green.

"Where've you been then Teal?"

"Had to take a poison bottle over to Windsor. Inspector asked me to."

"Right. Well I've had an interesting morning. I went to Windsor myself as you know to speak to the hospital about Kenny, one of the suspects at White Waltham. His story was backed up right enough but his sister had been discharged. I had this feeling that something was not right so I got her address... in Windsor, not far from the hospital...and went round there."

"Bit of alright was she Sarge?"

"I'm talking to PC Teal, Green, not you. Just get on with whatever you're supposed to be doing."

PC Green grinned but said no more.

"As it happens, she is an attractive woman. Red hair like her brother. But the thing is, her husband, Irish fellow by the name of Michael O'Brien, was there and guess what was outside the house?"

"I don't know, Sarge. A street?"

"Very funny Teal. There was a van, a small black van with Butler's Groceries painted on the sides. He's the driver for the Grocery. I asked O'Brien where he was on Saturday night. He said he was in the pub...get this...the Prince Harry pub in the town centre."

PC Teal whistled. "The same pub as sold the Pale Ale and where they said they'd seen the man in brogues. I think we might be getting closer Sarge. Did you arrest him?"

"Course not Teal...you need evidence. A hunch is not evidence but when Hawkins gets back from his jaunt to Oxford, I reckon we go over there, search the van and the house if necessary, see what we can find."

PC Teal thought for a moment. "You know, Sarge, at the back of my mind I've had this niggle since I spoke to the lady who found the paint tin in her garden. She gave me the tin and the brush but there was no lid. The fact that the paint went over one of her bushes suggests that it was thrown over without the lid. I wonder if that lid might still be in the van or maybe at the house?"

"That's what we'll be looking for then, Teal. Well done my boy, you're catching on."

"And by the way, Sarge, a couple of the young women at the air base were asking if they could visit Miss Hulett...you know the one we've got in custody who admitted to murdering that posh bloke."

"Has she written and signed her statement?"

"Yep. It's on the Inspector's desk."

"We'll need to get the boss to agree to it but I don't see any reason why they shouldn't though it's not usual. You'd better go and check on her by the way. Make sure she hasn't done anything daft."

"Will do, Sarge." PC Teal strolled along the blank corridor to the cells, whistling. Life was good and there was the prospect of going to Windsor again later, maybe earning some overtime. He unlocked the only occupied cell and swung the heavy door open.

He stopped and stared.

Laura Hulett was sitting on the bed slumped against the wall. Her head was on one side and she seemed completely inert. Was she dead? Should he call the Sergeant? What had happened? He snapped out of his frozen state and strode over to her. Carefully he lifted one arm and felt her wrist for a pulse. Nothing. His eyes opened wide with alarm. He moved his fingers slightly and then let out a huge breath. There was a pulse, a definite pulse.

"Miss…Miss…wake up. Are you okay?"

Slowly, she came to and turned bleary eyes towards him. "What d'you want?" she mumbled.

"Are you alright Miss? Do you want a cup of tea?"

She nodded. "Tea…yes please. So tired…didn't sleep last night."

PC Teal blew out a long breath. "Blimey, you gave me a fright then. Thought you were dead."

"I wish I were," she said in a monotone "This is a nightmare."

"You'll feel better after a cup of tea."

◆ ◆ ◆

"I think she would be better off if she were busy, Sir. Sitting around dwelling on it is doing her no good at all." Lizzie watched Trueman's face, trying to read his thoughts.

"You may be right, Lizzie, but is she in a fit state to do anything? Obviously she would have one of us in the aircraft but would it be a waste of time?"

"Let's just take it step by step. You could say we are going to do some theory work on...I don't know... navigation or something. That might distract her enough and then we could persuade her to get into an aircraft. Maybe there's something we haven't covered yet that could be explained."

"Such as?"

"Not sure, Sir. Perhaps it could be about following roads to find our way to places, using the sightlines from the cockpit to get directions, distances or something."

Trueman nodded slowly. "That would certainly be useful and worth a try. Please tell the others and see if Olivia will engage."

Lizzie left Trueman's office and walked into the lounge. "Right Girls, we're going to do some work on navigation this morning. Trueman has asked me to get you to the briefing hut. Kasia stood immediately, clearly glad to have something to do but Olivia looked pained. "Come on Olivia. You'll be much better off doing something. Dwelling on the situation will do you no good."

Olivia stood slowly. "But Lizzie, it will be a waste of time. I won't be able to concentrate."

Lizzie stepped close to her. "Olivia, you must make an effort. You're no use to Laura in this state. We need to be ready to help the Police find the real killer. That poison bottle...someone dropped it there. Now come on. Let's keep our brains active so we can think clearly."

Reluctantly, Olivia allowed Lizzie and Kasia to link arms either side of her and walk her to the briefing hut. All three were already in flying gear and Lizzie was hopeful that she would be able to entice Olivia into a cockpit even if she did not take off. Trueman was already there; the other two instructors were working with Mark Sanders, Parick Kenny and Graham

Swinburne out on the airfield, practising landings.

In the case of Mark Sanders, as he was an experienced pilot, he was being required to do a solo glide landing, cutting the engine some way from the airfield and bringing the aircraft down safely. The risk, if you got it wrong, was considerable as there was no second chance. With the engine cut, you could not pull up again. Lizzie had completed the manoeuvre successfully on several occasions. There was a wonderful sense of peace when the engine was killed, just an eerie screaming of the air through the wires, a sense of even greater freedom.

"Navigating in the ATA is an important skill as, on most trips, you will not have a navigator and will have to find your own way. Let's start by considering how to do that in good weather when you can see the ground." Trueman pointed with a stick to a large map on the wall. "This shows a good part of the South of England. We're here at White Waltham. If we wanted to get to...let's say Bristol...what could we follow?"

Oxford Police Station was impressive, a very large, mock-Georgian building on St Aldates Street which looked as though it had only recently opened. Its size suggested a large force was housed there. Hawkins parked in a side street called Floyd's Row and realised that it was not just the frontage of the building that was huge; it extended back from St Aldates quite a distance.

Inspector Hawkins showed his warrant card to the desk sergeant inside the Station. "I'd like to speak with someone who might be able to tell me about a case that happened five years ago...early May 1935."

"I'm afraid the Super and Inspector are both out at the moment, Sir, but I might be able to help you. Sergeant Baines, Sir, at your service." The Sergeant's smile was bright and he clicked his heels together as he said his last few words. He had fair hair that threatened to go out of control and was probably mid-thirties. An officer with a future.

"I would like to know about a case that perhaps didn't come to court involving a young woman by the name of Grace Upton."

"Grace Upton?" His face darkened. He turned away from the desk and called for a Constable to take over. "Think we'd better go somewhere more private, Sir."

The interview room was like all such rooms in Police Stations, bare, cold, windowless, intimidating. Hawkins pulled out a chair which scraped on the hard floor. When they were both seated, Hawkins began. "You obviously remember the case Sergeant."

"I do, Sir, but may I ask what your interest in it is? I mean you being from Maidenhead."

"I'm investigating the murder, Sergeant, in Maidenhead of a young man called Edward Melford." The sergeant's mouth narrowed, his brows lowered and his eyes turned hard. "We believe that he may have been killed because he attacked a young woman...probably a case of self-defence. I need to establish his character, whether such an attack is credible. I have visited St Augustine's College, that was his college when he was up at the University, and was given this name by...someone. I know nothing more than the name."

"I worked on the case Inspector. Terrible it was. Are you familiar with The Bullingdon Club?"

"Yes, I am but only the name."

"It's an unofficial club – not recognised by the University – that in the distant past began as a sporting club... cricket and horse-racing mainly. Membership is by invitation. You have to be male, very rich and have gone to one of half a dozen top private schools. The Club meets occasionally, usually to go to dinner somewhere. They get very drunk and usually cause significant damage which they often pay for in cash. Doubtless they regard themselves as having innocent fun but there is a darker side."

Hawkins took out his notepad.

"Not sure how much you should write down, Sir."

"Don't worry, Sergeant, it's for my own use only."

"It was after the May balls, they happen on the evening before the first of May, the Bullies as they are called met at a restaurant in the City. One of the waitresses was a young girl called Grace Upton who was still at school doing her Higher School Certificate but earning a bit of cash on an occasional evening. The Manager sent her home at about ten-thirty as the bulk of the work was done. The Bullies left immediately after, rowdy and wanting some 'fun' as they would call it. They followed her...she lived in Jericho so she did not have far to walk...and they forced her to go to an area by the canal where a number of them raped her."

The Sergeant paused, swallowing and looking away. "It never went to court. She dropped the charges...paid off I should think...and they got away with it as they so often do."

"And Melford was among those who attacked her?"

"I think he was the ring leader."

"She could still press charges couldn't she?"

"Perhaps you should visit her and try to persuade her. I'd love to see that lot behind bars. Bastards."

"I'd like to do that but please let your Superintendent know that I am doing so. It's important to the defence of the young woman I have in custody that he had form...not just her word."

"I'll get the address for you."

CHAPTER 29

The theory session in the briefing room had gone well. Olivia was intrigued as were Kasia and Lizzie by the idea of navigating using roads, railway lines, canals and rivers as well as prominent landmarks such as church spires. She was much more positive and did not resist when Trueman said they would do some flying to demonstrate what one could do.

There was only one Tiger Moth available as Roger Carlisle and Stephanie Garrett were up with Graham Swinburne and Patrick Kenny. Trueman suggested he take Olivia up first and then Kasia. "Mark Sanders is up in the Miles Magister. When he returns, you take that up Lizzie but look at the notes while you're waiting. Good practice for when you're doing operational flights." He smiled. "Are you happy about that?"

"Of course. You know me...raring to go. If there's an odd Wellington bomber hanging about idle, I'll take that up."

"Yes I think you would too but best not to run before you can walk."

Olivia strapped on her parachute but, for a moment, it looked as though she was going to refuse to climb into the cockpit. She hesitated and looked around at Lizzie who smiled encouragement. Then she hoisted herself up and into her seat. Lizzie was pleased that she seemed to have pulled herself out of the trough of despair into which she had sunk. A flight on a fine day would make her feel much better she was sure.

She and Kasia watched as the aircraft engine was started and the Moth taxied out to the end of the runway. It was a lovely sight to see it accelerating over the grass and lifting gracefully into the air. Lizzie found the notes for the Miles Magister. It was a single-engined monoplane, faster and more manoeuvrable than the Tiger Moth. She was looking forward to flying it. There was nothing in the notes that suggested it was a difficult plane to fly. In fact, by all accounts it was easier than the Moth, less temperamental, more predictable and faster. Lizzie couldn't wait to take it up. It was powered by a one hundred and thirty horse power engine. Lots of pull in that.

When she had read through the notes, Lizzie returned to the apron where Kasia was talking with one of the ground crew. Lizzie scoured the sky, now impatient for the return of Sanders and the 'Maggie' as the aircraft was fondly called. At last, she saw it approaching the airfield, coming in faster than a Tiger Moth would have done but steady. The landing was perfect. Sanders had certainly taken to it and Lizzie was determined that her landing would be as good. She would make sure she explored it fully on her flight so that she was confident about the landing.

Sanders taxied the plane towards the hangars and cut the engine when it reached the apron. He jumped down and pulled off his helmet and goggles. "Brilliant," he shouted. "What a lovely aircraft to fly. She responds so well and is so much faster than the Moth."

"Trueman said I could take it up now. Is there plenty of fuel left?"

"Yep. It was full when I took her up and there's well over half a tank left so, unless you're planning a long trip, you should be fine."

Lizzie felt a flutter of excitement in her breast as she hoisted herself into the cockpit. Then she thought of something. "Oh by the way," she shouted down to Mark Sanders, "I found a couple of plants like the one you didn't recognise in a book in the lounge. Not sure which it is. I'll show you later."

The smile that had lit the face of Mark Sanders since he landed suddenly faded. He said nothing but turned away. Probably a bit fed up that I've found something he didn't know Lizzie thought. That pleased her even more; she had to admit that she enjoyed having an advantage over a man.

♦ ♦ ♦

Inspector Hawkins knew he was on dodgy ground, attempting to interview the victim of a cold case in a jurisdiction that was not his own, but something compelled him to do so. He despised Melford and he wanted to be able to say on Laura Hulett's behalf that the man had a past of attacking young women. If he could do that, it would perhaps reduce her sentence. But there was something else. Sergeant Baines had asked him to try to persuade the girl to go through with the case. Maybe she would be stronger now and, even if not, maybe he would gain an insight into how Melford and his rich friends worked. Did they buy her off? Did they threaten her?

Canal Street was narrow and lined with Victorian terraced houses whose doors opened directly onto the street. They were all quite small but well maintained. He parked the car and found number thirty-eight. Trim window boxes filled with spring flowers gave a welcome splash of colour to the building which boasted a yellow brick frontage offset with red bricks forming arches over the windows and door. It was an attractive house.

He lifted the brass lion's head knocker and tapped twice. He did not have to wait long nor repeat the summons before it was opened by an attractive lady of middle age. Her auburn hair was well groomed and she was dressed smartly, though not expensively, in a skirt, blouse and cardigan.

"Good afternoon, Madam. Is it Mrs Upton?" She nodded. "My name is Inspector Hawkins from Maidenhead Police." He lifted his warrant card for her to see. "I'm sorry to visit you without warning but I wonder if I could talk with you and your daughter if she is available?"

The woman's eyes shrank with suspicion. "What do you want?" The voice had a trace of an Irish accent.

"I would prefer to talk privately…inside…if you don't mind, Mrs Upton."

"I don't think we have anything to say to the Police unless…"

"Let me explain briefly. I am investigating the murder of a man in a place near Maidenhead but I think the murderer may have had good reason to do what she did."

"She?"

"Yes, Madam, she. The dead man was Edward Melford."

"Melford! He's dead? Thank God for that. He can't destroy anyone else then."

"Quite. But I need to know what he and the others did to your daughter so that the jury will understand what kind of man he was."

Mrs Upton stood back from the door and beckoned him in. "Grace, my daughter, is in the sitting room. If she starts becoming too distressed, you'll have to go," she whispered.

"Understood."

Grace stood up when they entered the room, not a gesture of politeness but the action of someone preparing herself for flight. "It's alright Grace, darling. You can sit down. This man is a police officer from Maidenhead but he has brought some news for us."

Hawkins took his cue but waited until Grace was seated again. "I have to tell you that Edward Melford, whom you encountered some years ago, was murdered on Saturday night."

Grace was on her feet again. "You can't think I did it, though I would have liked to."

"No, no, Grace. We have someone in custody. It's a young woman and she said that Melford tried to….to….force himself on her. When she is brought to court, I am sure that will be her defence. Although of course she has committed a crime and I cannot condone it, I do understand why she took the action she did and I want the jury to understand it too. If I can ensure they know what kind of man he was, her sentence will be much lighter…she may even be acquitted."

Grace sat down slowly. "What do you want from me?"

"I know Grace in broad terms what happened to you. I do not want to distress you by asking you to go through all the details but perhaps if I could understand how Melford and his friends operated it would help."

Grace sat still for several seconds. Hawkins saw the same hair colour as her mother and indeed her mother's features replicated in her though a younger version. She was a very attractive young woman but there was a haunted look in her pale blue eyes.

"I have buried this somewhere inside me for five years because it destroyed me and I could not think about it but perhaps I need to come to terms with it," she said, so softly that Hawkins had to lean forward to hear.

Quietly, without histrionics and with considerable dignity, Grace told the story of that night, how she had endured comments throughout the evening from the Bullies, how they had followed her, forced her to go past Canal Street to a snicket that led to the canal itself. "There were six of them I think and they held me so each of them could..."

"You do not have to give any details that distress you, Grace." Hawkins saw her agony and felt an anger growing inside him. How could anyone treat this lovely young girl in this way?

Mrs Upton had a tear in her eye. "I can't help it, Inspector, when I think that this was happening a hundred yards from her home. If only we had known, if only we had gone to the restaurant and walked her home. I blame myself..."

"Mrs Upton. You must not do so. The only people to blame are those young men. A girl should be able to walk home free from such appalling violence."

"All the same..."

"Mum, you must stop blaming yourself. Like the Inspector said, the only people to blame are those Bullies."

"You are quite right, Grace." Hawkins paused, judging if he could ask the next questions. "I am told by Oxford City Police that you decided not to press charges."

Grace looked away. "That's right."

"This is a delicate question but I have to ask it. Did anyone offer you money to drop the charges?"

Mrs Upton leapt in angrily. "Oh yes, they tried that alright. Some pompous oaf called General Melford came round here in his swanky car and offered money if Grace dropped the charges. I told him where to put his money. We can't be bought off like that."

"I expect you think I was wrong to drop the charges, Inspector, weak but..." She stifled a sob.

"It destroyed her, Inspector. She was confident and quite carefree before it happened but she's hardly been able to step outside the door since. It was a good six months before she would do so. She gave up school...such a shame as her teachers said she was doing well, could've gone to university perhaps, but now..."

"I couldn't face the idea of standing up in court, being questioned by clever lawyers, everyone knowing what had happened to me. They'd have called me a slut. It's always the girl's fault. 'She must have invited it' they'd say. I couldn't show my face anywhere, knowing people were talking and laughing and thinking I was a prostitute."

Hawkins watched Grace carefully. He understood it, he had seen it before the way people assume the girl is to blame, inviting sexual mis-conduct by looking pretty. It was utter nonsense of course but the likes of Melford and his chums made use of it. "I would like to ask you, Grace, if it will not be too distressing, whether Edward Melford was one of the group that attacked you."

"He was the one with the limp. Oh yes, he wasn't just one of the group, he was the ring-leader, suggesting what they should do, telling them how to hold me. Perhaps if he hadn't been there, the others wouldn't have done what they did."

"Anger can be very useful in these situations, Grace. It can support your sense of your own worth and I detect an anger behind your words."

"Oh I'm angry alright. If one of those bastards was here right now, I'd kill him."

"Language, Grace. Try not to be angry."

"I disagree with you Mrs Upton. Be angry Grace but use your anger to make things better, drive a determination to do something with your life. You do not have to be a victim. Fight it. Don't let it destroy you."

Grace looked at Hawkins curiously as if the idea that she could still have a fruitful life had not occurred to her before.

"You could still bring those young men to justice, though I understand what an ordeal that would be for you. I must leave you now, have to get back to Maidenhead, but I thank you for seeing me and for allowing me to ask you about such a distressing period in your life. You are a very lovely young woman, Grace, and you have a huge amount to offer the World. Please do not let that be wasted. You do have to fight it and it won't be easy but I can see you have courage and intelligence and that is a formidable combination. Goodbye, I hope we may meet again."

Grace stood and held out her hand which Hawkins took. Their eyes met and she smiled.

At the door, as Mrs Upton showed him out, she said, "Thank you Inspector. It's the first time I've seen Grace smile for years."

"I will say no more at the moment but there are some young women whom I think it would be good for Grace to meet. Let me see if I can set it up."

He stepped out into the street and turned. "Tell me Mrs Upton, do you have relatives from Ireland in this country?"

"I have a couple of cousins, one in London and one in... Windsor I think."

"May I know their surnames/"

"Kenny, Patrick Kenny, but my female cousin who came over not long ago is called Nancy O'Brien... she married."

"Thank you, Mrs Upton."

CHAPTER 30

Patrick Kenny! What a coincidence…or was it? Perhaps Sergeant Drake had been right. Perhaps there was something suspicious about him, not just that he was a red-haired man from Liverpool with Irish parents. It would make sense. But he already had a confession. Laura Hulett was clear about how Melford came to have a knife in his stomach and Hawkins was sure she was telling the truth…even more sure now that he knew beyond doubt that Melford was quite capable of attacking her as she had described.

He climbed into his car and started the engine. He was tempted to drive back to Maidenhead immediately to see if Drake had got anywhere with Kenny's sister but there was something he needed to do in Oxford first. He eased the Wolseley away from the kerb and found his way back to St Augustine's College. The Porter did not seem surprised to see him again.

"I'd like to see the Master please and thank you for your help."

"I'm sure I did nothing, Sir. The Master usually takes coffee in his rooms after lunch, Sir, so I'll have Purdey show you up. I take it the Master is not expecting you, Sir."

"No, he isn't. No need to let him know. I'll only keep him a couple of minutes."

Purdey led him through the same route to the Master's rooms and went through the same procedure of knocking, waiting and announcing him.

The Master was visibly surprised and concerned. "Inspector. How can I help you?"

Hawkins didn't wait for the door to close behind Purdey. "This morning I told you Edward Melford had been murdered probably by a young woman he had attempted to rape. Perhaps if you had taken a firmer stance with him and the other Bullies who raped that young girl five years ago, he would have learnt a lesson and not repeated his behaviour. He may still be alive. How many other girls have had their lives destroyed by those animals that you protected I wonder?"

Hawkins noticed with satisfaction that the Master had turned pale. He was standing with a cup of coffee in his hand, speechless, staring at him. "You could have…should have sent them down, given them a clear message that such behaviour was unacceptable and, even if the young lady was too humiliated to press charges, the message would have been clear. Instead, you allowed yourself to be bought by donations from the parents. This morning, you denied any knowledge of wrong-doing on Melford's part, yet you knew what they had done. Did you meet the girl? Did you see how it destroyed her? Five years on and she still hardly ventures outside the door of her home. You…" Hawkins jabbed his finger at him, " you are almost as bad as they are. You are despicable. If I were on my own turf, I would arrest you for obstructing a police officer in the line of his duty."

"But…but Inspector…you don't understand. I had to think about the reputation of the College."

Hawkins exploded. "The reputation of the college! The reputation of the College! That's more important than the life of a young woman is it?" His voice dropped to a threatening growl. "People like you disgust me with your fancy airs and privileged lives. I suppose she doesn't matter because she's not rich. I hope that I can persuade her to bring charges again and get the others convicted even if it's too late for Melford. We'll see how the 'reputation of the College' is after it all comes out in court. Good-day to you."

Hawkins turned on his heel and strode out, slamming the door behind him.

It took the whole drive back to Maidenhead to calm his seething breast. He had to admit he had enjoyed firing that salvo and that arrogant, pompous idiot had deserved every bit of it. He must now catch up with Drake and Teal and see where they had got to with the fire.

Both Drake and Teal were hovering, waiting to speak to him. He detected in them a degree of excitement. Perhaps there had been a breakthrough. Leaving Green at the desk, he called both Drake and Teal into his office.

"I've just returned from Oxford. Melford and his rich chums raped a young girl after one of their drunken outings. She was only seventeen… a waitress in the restaurant where they were dining – if you can apply such a civilised term to what they were doing. Attacked her on her way home, dragged her to a secluded place by the canal and took turns. I know we have to put Laura Hulett on trial for his murder but, frankly, my sympathies are with her not her victim."

Drake and Teal stood in respectful silence waiting for the tirade to cease. "Sorry, gentlemen, but to see that young woman, a lovely young woman, destroyed by those animals… five years on and hardly goes outside the house…monstrous!" Hawkins shook his head, trying to clear his anger. "Anyway, what have you got Drake?"

"Well, Sir, I went to Windsor. The ward sister confirmed that Kenny had visited his sister on Sunday morning but she was discharged today. So I got her address and went to see her. But here's the thing. Her husband, a man called Michael O'Brien, drives a small, black delivery van for Butler's Grocery. He says he was in the Prince Harry pub on Saturday night having a drink but I reckon we need to search that van for evidence of the red paint and perhaps the house too. Teal pointed out that the lid of the paint pot was not recovered…may still be in the van or at his house."

"And, if you remember Sir, The Prince Harry pub was the place that had sold some Pale Ale to a tall man who wears brown brogues. Also, I delivered the blue bottle to doctor Jarvis at the hospital who said he'd try to get it analysed as soon as possible."

"Good work both of you. I came across some

information in Oxford that will probably confirm your belief that Patrick Kenny may be involved in Melford's death. Both Mrs Upton and her daughter Grace – she was the one attacked by Melford's mob - had auburn hair, not as red as Kenny's but similar. Kenny and his sister…get this…are cousins of Mrs Upton."

"I knew it, Sir. There's something not right there."

"The fact they are cousins doesn't of course mean Kenny killed Melford in revenge. Cousins can be distant. Kenny may not even know about the attack on Grace. Besides which, we have a confession from Laura Hulett, though there is still something niggling me about that."

"Maybe she's taking the blame for her younger sister. People do that and she is very protective of Miss Olivia."

"Maybe, Drake, maybe. I think we have to work on certainties though. For the time being, she is our murderer." Hawkins glanced up at the clock. "Three o'clock. Let's get over to Windsor now. Let's start with Butler's grocery, see if the van is there. I want both of you with me in case we have to search the house."

"Sir, there is one other thing. When I collected the bottle, the young women from White Waltham asked if they could visit the prisoner…Laura Hulett. I don't suppose we can allow that can we Sir?"

Hawkins thought for a moment. "Has she written and signed her statement?"

"Yes Sir. It's on your desk."

Hawkins picked up the folder and read through the statement quickly. "I think we should allow the visit. That young woman must be in need of some kindness after the situation she found herself in. We cannot underestimate how terrifying it is for a woman to be attacked as she was."

"I'll let Commander Trueman know, Sir. Is it ok if I cycle over to Windsor Sir?" Both Hawkins and Drake looked at him, puzzled. "There's something I need to do after we check the van."

"That's fine by me. Twice in one day. You'll be fit as a

fiddle soon Teal."

"Already am, Sir."

Training for the day had finished and Mark Sanders agreed to drive Olivia, Kasia and Lizzie into Maidenhead Police Station to visit Laura. The three women were subdued and Lizzie wished Mark Sanders would stop trying to make light conversation. It was a short journey, however, and he said he would return in one hour to collect them. That was the time agreed with the Police.

All three of them were nervous but Lizzie could see that Olivia was troubled. She had managed the training session very well but now entering the grim surroundings of the Police Station had resurrected her fears.

PC Green showed them into the cold, bare interview room. "I'll fetch the prisoner."

The word fell like a blow. Laura had been reduced to a 'prisoner', no longer a human being. Sufficient chairs had been brought in for the three of them and Laura. They waited in silence. What state would Laura be in? Would they see a broken shell of the confident woman they had known only yesterday?

Lizzie was relieved to see that, when Laura entered the room, she was wearing an expression of confidence on her face but it seemed to her to be a mask. She detected the anguish that Laura must have been feeling and recognised she was putting on a brave face for Olivia who leapt up and, rushing over to her, threw her arms around her.

Laura held her. "Let's sit down. Thank you for coming to see me. Wasn't sure whether you would want anything to do with me."

"How could you think that? Melford was a monster...I'm glad he's dead," said Kasia.

"Have you...have you really confessed to stabbing him Laura?" Olivia's voice was choked.

"Yes. That's what I did. I slipped out of our room when I thought you were all asleep and I went to his room to tell him how much he had upset you, Olivia. He was acting very strangely but he came towards me. I thought he was going to attack me and I grabbed the knife - I didn't even know it was a knife when I picked it up. Then he sort of staggered and fell against me. The knife went into his stomach. I didn't intend to kill him...you could argue I didn't actually kill him but not sure whether a jury will believe it."

"So you did it because of what he had done to me?"

"No Olivia. You mustn't blame yourself in any way. I certainly intended to tell him what I thought of him but the murder was an accident."

"You're being very calm about it, Laura." Lizzie offered.

"Got to keep a stiff upper lip. I know I'll go to prison but what's done is done. Now let's talk about something else. How's the training going?"

"Before we leave the subject of Melford, Laura, we want you to know that Olivia and I found a small poison bottle this morning and it was lying in the border right beneath Melford's window. The Police have got it. It may of course have lain there for a while but maybe Melford was poisoned."

Laura looked at Lizzie for several seconds. "Maybe, but there's no escaping the fact that I was holding a knife which ended up in Melford's stomach. At first, I denied being in his room at all. May have got away with it except that man Kenny told Hawkins he had seen me knocking on Melford's door."

"You don't like Patrick Kenny do you Laura?" Kasia asked.

"There's a reason for that." Olivia looked at Laura for agreement to tell the others the background.

"You may as well tell them Livvy. Hawkins knows.... Kenny told him."

"Patrick Kenny was due to marry a much younger woman but she changed her mind. She was a friend of Laura's and Kenny blamed Laura for persuading her friend not to marry him. The truth is she just came to her senses…realised that marrying a man so much older than herself may not be a good long-term bet."

The conversation then turned to lighter matters and Lizzie was pleased that they were soon laughing and joking as they had been before the visit to the Café de Paris. But how things had changed in the short time since. There would be no laughing if and when Laura was taken into court to face a charge of murder.

CHAPTER 31

"Mr Butler? I'm Sergeant Drake and this is Inspector Hawkins from Maidenhead Police. We need to ask you a few questions about your van."

"My van? It's all legal and above board, Officer." Mr Butler had a trace of an Irish accent. His eyes, beneath heavy black brows, looked at Drake suspiciously.

"I'm sure it is, Sir. I assume you own it."

"I do indeed. Who else would?"

"Are you the only driver of the vehicle, Sir?"

"No. In fact most of the driving is done by someone I employ for that purpose. His name is Michael O'Brien."

"Does he have access to the vehicle out of normal work hours, Sir?"

"He has a set of keys so yes I suppose he does. Sometimes he takes it home but usually it's parked here."

"Does he keep a log of miles he's done and do you check it?"

"No. Why would I do that? I trust him. He's a reliable sort."

"Did you use the van on Saturday evening, Sir?"

"No, I didn't."

"And was the van parked here by the shop that night or did Mr O'Brien have it at his house?"

"Sorry Officer. I couldn't tell you that at all. I didn't notice it here but then again I didn't make a point of looking for it."

Sergeant Drake nodded. "Will Mr O'Brien be bringing the van back here and at what time?"

Butler glanced at a clock on the wall. "He'll be back

anytime now, I should think. He had a few deliveries to make but they wouldn't have taken him long."

"Right, Sir. We'll wait. We need to have a look inside the van you see."

"I can't imagine what you'd be expecting to see in it but if that's what you want to do…" Mr Butler shrugged.

Drake smiled but said nothing. He and Hawkins stood in the shop, receiving puzzled and in some cases hostile glances from shoppers who gave them a wide berth. Mr Butler went about his business but it was obvious their presence made him feel uncomfortable. Fortunately, they only had to wait for some ten minutes before the van pulled up outside the door. Michael O'Brien entered the shop, whistling a popular song.

"Have you locked the van, Sir?" Drake stood in his path.

O'Brien looked startled. "Oh hello. You again is it? No it's not locked. Why?"

"We just need to take a look inside."

Drake and Hawkins left the shop and began to search the van. Hawkins checked inside the cab, peering at the floor on both sides for any traces of paint. There was nothing. Sergeant Drake had opened the rear doors and was examining the floor with intense concentration.

Suddenly he stopped and bent over to look more closely. "Sir. I think I may have something."

Inspector Hawkins joined him and Drake pointed to the floor close to the side of the van. Hawkins stared at it, his face only inches away. "Dried red paint I think." Carefully, he put the tip of one finger at the edge of the drop. It was hard but definitely paint. Hawkins nodded to Drake who went back into the shop.

"Mr O'Brien. We need to search your house."

"What? My house? Why in God's name?"

"Please drive the van home. I'll accompany you and the Inspector will follow in his car."

Drake left him spluttering and climbed into the passenger seat of the van. A moment or two later, O'Brien came out.

"Don't you need a warrant or something to search my house?"

"No. We suspect a crime has been committed and that gives us powers to conduct a search. If you've nothing to hide, Mr O'Brien, you've nothing to fear."

"My wife has just come out of hospital. You can't go disturbing her."

"Just drive Mr O'Brien."

PC Teal was waiting outside number thirty-five Albany Road when the two vehicles arrived a few minutes later. O'Brien was still protesting about the intrusion, grumbling to himself, but he led the three officers inside and told his wife they were going to conduct a search. She seemed completely bemused by this turn of events.

"Where's your bin, Sir?"

"My bin?"

"Your dustbin."

"It's outside the back door."

"Could you please show me, Sir?" PC Teal waited for O'Brien to walk ahead of him down the hallway and through the kitchen to the back door.

As soon as they had left the sitting room, Inspector Hawkins smiled at Mrs O'Brien. "Sorry about this, Madam, but we have to check something. Can you tell me please if your husband was out on Saturday night?"

"Sure, I've no idea. I was in hospital."

"Oh yes, of course. I had forgotten. Does he sometimes use the van outside his work?"

"Well...you won't tell Mr Butler will you?" Hawkins shook his head. "He does sometimes earn a few extra shillings by doing little jobs for people...you know shifting things, that sort of job."

"Of course. That's to be expected. People would ask knowing he had access to a van."

"That's right. It doesn't happen often you know..."

"Sir. I think you should see this." PC Teal had entered

the room holding with the edge of an evidence bag the lid of a paint pot with red paint clearly on it.

Michael O'Brien was following him, his face ashen. "What's so interesting about that? 'Tis just the lid off a pot of paint."

Inspector Hawkins looked at the lid and nodded at Sergeant Drake who assumed his most severe face. "Michael O'Brien, I'm arresting you on suspicion of involvement in the fire-bombing of a shop in Windsor on Saturday night."

"What are you talking about?"

"This way, Sir." Drake turned to Mrs O'Brien. "Will you be alright on your own Madam? We'll be taking your husband to Maidenhead Police Station to question him about this matter. He may not be back tonight."

PC Teal was left to try to mollify Mrs O'Brien who was clearly distressed by this unexpected turn of events. "What on earth are they accusing him of. What does it mean 'fire-bombing' a shop?"

Teal sat her down and asked her if she wanted a cup of tea which she declined. "On Saturday night, a shop owned by a Jewish family was attacked. Someone threw a petrol bomb into it, breaking the window at the front. The shop of course caught fire. The family was upstairs but they managed to get out. Unfortunately, the elderly mother-in-law of the shop owner had to be taken to hospital where she has since died."

"She died. Oh my God. So it's a charge of murder?"

"Not necessarily, Madam."

Mrs O'Brien looked at PC Teal, her eyes full of fear. "What was the lady's name, Constable?"

"Mrs Bloom."

Mrs O'Brien put her face in her hands and uttered a strangled cry. "She was in my ward. Oh Mother of God, please don't let Michael have anything to do with this."

Brian Teal felt for the woman but he wanted to get away. He tried to calm her again, telling her that her husband had been taken in for questioning and it was usual to name the charge when someone was arrested.

"But surely, Sergeant, there's no need to keep her in your cell now. It's not as if she's going to abscond...she'll be at White Waltham with us." Lizzie knew how to flatter a man. They were, in some ways, so easy to manipulate. Give them a sense of greater importance than they have and they could be moulded. She could see her promotion of the police officer to sergeant had pleased him.

For a moment, PC Green wondered whether to let the error go but thought he'd better not in case it got back somehow to the Inspector. "Actually Miss, I'm a constable, Constable Green."

"I'm so sorry. You looked like someone with authority so I assumed you were at least a sergeant. But do you see my point? You could save yourself a lot of trouble if you let her come with us."

"I'm afraid I can't do that Miss. The Inspector will no doubt be back soon and perhaps he will agree to that but I can't. She has admitted murdering a man after all."

"Yes but by accident...and there is that poison bottle. She may not have killed him at all."

"It's far too serious a charge to allow her to be freed, bail or no bail, so I will not be releasing her."

Lizzie was disappointed. She rather prided herself on being able to persuade people – men especially – to do things they didn't really want to do but PC Green was sticking to his guns.

"The woman you have in that cell is my sister, Officer. It is completely unreasonable to keep her in such conditions when it would be so easy to make life more comfortable for her." Olivia's lovely face and gentle eyes would have persuaded a lesser man

"I'm sorry, Miss, but I've given you my answer and until the Inspector returns the answer won't change."

Lizzie, Olivia and Kasia pushed through the double doors of the Police Station silently. They had tried and failed. Mark Sanders was waiting in his car outside. "How is she?"

"As well as can be expected I think. Would you agree Olivia?"

"Yes. I feel relieved that we have seen her and that she seems to be coping well. What she will be like in the dead of night if she can't sleep though…"

That sombre thought subdued them all and they drove back to White Waltham in silence.

◆ ◆ ◆

O'Brien had maintained a surly grumbling all the way back to Maidenhead. Hawkins and Drake ignored him but Hawkins was determined they would get the truth out of him, however long it took. They took him into the interview room still handcuffed.

"Now then Mr O'Brien, what was a lid from a tin of red paint doing in your dustbin?"

"Because I painted something red."

"What? I didn't see anything red in your house."

"It was for a friend."

"So where's the tin? Where's the brush you used?"

"Must have thrown it away someplace."

"Where does this friend live?"

"In Windsor."

"His name?"

O'Brien looked down at the table a moment. "I don't know his name. He's just some fella I met in the pub."

"You described him as a friend."

"Well, you know...just a manner of speaking. An acquaintance perhaps I should've said."

"Which pub?"

"I don't rightly remember."

"But you said '*the* pub' which sounds like a specific establishment."

"Just a pub somewhere in Windsor. Sure how would I remember everything? 'Twas just a passing conversation and I went round and painted his door."

"Did you go round in Mr Butler's van?"

"No, I walked."

"So how do you explain the fact that we found a drop of red paint in the back of the van?"

"That must've come from a different tin. Perhaps Mr Butler had red paint in there."

"Bit of a coincidence isn't it?"

O'Brien shrugged.

Hawkins waited several seconds until O'Brien shifted on his chair. Always an indication of nervousness beneath the bravado. He turned and nodded to Drake who sat beside him. Sergeant Drake slowly lifted the two bags he had beside his chair and placed them on the table. "Now Mr O'Brien. In this bag here, I have the lid we found in your dustbin and in this one, I have an empty tin of red paint. I wonder if the lid will fit?"

Drake opened the first bag and carefully took out the empty tin with the brush still in it. He laid the brush on top of the bag and then, his eyes on O'Brien's face, took the lid from the second bag and laid it on top of the tin. "Now Mr O'Brien, you see that the lid fits this tin perfectly. The colour of paint is identical and I suspect that when we take your fingerprints and check the prints on the tin and the handle of the brush, we will find a match."

O'Brien cleared his throat. "So you found the tin of paint I chucked away. Not a crime is it?"

"Where did you throw it away Mr O'Brien?"

"I told you I don't remember."

220

"But somewhere in Windsor was it?"

"Yeah."

"The problem Mr O'Brien is that this tin and brush were thrown over a fence in Maidenhead on Saturday night."

O'Brien's face fell

At that moment the door of the interview room opened and PC Green put his head into the room. "Sorry, Inspector. Telephone call for you...a Doctor Jarvis...said it was important."

Hawkins stood. "I think Mr O'Brien, you'd better start talking. The more co-operative you are, the better for you when you're facing the judge."

He left the room and took the call in his office. "Doctor Jarvis, I assume you have news for me. But I have some for you too. We have a confession from Miss Laura Hulett to the murder of Edward Melford. She stabbed him although she is claiming that it was in effect accidental as she tried to defend herself."

"That's interesting Inspector. There's just one problem. As I suspected, the knife did not kill Melford."

CHAPTER 32

Brian Teal smiled at the thought of the surprise he would give Sheila, visiting her again so soon. It would show her that he was serious about her if nothing else. He leaned his bike against the front fence. Pity he was in uniform but that couldn't be helped. He glanced at his watch. Nearly five o'clock. Perfect timing. She should be up and would be having a meal soon.

He knocked on the front door and waited, his heart beating a little faster than usual. It was Mrs Brown who opened the door. She looked alarmed until she realised who it was.

"Blimey Brian, you gave me a fright. Saw your uniform and thought something terrible had happened to Sid." She put her hand to her chest and exhaled. "Come in. Sheila will be down in a couple of minutes. I didn't realise you were coming today."

"I had a job to do in Windsor this afternoon so I thought I'd drop in and say hello…if that's alright with you?"

"Why should I be bothered? You're always welcome Brian. I expect the neighbours'll be wondering what's going on…handsome young police officer calling at the house." She laughed. "Oh don't worry, I'll soon put 'em right. D'you want a cuppa?"

"That would be very welcome, thanks." By this time, they were in the small kitchen and Brian found himself a place to stand against the wall where he was most out of Mrs Brown's way.

"Lovely weather we're having. Makes such a difference doesn't it? Feels like Summer's already here. Mind you they say that means Hitler's lot are more likely to come over and drop bombs on us. I hope it doesn't come to that. They got much better planes than they had in the last war and much bigger bombs. It's terrible really. I mean why bomb innocent people?"

"It is terrible Mrs Brown but Hitler doesn't seem to care about anyone."

"You're right about that."

Mrs Brown busied herself making tea and was obviously preparing the family meal. Brain Teal looked around the small kitchen, everything neat and tidy and very clean. Mrs Brown was obviously houseproud. She opened a cupboard to retrieve the packet of gravy powder and, through the open door, Brian caught sight of a lemon. You couldn't get lemons in the shops. Teal remembered the brief conversation with Mr Brown about having lemon in his tea but Mrs Brown had said very deliberately that you couldn't get them. How did she get that one?

But when Mrs Brown returned the packet of gravy powder to the cupboard, Brian Teal saw something else that sent a shock wave through him. There were two bottles of Wethered's Pale Ale. Must be coincidence, must be. Mr Brown liked a pale ale. So what?

And then he remembered seeing the very expensive cigarettes sitting on the mantelpiece which Sheila had said someone gave her father. What was the brand again? He pictured the packet sitting by the clock and knew it was Du Maurier. Could it be that Mr Brown was one....? God he hoped not. If it were so, he would have to arrest Mr Brown. That, he knew, would end his budding relationship with Sheila. If it came to it, could he do it or would he keep quiet, say nothing, turn a blind eye?

He heard Sheila's steps on the stair; his heart sank. She was singing, a lovely, smooth voice; he recognised Tommy Dorsey's latest song, I'll Never Smile Again.

'Ours was a love song that seemed constant as the moon,
Ending in a strange, mournful tune.'

◆ ◆ ◆

"What do you mean, the knife didn't kill him?"

"Exactly what I said, Inspector."

"So what did?"

"I'm afraid I haven't got time to explain now...it's quite complicated. I only telephoned now to arrange a time to meet in the morning when I can talk you through everything."

"But I've got Miss Hulett in custody. What am I supposed to do with her?"

"If you trust me, Inspector, I would release her if I were you...unless of course you want to charge her with something else."

"But what did kill Melford?"

"Inspector, if I don't get home very soon, you'll have another murder on your hands. My wife and I are going to a performance of the local operatic society. Must eat, get spruced up...you know the drill. Let's say nine 'clock tomorrow morning at your Police Station."

"But..."

"See you tomorrow, Inspector."

Hawkins looked at the mouthpiece as if that would bring back Jarvis's voice. He sighed in frustration. And pressed the button to bring the telephone to life again. "Green, could you please get me White Waltham on the telephone. Commander Trueman if he's available." He would have to release Laura Hulett and have someone pick her up. His mind was racing. What and who had killed Melford? Was Patrick Kenny the culprit after all?

Laura Hulett was sitting on the bed in her cell, slumped against the wall. "Miss Hulett, you're free to go. Commander Trueman is sending someone to collect you."

She sat up and stared at him. "What do you mean free..."

"I am told by the pathologist that the knife that stabbed Mr Melford did not kill him. I will not know the full details until tomorrow morning but Doctor Jarvis was absolutely clear that the knife wound was not responsible for his death. I may charge you with wounding but I understand the position you were in...and, as you say, perhaps it was accidental. I'm sorry to have detained you overnight but you did, by your own admission, appear to be culpable."

She stood up, her eyes still wide with surprise. "Thank you Inspector." She took two steps towards the door and looked at Hawkins nervously as if this was a cruel joke and he may change his mind. However, he gestured towards the open door of the cell and she walked slowly through to freedom.

Hawkins walked with her out to the foyer. "I don't know who will be collecting you but you should be able to see the car pull in from the doorway...unless you prefer to wait outside."

"Thank you Inspector. I will wait outside."

Hawkins watched her walk down the steps breathing in the air like a drowning person coming to the surface of the water. He let the door swing closed. He was thoroughly fed up that a case he thought had been sown up tight now lay in tatters. Several angry steps returned him to the interview room where he resumed his seat and glowered at O'Brien.

"Any progress Sergeant?"

"Not really, Sir. Mr O'Brien is still maintaining he knows nothing about the paint tin being thrown over the fence in Maidenhead."

Hawkins started speaking in a quiet snarl but, as he spoke, his voice grew to an angry shout. "Frankly, O'Brien, denying it is not going to do you any good at all. We know that you drove with someone else from Windsor to Maidenhead on Saturday night. We know that one of you painted a large 'J' on the door of a shop using that red paint. We know that one of you threw a petrol bomb into that shop setting it on fire. An old lady was taken out of that shop and to hospital suffering from smoke inhalation where she died. Start talking."

"Died? Old lady? What're you saying?"

"I am saying that you will be facing a charge of manslaughter at the very least."

"Now hold on. I didn't kill anyone. I didn't..."

"Who were you with? What is his name?"

"It was just a fella asked me to give him a ride to Maidenhead. I don't know his name."

Hawkins shot to his feet. "Lock him up Sergeant. Perhaps a night in a cell will improve his memory."

"With pleasure, Sir. Come on you."

"But Inspector..."

"Shut it," said Sergeant Drake.

Lizzie, Kasia, Graham Swinburne and Patrick Kenny were waiting in the lounge at White Waltham to welcome Laura back. They all had drinks and the bar steward – not Mr Bloom who was still on compassionate leave due to his recent bereavement – was primed to get whatever Laura and Olivia wanted. Graham Swinburne was keeping an eye through a window for the car's arrival.

At last he swung round on the sofa arm and called in a stage hiss, "Here they come."

Olivia and Laura entered the lounge with Mark Sanders behind them. A huge cheer arose accompanied by clapping and Laura's usually stern face broke into a wide smile. So much prettier when she's smiling thought Lizzie. There was much hilarity. It was as if a cloud had lifted.

When the initial excitement of Laura's return had faded and the recruits had settled into armchairs and sofas to await the call to dinner, Lizzie perched on the arm of a settee on which Mark Sanders sprawled, a benign smile on his face. "Now Mark, let me show you the book in which I think I found the plant you didn't recognise." He looked at her and frowned. "You remember when we were walking around the airfield this morning looking at the wild flowers."

"Oh yes...I remember."

Lizzie put her drink on a low table nearby and jumped up to retrieve the book. She knew where it was and she had marked the pages with slips of paper. "Here we are. This is one of them. What do you think?"

"It certainly does look like the plant we saw. Difficult to be absolutely certain though because it's not yet in flower and certainly doesn't have berries as yet. We'll have to check it later in the year."

"I'm pretty sure this is it but this is the other one." She flipped to the second mark. "I'll take the book out tomorrow or even after dinner tonight and have a closer look." She flipped back to the first. "But see these long stems and the way the leaves grow out of them alternately not like most plants where the leaves grow either side of the stem from the same point. That is what that plant on the perimeter looked like I think."

"Agreed. I'd still like to see the flowers and berries. So how did you find the Maggie?"

The abrupt change in conversation made clear to Lizzie that Sanders was bored with the subject; she put the book back on the shelf and returned before replying. "I thought it was brilliant...easier to fly than the Moth and faster...I like that."

"I really enjoyed it too. I was a bit surprised that Trueman let us out in it solo first time we flew it."

"Getting us ready for operational flying. That's what we're going to have to do when we've finished our training."

"Yes...strange isn't it that they do that with us. They wouldn't dream of letting RAF pilots take up an aircraft until they had been fully trained on the plane."

"Needs must I guess. They need aircraft delivering and there aren't many of us. I think we'll be busy."

"That suits me. I get bored fairly quickly."

In another part of the room, Graham Swinburne was giving a detailed account of a stage play in which he had acted and which seemed to have been disastrous. In very theatrical fashion, hands soaring through the air to emphasise the points he was making, he described how the scenery flats, knocked by a careless actor backstage, began to fall forward onto the main character in the middle of his biggest speech. "Without batting an eyelid, he turned round, stopped the flats with his hands and shoved them back upright. He turned back to the audience and carried on but they couldn't hear him because they were laughing, clapping and cheering him so much."

Olivia was in fits of giggles, fuelled undoubtedly by the relief that Laura had been released and was no longer under suspicion of murder. Laura too was enjoying Graham's account. Kasia was listening, a slight smile on her face, but not allowing herself to laugh openly. Mark Kenny's eyes were smiling but perhaps age made him more reserved than the Hulett sisters or perhaps he recognised in Swinburne a good story-teller whose account may have been exaggerated.

At last Swinburne subsided into his armchair and lifted his glass. "I've just realised that we haven't drunk a toast to our Laura." He stood up and held his glass aloft. "So please ladies and gentlemen, be upstanding and raise a glass to Laura."

"To Laura," they choroused.

Graham Swinburne suddenly looked puzzled, a thought striking him for the first time. "The thing is, if Laura didn't kill Melford, who did?"

CHAPTER 33

"Let's pick up where we left off yesterday Mr O'Brien." Sergeant Drake was going to enjoy this. He'd get the truth out of O'Brien where Hawkins had failed.

"Before I say a word, I want to know if you told my wife you were keeping me here."

"We telephoned our colleagues in Windsor and they were sending someone round to your house. I'm afraid I can't confirm whether they actually did so."

"She's just come out of hospital after a major operation. She needs me at home."

Drake jabbed the table with his finger. "And if you'd answered our questions fully and truthfully yesterday afternoon, you may have been taken home. You've only yourself to blame."

Michael O'Brien muttered something under his breath which Drake chose to ignore.

"So let's start with the pub you went to on Saturday night. What time did you get there?"

"It would have been about eight o'clock, maybe half past."

"And what time did you leave?"

"About ten o'clock I'd say."

"Why were you taking this friend whose name you can't recall to Maidenhead?"

"He said he had a message to deliver."

"It was a bit late to be delivering messages. Why didn't you go earlier?"

"Because he didn't ask me until we were leaving."

"What kind of message was it and to whom did he deliver it?"

"I don't know. I dropped him off and waited for him. He walked off round the corner. I didn't see where he went."

"That's a likely story isn't it? Let's see if you can do better."

"I've answered the question. I've nothing more to say about it."

Drake eyed O'Brien carefully. Was that fear he detected beneath the apparently blank refusal to give anything away. Gently he said, "Who are you afraid of Michael?"

O'Brien looked up quickly and into Drake's eyes. "Afraid? Me? I'm not afraid." But the signs were there in the tension in his face, the hunch of his body, the restlessness of his eyes.

"We can protect you. Perhaps you were forced into doing this...threatened maybe?"

O'Brien squirmed in his chair, his cheeks reddening, but said nothing. Drake waited, watching him until O'Brien was in no doubt that he knew.

"You see Michael, we know that two men drove in a van to Maidenhead on Saturday night. They parked on High Town Road, close to the junction with Grenfell Road. They walked some way down Grenfell Road until they were opposite the shop where they stopped to smoke cigarettes. We have a witness who saw them. A short time later, a large red J was painted on the shop door and a petrol bomb thrown through the window. You know the result. A livelihood destroyed and a woman dead. Do you smoke, Michael?"

"Occasionally."

"What brand?"

"Anything...the cheaper brands."

"It must have been nice to be offered an expensive brand like Du Maurier."

The colour drained from O'Brien's face.

"You see Michael, what with the paint and everything

else we know, we can put you there on Saturday night. The question is...were you a willing partner or were you forced into it?"

O'Brien now leaned forward, his voice hoarse and earnest. "You have to understand that if I tell you, they'll get me back. These are nasty people. They may do something to my wife. I had no choice then and I have no choice now."

"Who are we talking about Michael?"

O'Brien sat in silence for a while. "Alright. I'll tell you as much as I dare. The fella in the pub offered me a few bob to drive him over. I had no idea what he was going to do but he had a bag with him which he put in the back. When we parked the car, he took out the pot of paint and a brush, opened it and handed it to me. He then took a beer bottle from the bag and we walked down Grenfell Road as you said. We had a cigarette and talked about football because a fella was coming by. When he had gone, I was told to go and paint the letter 'J' on the door. He then took the top off the bottle – it must have been loosened and put back on – pushed some cloth into the neck, lit it and flung it through the shop window. I had no idea he was going to do that. We left quickly and I threw the paint pot over the fence where we parked the van. I didn't know the shop caught fire."

"Thank you Michael. Now we're getting somewhere. All I need now is the name of this fellow in the pub."

Michael O'Brien shook his head. "No, you'll not get that from me. I'd rather go to prison." He sat back, folded his arms and looked to the side at the blank wall.

❖ ❖ ❖

There was an uneasy atmosphere in the briefing room. Swinburne's question the previous evening before dinner had subdued them. He was right. If Laura did not murder Melford, who did? It opened the possibility that the killer was still amongst them. No one seemed to want to meet the eyes of another. Lizzie cast furtive glances around the room; everyone seemed perfectly composed – no obvious signs of guilt. She was sure that poison bottle was the key.

She looked at each of her fellow recruits in turn. Laura had admitted being in Melford's room and the knife in his stomach had been explained though she said Hawkins had told her the knife did not kill Melford. Had he been poisoned? Was the position of the bottle coincidental? Poison may have been slipped into his food. Anyone could have done that…not just the trainees but one of the kitchen staff, Mr Bloom, even John Hale.

She was certain that Olivia was not responsible. She would have admitted it surely when Laura was taken to the Police Station. But Kasia…she was a possibility. There was that determination and hardness about her and she clearly did not like Melford. All the same, to kill someone because their views were offensive to you was quite a stretch. She knew instinct could be wrong but hers told her that Kasia was not responsible.

What of the men? None of them seemed to have anything against Melford. Again all three recognised that Melford had some unpleasant attitudes but none of them seemed unduly exercised by that. There was that male camaraderie that seemed to inhibit chaps from judging another man despite what he said or did.

Her thoughts were interrupted by Trueman. "Good morning. I realise that this awful business with Edward Melford is on our minds but we must press on with training. The ATA has an increasing workload and I need you to be passed as pilots as soon as possible so you can get to work. Roger, Stephanie and I think it is best if you are kept busy…keep your minds off it."

Lizzie sensed relief amongst the trainees; none of them wanted to be sitting around doing nothing. Trueman outlined the procedure for the day. She and Sanders were to be allowed to fly the Maggie again but both had to follow a course and identify key landmarks, in other words to complete the assignment set on Monday which was interrupted when the rudder on her Moth failed.

When Trueman asked for questions, Lizzie's hand went up. "I know this is a delicate matter, Sir, but I think it is important. You'll remember that the Moth I flew on Monday had rudder lines that had been cut. Has the culprit been established?"

"No Lizzie. We know that suspicion will fall on John Hale and he has been suspended from duty for the time being although I must stress that guilt on his part cannot be inferred from the suspension…it's standard procedure."

Olivia chipped in. "But, Sir, how do we know that other planes have not been damaged?"

"Very simply, Olivia. All our aircraft have been checked and double checked. Everything is working and the aircraft have been secured in their hangars since they were checked. I'm certain that we will have no problems on that score."

When the briefing ended, the trainees left the hut chattering. A degree of normality seemed to have been re-established for which Lizzie was grateful but, at the back of her mind, questions tumbled over each other. So many unresolved issues. The only thing they could be certain of was that the knife did not kill Melford.

Doctor Jarvis stood in the office of Inspector Hawkins as if he were on a stage. Information came slowly, a magician holding the audience in suspense. Hawkins was becoming impatient. He just wanted the answers so he could get on.

"As I said, Inspector, the knife wound did not kill Melford. The blade was short and it went in to, shall we say, a generous lining of fat around the stomach at an angle. Thus it did not penetrate any vital organs nor arteries. But that wasn't the reason there was so little blood." Jarvis smiled and looked at

Hawkins whose face was unmoving.

"So what did kill him Doctor? I do need to get on you know."

"When that knife went into him, he was practically dead...on his last legs literally. That poison bottle that was found proved to be the key to unlock the mystery. The ribs on it prevented us from getting fingerprints but I had the contents analysed. Our laboratory technician actually was pretty certain from the smell that he knew what it was. That allowed us to look for that substance in Melford's blood and, lo and behold, it was there."

"And what was it, this substance?"

"Atropa Belladonna, Inspector, or in common parlance, Deadly Nightshade. It's a plant that grows wild...not lots of specimens about but enough. Any part of the plant is toxic and the juice of about ten berries is enough to kill an adult. It is deadly stuff."

"So someone found this plant, squeezed the berries into the bottle and gave it to Melford?"

"Indeed they did. I suspect that it was put into the port glass from which he drank. There wasn't enough left in the glass to be sure but it certainly was not in the small amount of port remaining in the bottle of Sandeman's. The juice from the berries is sweet and dark red. Melford had consumed a lot of alcohol and, as you know, after a few drinks, the palate becomes very undiscerning. He probably would not have noticed the taste and certainly not the colour. But...and this is important...this cannot have been done on impulse. Atropa Belladonna is not yet in flower in most places and certainly the berries will not form and ripen until later in the year. The poison was collected last growing season and brought to White Waltham by the assassin."

"Pre-meditated then?"

"Indeed."

"That suggests an old grudge, something that happened well before the last week or so."

"That's correct Inspector. An exploration of the past

may reveal the murderer."

"You say Melford was almost dead when the knife went in. How did Laura Hulett think then that she was about to be attacked."

"May I read her statement?"

Hawkins lifted the folder from his desk and handed it to Jarvis who scanned it quickly, nodding his head in various places.

"This fits absolutely. The effect of Deadly Nightshade is quick if given in the quantity I suggested. The victim would become flushed, would be staggering, have slurred speech and dilated pupils. At first, he would have been talking and laughing but the poison disrupts the heart rate meaning that the vital organs – brain, lungs, heart do not have sufficient oxygen. Death is inevitable. I suggest Miss Hulett encountered him when he was very near the end,. Her description of his behaviour – the way he staggered against her especially - fits absolutely with poisoning by Atropa Belladonna."

"Someone therefore gave him the poison between Olivia Hulett leaving his room and Laura Hulett arriving. I wonder..."

"What Inspector?"

"Patrick Kenny was the person who saw Laura Hulett at Melford's door. She went away when he disturbed her and he said he went back into his room. Maybe he didn't. Maybe he went into Melford's room first."

"But why Inspector?"

"Because the daughter of his cousin – they live in Oxford – was raped by Melford and a group of his rich friends five years ago. The girl did not feel able to go through with a prosecution and dropped the charges. We have Kenny's brother-in-law in custody in connection with the fire at the shop on Saturday night. I think I need to question Kenny urgently."

CHAPTER 34

Sanders had suggested that Lizzie should take the Maggie up first and she was only too pleased to do so. She sat in the cockpit, the throbbing engine sending a slight vibration through the aircraft, waiting for the signal to take off. She smiled to herself when it came and opened the throttle. That surge of power was a thrill and more pronounced in the Maggie than in the Moth. Lizzie breathed deeply; it was such a relief to be away from the intensity of the air base. The last few days had been a nightmare.

It was a smooth take off which pleased her as she knew fellow trainees and especially Mark Sanders were watching from the apron in front of the hangars. Her route was the same as the one she had started on Monday so she found Henley very quickly, the Thames taking a long, slow curve from its East West direction to flow South to North. There was the church by the old stone bridge and the sun brushing the buildings with a golden light. It looked idyllic.

From Henley, she headed South West towards Reading. She could have followed the river which described long curves between the two towns but flying slightly further West of it gave her a more direct line. Lizzie knew it was her competitive nature at work; she wanted to complete the course more quickly than Mark Sanders, not because she had anything against him but because she would derive considerable satisfaction from beating a man. The ATA was a very egalitarian organisation but she knew that a woman always had to prove herself in ways that a man did not.

She was soon flying over the lakes to the North West and could see the way the railway lines cut the town in two.

Perhaps the island in the river a little North of the railway line would be a suitable landmark to give. The town seemed rather nondescript from the air...not much to identify it except perhaps the large factory she could see...or even better the high brick walls and the giant cross shape of Reading Gaol. She remembered a teacher at school telling them about Oscar Wilde but becoming very embarrassed when pressed on why he was in prison.

Lizzie was in her element. She loved flying and the Maggie was an absolute delight. It was so responsive to the controls and faster than the Tiger Moth. She threw it around rather more than was necessary simply for the joy of flying it. And so she continued her assigned course finding Farnborough – the airfield was unmissable – Weybridge, flying over Hampton Court Palace to Kingston upon Thames and then following the river roughly Westwards again to pass close to Slough. Then it was a simple heading over the river to Maidenhead.

But before Maidenhead came Windsor. The Castle dominated the town and looked splendid in the hazy morning sunlight. The paths across the parkland lay neatly on the grass and the long avenue, double lined with trees, stretched away to the South. It was called 'The Long Walk' she remembered and long it certainly was.

She flew over Maidenhead and began to descend as she passed the centre of the town. Just as with the take-off, she wanted the landing to be very smooth. It was...a perfect touchdown, no bounces and no deviation from the centre line of the runway. When the plane had slowed, she taxied back to the apron, switched off, and checked her watch. The time brought a smile to her face. Let Mark Sanders beat that! She climbed down, removing her goggles and flying helmet as she did so.

Mark Sanders approached her. "You've certainly got the hang of it."

"I think so. It's such a joy to fly...so responsive."

"It certainly is. Did you find everywhere?"

"Naturally. Best of luck with your flight."

"Thanks. I'll see you back here before too long."

"I'll be checking the time." She smiled at him but he seemed baffled by her remark.

◆ ◆ ◆

Commander Trueman seemed relieved when Inspector Hawkins arrived. "Thanks so much for coming, Inspector."

"I needed to come out here anyway."

"I'm not too sure what General and Lady Melford should be told. Perhaps you would…"

"Of course. It's a Police matter so it's right that I talk with them. The revelation from Doctor Jarvis that Melford was poisoned rather than stabbed to death is tricky but I think we have to be frank. They don't even know that he was murdered yet do they?"

"No. I've told them nothing other than he is dead. I think they will be assuming there was an accident."

Inspector Hawkins looked out at the activity on the airfield. "I will need to interview Patrick Kenny again, Commander. Is he flying at the moment?"

"Not sure if he's actually in the air but he is on the training session. You'll be able to catch him when the session ends."

There was no time for further discussion as the arrival of General Sir Gordon and Lady Melford was announced. After introductions were made and coffee served, General Melford put his hands on his knees and sat erect in his chair. "Right Trueman. Let's have the facts. How did my son die?"

"Inspector Hawkins will give you as much as he can, General."

Hawkins felt Melford's unwavering gaze on him but he would not allow himself to be intimidated. "Firstly, let me say that I am sorry for your loss. This must have come as a huge blow to you. I'm afraid to say that Edward was murdered."

"Murdered?" General Melford shot to his feet and Lady Melford's hand went to her open mouth.

"I'm afraid so, Sir."

"Who on earth would want to murder Eddie?" Lady Melford said. "He was always very popular with everyone."

"His body was found before lunch on Sunday, just before Commander Trueman telephoned you in fact. A small silver knife, which we believe is a letter-opener, was protruding from his stomach but that did not kill him. Tell me, was your son prone to…shall I say…force his attentions on young women?"

"Force his attentions…" Lady Melford's outrage was very evident. "How dare you suggest that! Edward was a perfect gentleman. He went to Winchester School and then St Augustine's, Oxford. What makes you think he would behave like that to a lady?"

"On Saturday night, your son went with the other trainees to a club in London. One of the trainees is a very beautiful young woman who obviously attracted Edward's attention. He invited her to his room where he attempted to rape her."

"This is ridiculous. Edward would never do that." General Melford glared at Hawkins who did not flinch.

"The evidence of it was in the buttons ripped from her dress and her very distressed state. Fortunately, she managed to get away…he was fairly drunk by all accounts. But, her elder sister who is also a trainee went to his room later to remonstrate with him about his behaviour towards her sibling. He went for her too and, fearing for her safety, she grabbed the knife. According to her account, she had no intention of stabbing him but he seemed to stagger and fall against her."

"So you've got the culprit. Good. She'll hang for it."

"There is more, Lady Melford. But before I proceed, could you tell me whether there were any incidents in the past in which Edward was accused of rape or attempted rape."

"Of course not. I've already said he was a perfect

gentleman."

"Are you aware of anything General Melford? Anything at Oxford perhaps?"

Melford looked for a moment as though he were about to refute the allegation vociferously but he saw the look in Hawkins' eyes and suddenly sat down. "There was an allegation made at Oxford but the girl withdrew her complaint so there was nothing in it. She was probably after money."

"The girl is called Grace Upton. She was seventeen at the time when your son and a group of his rich cronies attacked her as she walked home. They held her while each of them took turns to do their sordid business."

Hawkins paused and saw with satisfaction the horror and disbelief on Lady Melford's face. "She did not proceed with the complaint because she could not face having to relive the ordeal in court. She knows that in the court of public opinion she would be blamed, branded as a whore. So your attempt to buy her off, General, was unnecessary."

"Buy her off? What is this Gordon? Why are you letting this man make these ridiculous allegations?"

Melford stared at the floor for some seconds before turning to his wife. "Because that is what happened. It cost me a large donation to the College funds to ensure that Edward was not sent down. The other parents did the same."

"But…but…Edward would not have been involved in such a thing."

"I fear Lady Melford that Edward believed he could act as he wished with impunity. You may wish to reflect on what in his up-bringing gave him that conviction." Lady Melford glared at Hawkins with unconcealed hostility. "The pathologist has of course examined the body and discovered that Edward was actually poisoned. By the time the young woman had raised the knife to protect herself, he was almost dead. His heart was beating its last."

"Poisoned?"

"Yes. It is clear that this was a pre-meditated act. Someone brought the poison to White Waltham. I need to ask you therefore whether Edward had any enemies. Was there anything else in his past that may have made him a target for murder? In particular, perhaps you could tell me about his activities as a member of the British Union of Fascists."

"The BUF? Sir Oswald Mosley is a personal friend of mine. We went to school together. I knew Eddie was a member but I'm not aware that he was active in any way."

"There is evidence that he had anti-semitic views."

"What evidence?"

"Comments he made to others here."

"He may have had such views, Inspector, but he would not have acted upon them."

"How can you be so sure, Lady Melford?"

"Well…as I said…he was a…"

She did not finish the sentence and Hawkins did not press her. He felt for them even though they had brought this upon themselves. Turning a blind eye to their son's mis-demeanours when younger, covering them up, clearing up the resultant mess had resulted in this. There would be something in his past that would account for his murder but he did not feel that General and Lady Melford were sufficiently aware that they had created a monster. There were probably numerous things and it could take months to discover what led to his death. He said nothing of course about Patrick Kenny's relationship to Grace Upton's mother, now his most likely lead.

"I'm afraid your son's body cannot be released for burial until the Coroner gives the word. I am sorry. I realise that our meeting today has given you some very unpalatable information and raised serious concerns. I trust your son's soul will rest in peace." Hawkins stood and shook hands with general Melford. He offered his hand to Lady Melford but she turned away pointedly and did not lift her own. "I assure you, Lady Melford, that any views I might have about your son's conduct are completely irrelevant. I will find his killer and bring him or her to justice." She turned away without speaking.

◆ ◆ ◆

Since arriving at the Station, Brian Teal had been trying to have a word with Sergeant Drake. He had spent a dreadful night agonising over what he had seen at Sheila's house. Could it be that Mr Brown was the other man who had attacked the shop in Grenfell Road? He knew that duty required him to raise his suspicions with his seniors but his admiration and affection for Sheila constantly fought it. In the end, he knew that he must do his duty but it gave him no pleasure. The thought of losing that beautiful young woman was unbearable.

The last time he tried to talk to the Sergeant, Drake said he had to make a telephone call to the British Union of Fascists on behalf of Inspector Hawkins. Brian Teal now watched the Sergeant's face turning redder, heard his voice rising in volume and noticed the Welshness of his accent becoming more pronounced. At last he slammed the handset down on the cradle.

"Bloody people. They should be jailed the lot of them, banned, closed down."

"No luck then Sarge?"

Drake mimicked badly a posh British accent. "I've been meaning to return your call but I've been so busy. We don't have any members in Maidenhead or Windsor. Sorry I can't be of any help." Drake raised his fist and shook it. "That's a bloody lie I bet. I told him we'd get a search warrant, turn the place over. They'll have members around here."

PC Teal waited until the volcano subsided. "Sarge, you know I've been walking out with a girl in Windsor?"

Sergeant Drake looked up. "Have you? Very nice for you."

"The thing is Sarge, yesterday, when I went round there after we searched O'Brien's house, I happened to notice two bottles of Wethered's Pale Ale in the cupboard and a lemon. You can't buy lemons in the shops. The other day, I saw a packet of Du Maurier cigarettes on the mantelpiece. I think my girl's father might be the other man."

Sergeant Drake sank slowly onto a chair. "Bloody hell. So we might not need the BUF after all. Well done Teal. I'll contact Hawkins and we'll investigate further."

CHAPTER 35

Inspector Hawkins eyed Patrick Kenny carefully. He seemed fairly relaxed as if he had nothing to hide. "The reason I need to speak with you again, Mr Kenny, is that I think you omitted to mention something very important when Sergeant Drake interviewed you."

Kenny looked puzzled. "Did I?"

"You have a cousin I believe."

"When you come from an Irish family, you tend to have lots of cousins. Are you asking about a particular cousin?"

"Mrs Upton who lives in Oxford."

"Yes. It's been a long while since I've seen her. We exchange Christmas cards that's about the extent of our contact."

"You know she has a daughter though."

"I believe so…and a son I think. I can't remember what ages they would be now."

"Grace, the daughter is twenty-two. Do you remember what happened to her when she was seventeen?"

Kenny looked at Hawkins blankly. "She became a year older than when she was sixteen I suppose. I don't know of anything in particular."

The certainty of Kenny's involvement in Melford's murder that Hawkins had felt earlier when he was told of the poison started to melt away like snow. Was this another false trail? He watched Kenny's face for the slightest change that may suggest he knew more than he was saying. "When she was seventeen, Grace was attacked on her way home one night by a group of young men. As I'm sure you understand, it destroyed her. She has hardly ventured outside her home since. That's five years…five years of misery, the desire to end her life probably present every day."

Patrick Kenny's face fell and his eyes stared in horror. That could not be faked surely? "I had no knowledge of this at all. I was never told. Did they catch the perpetrators?"

"Yes, but Grace could not go through with the prosecution. She was utterly humiliated, could not face re-living that ordeal so, without a witness, it never went to court."

"That's terrible. And how is she now? Why didn't my cousin let me know? Perhaps I could have done something."

"Grace has no self-confidence left and I suspect she wanted it kept quiet. She did not want people to know about it, felt that she would be blamed for inviting it…felt humiliated I'm sure. So that gang of young men got away with it."

"If I knew who they were," Kenny shouted, his face reddening," I'd make sure they didn't get away with it. I'd…"

"What would you do Mr Kenny? Kill them?"

"No…of course not, but I'd find a way."

"Perhaps you would murder them with poison."

"Poison…that was how Melford was….wait a minute." Hawkins watched Kenny's face as he realised the connection. Was Melford one of the attackers?"

"Yes Mr Kenny. He was the ring leader in fact."

"And you think I killed him to give Grace justice?"

"Well did you?"

"Of course not. I've told you I didn't even know what had happened to Grace."

"What do you know about poisons Mr Kenny?"

"Nothing. Why should I know anything about poisons?"

Hawkins raised an eyebrow. "What was your work before you entered the ATA?"

"Oh I see where this is going. I was a pharmacist but we did not deal with poisons."

"But your training would no doubt have covered toxic substances? The effects of things accidentally ingested for example?"

"Yes but...this is ridiculous. I had no reason to kill Melford. This is the first I've heard about Grace."

"You see, Mr Kenny, you told us about seeing Laura Hulett knocking at Melford's door and then she left after the words exchanged between you. Perhaps you did not go back inside your room after all. Perhaps you went into Melford's room, administered the poison and slipped back to your own room so that, when Laura Hulett returned, she did not see you."

"This is ridiculous." Kenny leant forward over the table, glared at Hawkins and stabbed the desk with his forefinger. "I did not kill Edward Melford. I didn't stab him, I didn't give him poison. I didn't particularly like him but I had no reason to kill him." He sat back and clamped his mouth closed, breathing heavily. "I'm not saying another word until you drop that accusation. You couldn't pin it on Laura so now you're trying to pin it on me. Who's next I wonder? Why not just accuse everyone?"

Hawkins waited until Kenny had subsided and then spoke in a calm, reasonable way. "I have a murder to solve Mr Kenny. You must admit that, with the knowledge of what happened to Grace, it is a reasonable conclusion to draw." Kenny said nothing. "Let me just repeat Mr Kenny that, for the time being, you are not to leave White Waltham without my express permission."

Patrick Kenny stood up abruptly and left the room without another word.

◆ ◆ ◆

Lizzie and the other trainees were sitting in the lounge when Patrick Kenny returned. His face looked like thunder. Lizzie rose to meet him before he had taken many steps into the room. "What was that about Patrick? You've already been interviewed."

"Oh it's quite simple. Because they couldn't pin the murder on Laura, they've now chosen to accuse me. Hawkins has dug up something that happened to the daughter of one of my cousins. Mind you, had I known about it, I would have been tempted to murder Melford."

"Why. What did he have to do with your cousin?"

"Apparently he was the ringleader of a group of young men who attacked my cousin's daughter in Oxford five years ago. But I was never told about the incident...only just found out from Hawkins now. The bastards got away with it. The poor girl was too ashamed to go to court."

Mark Sanders who was standing nearby heard the exchange between Lizzie and Patrick Kenny. "Good God. The man was a monster. Perhaps he deserved what he got."

"Perhaps, but you can't go round murdering people can you? I mean we have to let the law take its course otherwise there'd be anarchy."

"I suppose so, Lizzie, but if the law doesn't do its job, maybe..."

They all sat down again and the conversation rattled on about justice, the law, the courts. Lizzie let it wash over her. From her seat, she could see the office door where Kenny had been interviewed and she watched it for Hawkins to appear. She wanted to talk to him about the poison and she had a suggestion to make to him. At last, the door opened and a tired looking Inspector walked out. The confident, authoritative figure who first addressed them on Sunday seemed to have been replaced by an uncertain, contemplative man. She could understand that. There seemed to be no positive leads and the case against Laura had fallen apart.

She stood and walked out of the lounge. "Inspector, I wondered if I could have a word please?"

He looked up and smiled weakly. "Certainly Miss Barnes."

"I know you'll probably tell me to mind my own

business but the more I think about it, the more I think that Melford may have been a German agent or spy."

"Why so?"

"It's the views he had about Jews. There was no doubt he shared Hitler's view of them. So one wonders what other views he may have shared. It's also the poison. Murder like that is the stuff of spy stories." Hawkins looked at her but said nothing so she continued with a short laugh. "I remember my school friend and I used to play at spies, pretending that the other kids and the teachers were enemy agents. We used to do things like write notes in code and even one time we wrote notes to each other in lemon juice. It was great fun because the teacher thought we were exchanging blank sheets of paper."

Hawkins looked at her with keen interest but still said nothing.

"Oh I know that's ridiculous but I think the spy thing is an avenue that's worth exploring if you...but you probably already have."

"Lemon juice? Why lemon juice?"

"I thought it was well known. If you write something in lemon juice it doesn't appear on the paper until you put it on something hot. Then it appears as if by magic and fades when the paper cools again."

Inspector Hawkins suddenly came to life as if he had been charged up. "Thank you Miss Barnes and thank you for keeping your eyes open and finding that poison bottle. I must make a telephone call." He strode back into the office, closing the door behind him and leaving Lizzie staring at the closed door.

◆ ◆ ◆

"Get Sergeant Drake to the telephone please Green." Hawkins tapped the desk impatiently until Drake came on the other end of the line. "Drake, that blank sheet of paper I took from Melford's room. It's in the evidence store. Please get it now, boil the kettle and put the piece of paper against it. Be ready to read what it says. I'll hold the line until you've done that so be as quick as you can."

Hawkins could imagine Drake's facial expression and what he would be muttering to himself as he carried out the task. He pictured him collecting the key to the evidence store, going in and sifting through the few pieces of evidence they had gathered on the Melford case. He would then go to the small kitchen, fill the kettle, put it on the burner and wait. A watched kettle never boils of course. Hawkins tried to maintain his patience and tried to guess what was on the paper...provided Lizzie Barnes was right and there was something.

After what seemed an age, Sergeant Drake's excited voice came on the line. "Sir...it's amazing. Writing appeared. It said 'We'll do the shop on Saturday night!' That's all but that must be from O'Brien and his accomplice..."

"To Melford yes. Melford was the organiser. He was part of the plot to bomb that shop. He may not have been there but he was complicit in the death of Mrs Bloom. He probably suggested the trip to the Café de Paris to make sure he had an alibi. Clever bastard!"

"You know the chef and Mr Bloom said Melford came into the kitchen on Friday I think it was...stood by the oven range. I bet that was what he was doing...heating up the paper to read it."

"And Bloom saw him didn't he? I wonder if he was able to read the message and then after the shop was bombed put two and two together."

"That's it, Sir. That puts Bloom in the frame for Melford's murder doesn't it?"

"Yes, except he was probably still at the shop when the poison was given to Melford. Perhaps he had an accomplice."

"That Polish woman at White Waltham is a Jew. Perhaps it's her, Sir."

"And one of her hairs was found on the carpet in

Melford's room. You get over to Grenfell Road and interview Bloom again and I'll…"

"Sir I think there's something more pressing. I've just had PC Teal tell me that he suspects the father of his girlfriend might be O'Brien's accomplice. He saw a packet of Du Maurier cigarettes on the mantelshelf the other day and yesterday he saw there were a couple of bottles of Wethered's Pale Ale in the cupboard…oh and there was also a lemon."

"Right Drake. Bloom and Miss Michalski won't be going anywhere so we'll deal with Teal's suspicions first. Get the address and I'll pick you up in a kew minutes."

"PC Teal asked if it would be possible for him to be left out…doesn't want his girlfriend to know he shopped her Dad."

"Of course. I'm impressed by his integrity giving us that information. We can tell the father that O'Brien gave us his name. Nothing like driving a wedge between accomplices. What's the man's name?"

"Sidney Brown, Sir."

CHAPTER 36

"PC Teal, I want to thank you for providing the information about Sidney Brown. Your observation of details was impressive but even more so, the integrity and sense of duty you showed in giving that information when it may have and of course may still compromise your relationship with the young lady were admirable. I know you don't want a big thing made of it but I like to give credit where it's due. You need have no fears about the young lady knowing your part in it. We said we had been given Brown's name by O'Brien and we made sure that we searched the house to find the items you mentioned. You may be interested to know that we also found a pair of expensive brown brogue shoes in the cupboard under the stairs."

Sergeant Drake's eyes lit up with boyish glee. "It was great you know boyo. Brown tried to deny it but we just took him through everything we knew including the pub he met O'Brien in, you know the Prince Harry, the cigarettes and everything. He admitted that the stunt had been organised by Melford. That's obviously why Melford wanted to be out on Saturday night so there was no danger of him being placed at the scene. Slimy bast…"

"Quite Sergeant. That's one mystery solved. Drake, you can get up to Grenfell Road and tell Mr Bloom that we have found the culprits and they will be in custody until put before the court. See if you can get anything from him about Melford, especially whether he saw the writing on that note."

"Will do Sir."

"I'm going back to White Waltham. I'm going to see Swinburne first. He saw Kasia Michalski on the Sunday morning remember. I want to know if Bloom was up there too. I'll then put pressure on Miss Michalski. She may have given Melford the poison the night before. Miss Barnes said she was asleep but she could have been faking it."

It was lunchtime when Inspector Hawkins arrived back at White Waltham. He paced in the corridor outside the dining room, not wishing to pull Graham Swinburne out in front of everyone. He was only too aware from what Lizzie Barnes had said that it looked as though he was desperate, flinging accusations in all directions. At last Swinburne came out chatting to Mark Sanders.

"Mr Swinburne...a word if you please." Hawkins led him into the office he had been using. "When I spoke with you immediately after the discovery of Mr Melford's body, you told me that you thought you had seen Miss Michalski on Sunday morning going down the stairs but she appeared to have been coming from the men's corridor not the ladies."

"That's correct. I can't be sure it was her...I didn't see her face."

"Are you sure you did not see anyone else on Saturday night or Sunday morning near Melford's room?"

"I am sure. I saw no one else."

"Not a member of the staff?"

Swinburne coloured. "Oh I didn't think you meant..."

"Not important enough to mention perhaps? Just a servant! Who was it Mr Swinburne?"

"Well now you mention it, Bloom, the steward, was along the corridor. Looked as though he was doing something in the linen cupboard."

"When was this?"

"It would have been Sunday morning...at the same time as I saw Kasia...Miss Michalski."

Hawkins nodded. "Thank you Mr Swinburne, that will be all for now. I wish you had mentioned that before."

◆ ◆ ◆

Mr Bloom's face was dark. He looked at Sergeant Drake with tired eyes full of distrust, holding the door half open. "What is it?"

"I said I'd come back when I had some news to give you...about the shop and your Mother's death." Bloom said nothing and did not move. "Perhaps it'd be better if I came in, Sir."

Bloom stepped to one side and let Drake pass, closing the door behind him. He walked into the sitting room and stood in front of the empty fireplace.

"I thought you'd like to know, Sir, that we have found the men who bombed the shop. They are in custody and will be going to court facing charges of criminal damage and manslaughter. They are insistent that they did not want anyone to get hurt so a charge of murder will be very hard to make stick."

Bloom turned and sat down, his breath leaving him in a long slow exhalation. His body slumped on the chair. "Why? Why did they do it?"

"I'm afraid, Sir, it was a result of their anti-Jewish feeling. We believe they were put up to it by a member of the British Union of Fascists who gave them money, expensive cigarettes and all sorts."

"Melford?"

"We believe so, Sir."

"I knew it."

"You may remember Sir that Mr Melford came into the kitchen last Friday and you saw him by the oven range. Did you see the piece of paper he had?"

"Yes. He held it on the range and I saw the words that appeared. They meant nothing to me then but late on Saturday I knew what they referred to."

"I have to ask you, Sir, did you go to White Waltham that night, after the fire?"

Bloom looked at Drake sharply. "No Sergeant I did not. I told you. I went early Sunday morning."

"It's just that..."

"I know what you're thinking. I killed him in retaliation for the fire but I did not."

Drake paused, made uncertain by the ferocity of Bloom's response. "How well do you know Miss Michalski, Sir?"

"I know who she is...nothing more."

"She is Jewish too I understand."

"Yes, I believe so."

"Would she have done something on your behalf...you know...people stick up for their own kind."

Bloom was on his feet, his voice like a steel blade. "I thought you came here to inform me about my Mother's killers. Now you seem to be accusing me of being in league with Miss Michalski to kill Melford. This is outrageous. I am the injured party here not the culprit."

Sergeant Drake took a step backward, shocked by the sudden intensity of anger. "We're just trying to establish how Mr Melford died, Sir. I'm not accusing you of anything."

"Thank you for the information about the fire but you can leave now. Good day to you."

Hawkins did not smile when he sat Kasia Michalski on the chair opposite him over the desk. She was a hard nut to crack, inscrutable, unflinching, deep. But he was determined and he would do whatever it took. "Miss Michalski, you told me that you were not in the men's corridor on Sunday morning though Mr Swinburne was sure he saw you."

"You said he *thought* he might have seen me but only saw the back of someone's head. Why you assume it was me? I told you what I did...I came from our room and went down the stairs."

"Yes you did say that. Did you see Mr Bloom, the

steward at any time on Sunday morning?"

"I saw him when I went into the mess for breakfast."

"You should bear in mind what I might already know Miss Michalski. Lying simply leads me to think that you are covering something up...like murder."

"Don't be ridiculous."

"You told me that you had not been inside Mr Melford's room and that the hair we found which is certainly yours must have attached itself to him when you were dancing on Saturday night. But I was told by witnesses that you did not dance with Mr Melford on Saturday night."

Kasia shrugged. "You pay too much attention to a hair. It may have come from a cleaner or from the last person to use that room I don't know."

Hawkins decided to change tack. "How well do you know Mr Bloom?"

"I know who he is that's all."

"But you have something important in common...you are both Jews."

"I don't know every Jew in the country."

"You see Miss Michalski, Mr Bloom was also in the men's corridor on Sunday morning." Hawkins took a risk. "He acknowledges that you were there too."

For the first time, Kasia looked unsettled. She cleared her throat. "He must be mistaken."

"Oh no. There's no mistake. You see you told him what Melford had said about that young man at the Café de Paris and Mr Bloom discovered that Melford had probably been the organiser of the attack on his family's shop on Saturday night. Powerful motive for revenge I think. Perhaps on Sunday morning the pair of you were checking to make sure Melford was dead or perhaps you went to his room on Saturday night and..."

Kasia stood up and shouted. "Just as I thought, blame the foreigners. You don't know who killed Melford so you blame it on me. Why don't you just lock me up now? Come on." She thrust her joined hands in front of her.

"Don't play that card with me Miss Michalski. I don't care what nationality or faith people are. I just follow the evidence. You were in that room weren't you?" Hawkins now shouted in return, "Weren't you?"

"Alright, alright, if you know already why ask? I spoke with Mr Bloom on Sunday morning early and told him about what Melford had said. He then told me about the fire and his mother being taken to hospital. We decided to have it out with Melford. He had been too drunk the night before to see reason. We went to his room but he was lying dead on the bed. There was nothing we could do, so we left."

"Why on Earth did you not report it then?"

"Because we knew we would be accused of his murder...just as you are doing now. What else could we do?" Kasia sank onto the chair. "We did not touch him. I was shocked by what I saw. Mr Bloom put his arms around my shoulders. A strand of my hair must have caught in his hand or fingernail or something and it must have fallen on the floor."

Inspector Hawkins looked at the crumpled figure in front of him, no longer defiant, no longer confident. He stared out of the window for several seconds, his mind yet again turning over the evidence. The problem was that he believed her. Another lead coming to a dead end. Would he ever solve this case?

◆ ◆ ◆

When Lizzie saw Kasia, upset, broken, she was furious. What was Hawkins playing at? He seemed to be accusing everyone at random; when one lead came to nothing, he attacked someone else. She felt protective of Kasia knowing the hardships she had faced. She was not going to allow her to be browbeaten by Hawkins or anyone else. When Hawkins emerged from the office looking again rather forlorn, she put her natural sympathy aside and went for him.

"Inspector Hawkins. What are you doing accusing Kasia of murder? What evidence do you have? You can't just keep accusing everyone."

Hawkins turned his tired eyes on Lizzie. "Things would be a lot easier Miss Barnes if people told the truth in the first place. I have a job to do and if it means that a few people get upset along the way, so be it."

"If you were to be open about what evidence you do have and what you need to know more about, we might be able to help you."

"I doubt it Miss Barnes, I doubt it."

"Try us. Before we go for the afternoon training session, please tell us where things stand. You don't have to give away crucial bits of information but..."

Commander Trueman who was nearby stepped in. "Lizzie, the Inspector must be allowed to conduct his investigation as he sees fit."

Lizzie said nothing but she looked hard at Hawkins, ignoring Commander Trueman's remark.

"I suppose it is only fair to let people know what I can. No reason for them to be completely in the dark. Can you get everyone together in the lounge Commander?"

"Of course Inspector, if that is what you wish."

Trueman walked away and Lizzie turned to follow him when Inspector Hawkins spoke.

"Actually Miss Barnes. I wanted to speak with you briefly. I wonder if you and the other female trainees might do a great service for someone...if she is willing that is?"

Lizzie turned to face him. "If we can, I'm sure we'd be happy to. Who is it?"

"There is a young lady, about your age, who five years ago had a dreadful experience. She has hardly ventured outside the house since. If she can be persuaded to come to White Waltham, I think meeting a small group of independent, confident young women may help her."

"What happened to her?"

"I don't think I should disclose that. Perhaps if she does agree to meet you, she may tell you."

"I am certainly happy to meet her and I'm sure the others will be too."

"Thank you. And now to face the lions." Hawkins smiled wryly.

"We're not that bad are we?"

"I'll tell you in ten minutes!"

CHAPTER 37

The trainees and instructors assembled in the lounge wearing flying suits ready for the training session immediately afterwards. Lizzie hoped that Hawkins would tell them something and not just fob them off. There was growing anger at the way he had accused various people and frustration that the case had not yet been solved. They needed this sorted so they could focus on the job of learning to fly.

Inspector Hawkins did not keep them waiting; he had Sergeant Drake with him. Hawkins looked a little nervous and very different to his first appearance before them. He cleared his throat.

"Thank you ladies and gentlemen. I will not keep you long because you have a training session to complete. I have been asked to tell you as much as I can about our investigation but you will appreciate that, until we have solved it, some things must remain confidential. I must first apologise for the length of time the investigation is taking and for the distress that has been caused to some of you. We have been dealing with another serious issue which is connected to Mr Melford and Sergeant Drake will brief you on where we have got to with that."

Sergeant Drake stood a little taller, his chest thrust out. He was clearly going to enjoy his moment in the limelight. "Thank you Inspector. Some of you will know that a fire was started deliberately on Saturday night in a shop owned by a Jewish family in Maidenhead." Lizzie glanced sideways at Kasia whose face was full of thunder. "I am pleased to say that we now have two men in custody who have been charged with criminal damage and manslaughter. You may not be aware that an old lady who was living in the house died in hospital as a result of smoke inhalation from that fire. That lady was the mother of Mr Bloom who is the steward here. We have evidence that Mr Melford was the person who organised that dreadful deed and, of course, that or other anti-semitic activities must be considered a possible motive for his murder."

"It's good that he is dead then!" Kasia's eyes were hard and her mouth drawn tight with anger."

Hawkins ignored the comment. "Thank you Sergeant. It is clear that some aspects of Mr Melford's character may well have generated hatred of him. But our job is to find out who murdered him not to make a judgement on his character." Hawkins looked at Kasia who stared back at him, unflinching. "Edward Melford was poisoned in the early hours of Sunday morning, probably around one o'clock. The knife that Miss Laura Hulett admits she was holding when Melford staggered against her did not cause his death. The wound was fairly superficial and the pathologist says he was already nearly dead when he was stabbed."

Inspector Hawkins looked around the room, shrewdly assessing the responses of everyone, searching for that tiny narrowing of the eyes, shuffle in the seat that might indicate guilt. There was nothing.

"This morning, Edward Melford's parents travelled here from their home near Cheltenham to find out how their son died. That was not a pleasant conversation for them and nor indeed for Commander Trueman and me. I think it is fair to say that they had – perhaps still have – a very different view of their son to the one that has emerged in our investigations. We are certain that his death will be connected to something in his past, something he did that caused serious offence. The problem is discovering what that might be."

Cheltenham! Lizzie felt a cold shiver down her spine. She stood up, hardly daring to ask the question in her mind. "Excuse me Inspector. May we know what poison was used?"

"No reason why not. It was Atropa…"

"Belladonna or Deadly Nightshade." Lizzie finished the

sentence.

"That's correct. How did you know?"

Lizzie did not answer. She turned slowly, her eyes roving over the assembled faces but he was not there. "Where's Mark Sanders?"

Everyone stared at her but then looked around. "He's not here," said Trueman. "Where…"

"Mark Sanders is the killer. He has an interest in wild flowers and knows everything there is to know about them but pretended he could not identify one plant growing in the long grass at the edge of the airfield. He knew what it was of course. It was Deadly Nightshade. I heard him tell Graham Swinburne that he grew up near Cheltenham. We must find him."

At that moment there was the scream of an automobile engine at full throttle and a car flashed past the windows. "That's his car," shouted Patrick Kenny.

"Quickly Inspector, you've got to follow him." Lizzie rushed out of the building with Hawkins and Drake in hot pursuit. "You follow in the car, I'll be your spotter in the air. I'll keep above him so you'll know where he is all the time."

"What do you mean?" yelled Hawkins at Lizzie's fleeing back.

"No time to explain. Just get after him." Lizzie raced to the hangars. "Is that Maggie fuelled and ready to fly?" she yelled to the ground crew.

A startled engineer gave her a thumbs up.

"Start her up." Lizzie grabbed flying helmets, goggles and parachute from the racks at the side of the hangar and pulled them on. In seconds she had hoisted herself into the cockpit and the engine was started. She taxied the aircraft out to the runway as fast as she could, bumping over the grass. She did not wait for a signal to take-off but, as soon as she was lined up with the runway, pulled the throttle back and felt the plane rush forward.

The big Wolseley surged away from the building and headed for the barrier at the edge of the airfield. There was no sign of Sanders. Hawkins screeched up to the barrier, stuck his head out of the window and shouted to the guards. "Get this barrier up immediately."

The guards responded quickly and Hawkins shoved his foot hard on the accelerator. "Which way now do you think Drake?"

"That aircraft Miss Barnes took off in is over to our right, Sir. That's where he'll be. He's heading for Twyford I bet. Didn't want to take the road into Maidenhead 'cos he wouldn't be able to put his foot down. "

"She is quick thinking that Lizzie Barnes. She'd make a very useful detective."

"Yes, Sir." Sergeant Drake held tight to the edge of his seat with one hand and to the holding strap above the door with the other. The car bucked and swayed as Hawkins took the bends in the road. He slowed a little passing through White Waltham village but the car raced forward again like a leopard eager for its prey.

They could see the Miles Magister in the air. Lizzie seemed to be crossing backwards and forwards over the road. "Why's she doing that, Sir?"

"Because the aircraft is much faster than the car. If she flew straight along the road, she would be miles ahead of it in no time. We're bound to catch him. What's he driving? A small Morris or something?"

"Something like that, Sir."

"No match for this."

Drake turned his head slightly and saw the concentration and determination on his boss's face. He started to feel a little queasy as if he were in a boat on the sea and he hoped they would catch Sanders soon. He didn't think his stomach would take much more of this.

Lizzie kept the Morris in sight by looking back at the road each time she turned. She did occasionally fly parallel to the road for a short distance but she outpaced the car too quickly and risked losing sight of it. Each time she saw a side road in the distance, she was alert to the possibility that Sanders would turn off. As he approached Twyford, she wondered if he would join the Bath Road. He didn't. He crossed it and headed North.

Lizzie was glad she had already had two flights in the Magister. She felt entirely confident about throwing it around, enjoying turning it tightly at the end of each pass over the road. She looked for Hawkins. He was not far behind and gaining slowly on the Morris. She wondered what Sanders was thinking. Perhaps it would be better if she flew away from the road so he would think he was not being followed. He may slow down and allow Hawkins to catch up. But it was too risky. If she lost sight of him, there would be no way of finding him again in the tangle of country lanes that lay on the landscape.

She wondered if she should fly very low over the car to spook him. Perhaps that would make him give up. On the other hand, as an experienced pilot, he knew there was nothing she could do on country roads like this. There were far too many bends, too many trees, so low flying would be an extreme risk. She must hope that Hawkins would catch him before he had fled too far.

He was guilty, she knew that, otherwise he would not have run. He must have thought that Hawkins gathering everyone together was the final reveal in public like they do in detective stories: all the suspects and witnesses gathered in a big circle while the expert detective reveals everyone's secrets before pointing the finger of blame and providing the evidence. The question was why had he killed Melford? What secret lay in his past, what had Melford done to him? Sanders had always seemed so calm, so untroubled by everything and yet there must be something in his past near Cheltenham.

Lizzie could see the River Thames snaking its way towards the road Sanders was on. She looked North and could see the river ran beside the road until, in the distance, both road and river passed into a town. Henley. She recognised it from her previous flight in the Maggie. Where would he go after that?

She turned the aircraft to starboard and looked down at the road to check the car's position. She could not see it. She scanned the road in both directions but there was no sign of it. It had been approaching a section with woodland either side, thin on the river side but fairly large on the other. He must have turned off and stopped under trees. Blast! If only she had a radio to communicate with Hawkins. All she could do was to keep flying over the spot where the car had probably reached and hope that the pursuers on the ground would realise Sanders had gone to ground at that point.

What if he left the car and disappeared into the woodland on foot? He could make his way unseen into Henley and take public transport to wherever he was heading. They would lose him. "Damn!" Lizzie shouted. "I take my eyes off him for a few seconds and I lose him."

"What do you suppose she's doing Sergeant? She seems to be flying backwards and forwards over the same spot."

"Perhaps he's stopped, Sir. Might have realised it's hopeless with someone in the air and us on the ground."

"He perhaps doesn't realise we're chasing him...he'll have seen only the aircraft."

"That's true, Sir. We'd better keep our eyes peeled. He may not have stopped on the road...may have turned off."

Hawkins allowed the Wolseley to slow. Just North of Wargrave, the river twisted away from the road again and a turning on the left followed its course. Hawkins let the car ease to a halt. "What d'you think Drake? Will he have gone down there?"

"Impossible to say, Sir, but Miss Barnes is flying a bit further on...suggests he's up the road a bit."

"Yes, if I remember rightly, the river joins the road again a little further on. Let's stick to the main road."

The car purred as it cruised forward, both officers searching the sides of the road intently, looking for any telltale signs of car tracks in the soft woodland ground. They could not see the plane, just an occasional glimpse in the gaps between the trees but they could hear it as it passed over the road and knew they were closing in.

Suddenly Drake pointed. "That little track there, Sir. It's right under where the aircraft is flying. Let's try it."

Hawkins slowed and turned the Wolseley onto the woodland track. There were car tracks in the softer ground and, after a couple of bends, they saw the Morris standing silently under the trees. Hawkins stopped a little way off, turned off the engine and both officers climbed out. They walked forward and Hawkins nodded at Drake who hovered ten yards behind the car ready to give chase if Sanders made a run for it.

Hawkins stepped cautiously up to the driver's door. Sanders was inside, his eyes staring ahead, seeing nothing. Hawkins tapped on the window but he did not move.

CHAPTER 38

Brian Teal once again leant his bicycle against the garden fence. This would probably be the last time he visited the house. He had wondered whether to change out of his uniform before cycling over to Windsor but he had decided that there was no use pretending he was not a police officer; besides which, he was still on duty. He had slipped out of the Station in the absence of Hawkins and Drake. Told Green he had a job to do in Windsor. That wasn't a lie, just not strictly Police business. Sheila probably would not want anything to do with him now and Mrs Brown would, as likely as not, turn him away.

He looked at the front door and braced himself. He wasn't going to pretend he did not know what had happened - that would be implausible – but he was not going to reveal that he had been the person who identified Mr Brown as the possible fire-bomber. He walked the few steps up the path and knocked on the door. It was still fairly early and Sheila may not be up.

The door was opened and Sheila was facing him. In that first instant, he searched her face in the hope he might read his future but he had no time. Her arms went around his neck and her face was on his shoulder. "Oh thank God, Brian. I didn't think..."

He held her for several seconds, feeling her warmth and softness and savouring the sweet scent of her hair. "Shall we go inside?"

She led him into the kitchen. "It's Brian, Mum."

"Brian. Hello love." Mrs Brown's face was drawn, her eyes not meeting his own. "I suppose you know about..."

"Yes Mrs Brown. I was at the Station when Mr Brown was brought in. I am so sorry."

"How could he do that? How could you deliberately destroy someone's business and home. What sort of man have we been living with?"

"Now, now, love. Maybe there's an explanation. Maybe he was forced to do it by the other man he was with. I don't know. Will he hang Brian?"

"Oh my God." Sheila's hands went to her face and her horrified eyes fixed on Brian, waiting for the answer.

"I don't know…but it sounds as though they weren't trying to kill anyone so the charge will perhaps be manslaughter."

"He'll go to prison then?"

"I'm certain he will, yes, Mrs Brown."

"And so he should. I can't believe it. She was a dear old lady. I nursed her during her final hours and never even dreamed that my father could do such a thing. Well he's not my father, not any more."

Mrs Brown sighed. She looked and sounded very tired. "Now you two go into the sitting room and I'll make a cup of tea."

The British answer to everything…a cup of tea! But it was very welcome and Brian Teal felt his heart lift as he nestled close to Sheila on the settee. She had not rejected him, did not appear to blame him and, quite rightly, was appalled at what her father had done. She was a good person, a kind, loving, beautiful person.

"I don't think I can look anyone in the face ever again. What am I going to say to Matron and the other nurses? I may have to resign."

Brian slipped his arm around her and gently pulled her head onto his shoulder. "You are not your father, Sheila. You have nothing to be ashamed of. If it were the other way round and you had done something awful, your parents should feel ashamed. But you didn't bring up your father, you didn't shape his views, you didn't allow him to become unfeeling. You are not to blame in any way. You're a truly lovely person, Sheila, and I am very fond of you."

She lifted her head and looked into his eyes. "And I'm very fond of you, Brian." Slowly, her mouth moved closer to his and their lips met. His part in her father's discovery would always be a secret locked inside his mind. And so it is with many relationships: one or both parties keeps close something from the past.

◆ ◆ ◆

Hawkins had feared the worst but Sanders was not dead, merely shocked by being discovered. He had driven him back to the Station, handcuffed, though that did not seem necessary, so tranquil was he. It seemed not a quiescence arising from callousness but from being stunned, as if he had suddenly come to his senses and realised what he had done.

Drake had driven the Morris back to White Waltham and collected his bike. He now sat beside the Inspector who addressed the prisoner calmly. "Did you kill Edward Melford?"

"Yes I did."

"Could you tell us in detail how you did that?"

"I think you know most of the details of what happened on Saturday night. I was chatting with Swinburne in the lounge until late and I followed him up to bed…a minute or so after him. It must have been about a quarter to one. No one was about. I had with me a small bottle of poison, the bottle that Lizzie Barnes found. I tapped gently on his door and went in. He was in a fury because Olivia Hulett had just got away from him. He was of course drunk. He was going on and on about how dare she refuse his advances – though he spoke more bluntly than that – saying things like 'She should be glad that I'm interested in her' and 'Who does she think she is?' That sort of thing." Sanders paused as if remembering the scene.

"Do go on Mr Sanders."

"I saw the opened bottle of port there and two glasses. I

could see one had been used by a woman, presumably Olivia, so I commiserated with Melford and poured him another drink. He was ranting over by the bed so it was easy for me to tip the poison into the glass. He didn't even notice it. He tipped the glass up and swallowed the lot; he didn't seem to taste the additional sweetness in the port. I waited until the effects were clearly visible."

Sergeant Drake looked up from the pad on which he had been making notes. "Where did you get the poison, Sir?"

"My passion, Officer, is horticulture, more specifically, wild flowers. Last Autumn, I collected berries from a Deadly Nightshade plant I found, and made juice from them. I brought the poison with me."

"So you intended to kill Mr Melford?"

"Oh yes. I saw his name on the list we were sent and thought this was my opportunity. Anyway, when I knew the poison was taking effect, I opened the window and dropped the bottle out – didn't want to risk having it found in my possession. Then I went back to the room and went to bed."

Hawkins spoke. "You seem very calm about the whole thing Mr Sanders. Do you not feel any remorse for killing another human being?"

"Yes I am calm about it because I have at last carried out something that I've needed to do for many years. And no, I do not feel any remorse. In fact, I am very glad. I have removed someone who was a monster, someone who had no regard for others nor for the consequences of his actions. He was evil, Inspector, thoroughly evil."

"What brought about such hatred for him?"

"You will not know but my father was an under butler for General and Lady Melford. Even though I say it, he was a lovely man my father, utterly loyal and a man of absolute integrity. When Edward was fifteen – ten years ago – I was of course in my early thirties and had long left home - Edward was careering around the house one day and he knocked over an extremely valuable Chinese vase. It shattered, was destroyed beyond repair.

My father cleaned up the mess and threw the fragments out." Sanders breathed long and slow as if trying to control a powerful emotion.

"Some week or so later, Lady Melford noticed the vase missing and asked my father about it. He started to explain but Edward was there and he accused my father of stealing it, said he had seen him with it. My father tried to explain what had really happened. Lady Melford asked Edward if he had broken the vase but he denied it and repeated the allegation against my father. Lady Melford refused to believe that her son would lie to her and demanded that my father be sacked. He was...on the spot...without any notice nor payment in lieu. The job of course came with a house on the estate and my parents had to leave immediately."

"And this was ten years ago?"

"Yes. My parents found a place to rent and they had some small savings. I of course helped out. My father did find various jobs but none seemed to last long. I believe that Lady Melford told people what he was supposed to have done and they felt obliged to let him go. My parents struggled on for some three years. One weekend, I was visiting them. When I arrived my mother was out. I knew instantly that something was wrong. There was a strange stillness about the place." Again Sanders paused for several seconds this time trying to maintain his composure.

"I searched through the house...no sign of anyone. Then I went outside. There was a large shed in the garden with a ridged roof. I approached it with dread. Somehow I knew what I would find and indeed I did. My father was hanging by the neck from the tallest beam. He was dead. You see, there is only so much a man can take. Edward Melford destroyed my father. He took away his good name – more precious than anything else – and his livelihood. He was a broken man after he was dismissed, no confidence, no spirit, no interest in life. Imagine what his death did to my mother."

Mark Sanders sat still, his story told, his energy spent.

Inspector Hawkins let the silence grow until he said very gently, "I sympathise with you Mr Sanders and what your parents suffered but murder is murder and our job is to bring perpetrators to justice."

Sanders looked up. "Of course Inspector. I understand that. But don't expect me to shed any tears for Edward Melford. You saw the way he treated Olivia Hulett, trying to rape her. He seemed to believe that he had a right to everything he wanted and that his privileged upbringing gave him licence to do anything he pleased. This war is a fight against tyranny on a grand scale but there are tyrants even in everyday life and Edward Melford was a tyrant. I know I will have to pay for what I did, perhaps with my life, but I can go to my grave knowing that I did not fail my father." He gave a short laugh. "Bit like Hamlet avenging his Dad really."

Sergeant Drake again looked up from his notes. "On Monday, Mr Sanders, one of the aircraft at White Waltham was sabotaged. One of the ground crew is under suspicion. Do you know anything about that?"

"Yes. John Hale is not responsible. It was me. On Sunday morning, as well as walking around the airfield, I slipped into the hangar. It being Sunday, no one was about. I cut the rudder lines so they would break when put under strain."

"Was that a second chance to kill Melford if the poison failed?"

"No. I knew the poison had worked. No it was to divert blame. I'm sorry for that but when engaged in revenge, such tactics seem necessary."

"An innocent person could have been killed and an innocent man could have lost his job."

"It is perfectly possible to fly a plane without a rudder as Lizzie Barnes demonstrated. She is already an experienced pilot – on Tiger Moths anyway – and any one else flying that plane would have had an instructor who could have taken over control. John Hale has a worthy reputation, but...but I had to throw you off the scent and...."

Hawkins again left a pause ensuring that Sanders had nothing else to reveal. "Please stand up, Sir." Sanders slowly rose to his feet as did both Inspector Hawkins and Sergeant Drake. "Mark Sanders, I am charging you with the murder of Edward Melford. You do not have to say anything but anything you do say may be written down as evidence. Do you understand?"

"Yes Inspector, I do."

CHAPTER 39

Lizzie, Kasia, Olivia and Laura were waiting in the lounge. Since the dramatic events of the previous Wednesday, camaraderie, joy, fun had replaced the oppressive suspicion that had lain over everyone at White Waltham. Olivia seemed to have regained most of her vivacity though Lizzie knew from her own past that the experience with Melford would always be a shadow stalking through the recesses of her mind. Saturday lunch had been a happy occasion, a glass or two of wine and much hilarity because the four young women had been excused training for the afternoon.

For now they had an important assignment. Lizzie was watching out of the window for a visitor. On the dot of two-thirty, the black Wolseley of Inspector Hawkins slid into a parking space outside the building. Lizzie watched as the Inspector stepped out and opened one of the rear doors. A very attractive young woman with auburn hair, tied neatly away from her face, stepped out of the car and smiled at Hawkins. She held a handbag in both hands in front of her and looked nervously around her. From the other side, an older woman walked around the rear of the car. She had the same auburn hair, the same features. Inspector Hawkins gently put a hand on the younger woman's elbow and steered her towards the building.

This was Lizzie's cue. "She's here, girls. I'll go out on my own to meet her."

Lizzie stood in the foyer and watched the visitors enter the building. The young woman seemed even more uncertain, glancing at both walls of the foyer as if looking for an escape route. Lizzie recognised the sense of vulnerability and her heart went out to her. She walked forward, smiled and, without asking, put her arms gently around her. The hug was brief and not reciprocated. Lizzie understood that and was not offended.

The older lady was treated more formally with a handshake. It was warm and Lizzie saw in her eyes that she had been troubled. She and the others would do everything they could to relieve that trouble.

"I am so glad to meet you Grace and Mrs Upton. Grace, are you happy to come in the lounge...it's just us four girls in there, no one else. We can have some tea later...might even be cake." Lizzie took Grace's arm and softly moved her towards the lounge door. She felt a little resistance but her plan was to get her in there before she had a chance to object.

"Mrs Upton, your cousin Patrick is waiting in this room along here. I know he is very keen to talk with you." Inspector Hawkins led Mrs Upton away. She glanced towards Grace but the two young women had already disappeared inside the lounge.

It was difficult at first with Grace as she was like a small, frightened animal but the four ATA women were gentle and did not ply her with questions. They had decided to show her around the air base. The briefing room was first and she looked with wide-eyed wonder at the huge maps that adorned the walls.

When they went to the hangars, Grace was agog. "You actually fly those things?"

"Of course," Olivia laughed. "They're really quite fun and not as difficult as you might think."

"Do you want to sit in one?" asked Kasia.

"Is that allowed?"

"Absolutely. They wouldn't dare to tell us not to... they'd be scared. Four young women are a match for any man!"

"Well said, Laura. Here, let me help you up." Lizzie showed Grace how to mount the wing and climb into the cockpit.

"Perhaps you'd like to go for a flight?" Olivia called from the ground. "We've got permission to take you up, or at least

Lizzie has."

Grace looked terrified. "Oh no...I couldn't possibly do that."

"Tell you what. Why don't we just taxi around the airfield so you get something of the sensation of being in a plane?"

"Ok, I'm alright with that."

"Great but you have to put on the helmet, goggles and parachute. It's the rules even if you don't leave the ground." Laura smiled at the others without Grace seeing. "So hop down again, we'll get you kitted out and then Lizzie will take you for a drive."

Once the Moth had been started, Lizzie taxied out and took the plane across the grass to the start of the runway. "Are you ok?" she shouted.

"Yes. It's quite noisy isn't it?"

"It is but it's better when you're flying because some of the noise is left behind."

"I see."

"Shall I open the throttle a bit as if we were going to take-off and then you can see how exciting it is. It will be a bit bumpy I must warn you."

"Ok but not too fast."

Lizzie opened the throttle and the Moth surged forward. "Ok?" she yelled.

"Yeees. It is bumpy."

"Soon put a stop to that." when Lizzie had gained enough speed, she eased the joystick back and the Moth lifted into the air. She waited for the shout of protest but it did not come. She did not take the Moth very high but flew in a large circle centred on the airfield. On the second time round, she dropped altitude and speed and lined up on the runway. They raced over the grass in a perfect landing and Lizzie taxied back to the hangars. It was a risky tactic she knew. If Grace hated it, Lizzie would have destroyed trust. On the other hand, if Grace loved it, her confidence would be lifted. Lizzie jumped down from the aircraft and helped Grace down. The others were on hand to take off the parachute and other kit.

"What did you think of that?" Olivia asked, hoping to convey excitement in her voice and smile.

Grace was almost speechless, her eyes wide with excitement. "I can't believe I've just flown in an aircraft. It was wonderful."

"Would you like to go up again for a longer flight sometime?"

"Yes please, I'd love to."

Grace appeared transformed. All of them knew that major catastrophes in someone's life are not solved by one act nor event but this may be the start of restoring Grace to greater confidence. She needed something to aim for, something that would give her belief in herself.

The five young women walked back to the lounge. And Kasia went to find Mr Bloom to ask for tea. He came soon after with tea and a very welcome sponge cake.

"Mr Bloom," Laura said, "All of us are very sorry to hear about your mother. It is so disturbing that people can act like that. We know how hurtful even comments are to someone who has come from another country or who is of a different religion. Kasia has told us what it's like. We want you to know that many people in this country welcome refugees and would never wish to harm anyone of your religion or race."

Bloom stood holding the tray. He made a small bow. "Thank you Miss. It is very kind of you to say. I cannot approve of murder whoever is the victim but I cannot help but think the World is a better place without such men as Melford."

He turned and left and did not see the sudden change in Grace's face. "Did he say Melford? He was here?"

"Yes."

"He was..." She stopped suddenly and a tear rolled down her cheek.

Lizzie's arm slipped around her and her voice was hoarse in Grace's ear. "He cannot harm you or anyone else ever again

Grace. We do not know what you have endured and do not wish to know unless and when you want to tell us. But please know that I and others here have endured the animal desires of men. I hope one day that you will become angry and use that anger to achieve what you want to attain as I have done."

Grace wiped away the tear and looked at Lizzie with wonder. "You have been…"

Lizzie nodded. "Like you, I don't wish to talk about it but I have used it to make me stronger."

It took a little time to restore the atmosphere generated after the flight but Grace rallied and Lizzie felt that she was spirited enough to begin to put her life back together. "Perhaps Grace, if you enjoyed flying, you should think about joining us here."

"Me? Learn to fly?"

"Why not? We're all learning," said Olivia.

"It gives you a wonderful sense of freedom. I'm sure you felt that even in that brief flight," said Kasia.

"I did…I know what you mean."

"Freedom…it's a strange thing. It's so important to be free to do what one wants…without hurting anyone else of course… but it's also the freedom from things that might do us harm. Freedom from the tyranny of Hitler and his henchmen. Freedom is like breathing clean air, it's the feel of the wind in your face; it is absolutely essential to happiness…to everything in fact."

"You are so right Lizzie. The freedom from men who think they have a right to our bodies, from people, usually men, who want to tell us what we should do. But we need to be strong. We need to resist that. That incident on Saturday night has shown me that." Olivia looked at Grace. "Melford tried to…attack me. I managed to get away."

Grace turned an astonished face to Olivia. "It seems to happen a lot."

"With some men. Others are perfectly nice." Laura seemed tentative in that assertion and Olivia looked at her keenly.

"It's alright, Livvy. I talked with Patrick Kenny. I think he now accepts that I had nothing to do with his fiancée jilting him. We might even be friends from here on."

"Oooh Laura," teased Olivia, "are you falling in love?"

"Not likely."

The five young women laughed and, at that moment, Patrick Kenny brought Mrs Upton into the lounge. Lizzie could see the delight in her eyes that she found Grace laughing too. It had probably been a long time since she had seen that.

Commander Trueman entered soon afterwards and smiled. He pinned a notice on the board and left again. Laura went up to read it.

"What does it say Laura? Read it out."

"It says: 'All women pilots should remove their trousers immediately upon landing.' This produced a wave of laughter. "Do you think we have to take our trousers off even before our parachutes?"

"Perhaps they want us to walk about in our underwear." Olivia's eyes opened wide with mock outrage.

When the laughter had subsided, Kasia spoke. "I have always wondered what the ATA motto means...you know the words above the noticeboard."

"I can help there." Patrick Kenny stood up. "My childhood years were spent in a Jesuit school where we had Latin drummed into us. The motto in Latin reads 'Aetheris Avidi'. It means 'Eager for the Air.' I guess that's all of us."

HISTORICAL NOTE

The Air Transport Auxiliary (ATA) was formed in September 1939 as an adjunct to the British Overseas Aircraft Corporation (BOAC). It was a civilian organisation and its headquarters were at White Waltham Airfield from February 1940 until 1945. The ATA was hugely successful in its designated task of ferrying aircraft from factories to operational bases for both the RAF and the Royal Navy.

The ATA trained and used pilots who were too old or unfit for the regular services and, from its very early days, it employed women. The task facing aircrew in the ATA was daunting. Once they had been deemed able to fly one aircraft in a category, they were asked to fly any other aircraft in the same category, Thus they often flew planes they had never flown before and were provided with notes to do so!

Of the 1250 staff it employed during the war, 168 were women, most of them pilots. In 1943, women were granted pay parity with men, one of the first organisations to do so. The ATA Museum based at the Maidenhead Heritage Centre is small but superb and well worth a visit.: https://atamuseum.org/

Eager for the Air takes place in May 1940 when Winston Churchill became Prime Minister and Germany invaded Belgium, Holland and France on 10th May. The novel refers to a newspaper article published in the Daily Express on 13th May which suggested that refugees from Germany and Austria in Britain were actually German agents; the article prompted calls for all German and Austrian refugees to be interned. There were significant acts of anti-semitism too and Oswald Mosley's Blackshirts had for some time terrorised Jewish neighbourhoods. On 16th May 1940, large scale internment of aliens began and was followed by the Treachery Act on 23rd May. On the same day, Sir Oswald Mosley was detained and, later that year, the BUF was banned.

ALSO BY KEVIN O'REGAN

The Lizzie's war Series
New Swan Stone February 1943: Can Lizzie's powers of observation help find the murderer of a young civilian girl at RAF Silverstone despite the ghosts of her own past?

Meteor March 1943: RAF Cranwell in Lincolnshire. Can Lizzie help discover the mole relaying information to the Germans and also the murderer of a young airman?

Highball May 1943: Lizzie is tasked with flying some VIPs to the West coast of Scotland to witness testing of a new bomb. What does she find there? Due for publication in 2025.

The Dresden Tango
It is 1889 and a ship, The City of Dresden, carrying nearly 1800 poor Irish migrants, arrives in Buenos Aires after a nightmarish journey with inadequate provisions. Rose is coerced into prostitution whilst Patrick, a young priest, accompanies some 300 migrants to an area 400 miles South of Buenos Aires to found a farming community. Both suffer unbearable hardships and meet again in Buenos Aires. Can they restore each other's self-worth?

All available now on Amazon as e-books or paperbacks.

ACKNOWLEDGEMENTS

I first came across the important role that the Air Transport Auxiliary (ATA) and especially its female pilots played in World War II when reading 'Spitfire Women of World War II' a non-fiction book by Giles Whittell. I am very grateful to the Air Transport Auxiliary Museum for providing such a wealth of information on their web-site (www.atamuseum.org) and at the museum itself, which, though small, is well worth visiting.

For this novel, I made particular use of a dissertation by Anna Peterson (now Cole), available on the ATA web-site, in which she provides very valuable information about how the ATA women viewed themselves and were viewed by others. She provides evidence that they wanted to preserve their femininity and demonstrate that a woman could be successful in what was regarded as a male environment whilst retaining those qualities that made her a woman. I hope this novel captures that balance.

I am indebted to those who have once again read an early draft of the novel and provided such valuable feedback: Patrick Sanders, Mark Kenny and Laura Boggeln. I am also grateful to them for allowing their names to be used as characters, albeit in altered form. I would like to thank my publishers for their continued belief in the value of the Lizzie's War series and for bringing another book to public attention. Finally, thanks to my wife, Carrie, for her patience, encouragement and support.

Printed in Great Britain
by Amazon

49917577R00165